TWISTED METAL

TWISTED INTENTIONS #1

SAVANNAH RYLAN

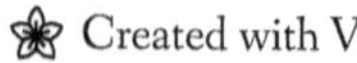 Created with Vellum

1

NAOMI

"What do you mean, you work on Saturday? What about the cookout!?"

My head tilted toward the ceiling as my tired eyes fell closed. "What cookout?"

My fiancée, Gordon, apparently didn't like that question. "Seriously, Naomi? You forgot again?"

I whipped around on that asshole so fast. "Forgot? You never tell me about anything like this. You never tell me when I need to know what days I need to take off with my schedule."

He threw his hands into the air. "Well, it's not my fault if you keep forgetting things. I told you about this cookout. The guys have been planning it for weeks!"

"Had you told me about it," I said as I tried to keep my voice even, "I would have taken off for it. You know I need three weeks' notice for stuff like that."

"When in the hell does anyone know three weeks in advance about a cookout?"

"Then it must not be a very important cookout. I have to work, but give everyone my best."

He charged me, pointing his finger into my face. "You will

not embarrass me this time. Everyone already thinks you're nothing but a workaholic. All I'm asking is for a Saturday afternoon."

"I'm a nurse in the middle of a pandem--."

"The pandemic is over, Naomi! You can't keep using that as an excuse to not get together with me and my friends! I get that they're not your cup of tea, but I stomach entire weekends with you and your father sitting there doing absolutely nothing but watching television and laughing at Judge Judy. You'd think you'd be excited to get together with people your age!"

I folded my arms across my chest. "I can't just take off for a three-hour cookout I knew nothing about beforehand. I'm a nurse--."

He nodded. "That's right. You're a nurse, not a doctor. They'll find someone to cover for you."

His words took my breath away. "Well, if you want to play that game this morning, then why don't we start with the fact that it's my paycheck that pays for this massive house you wanted?"

"Don't start with me."

I barked with laughter. "Start with you? Start with you!? I'm not the one who dropped a bomb about my schedule on me before my first cup of coffee, Gordon! Start with you? I'm not the one who constantly makes last-minute plans and then expects my partner to pivot around them as if my life doesn't matter!"

He gripped my upper arms. "All I'm asking for is an afternoon. Why is that so hard for you to give me? Do you know how many sick days I've called in without question because you wanted me at the house? Can you really not repay the favor, just once?"

I tried not to let the guilt flood me. It was his go-to tactic, after all. Guilt-tripping me into bullshit like that. But it wasn't as if he didn't have a point. Every time I needed him there, he was always there, no matter the consequence to his job.

Especially over these past few months, with Dad's health deteriorating so badly.

"I'll have to call someone, but I think I've got a couple more sick days to use up," I said.

He sighed as his hands slid down to mine. "Thank you. Was that so hard?"

I ground my teeth together to keep from legitimately biting his head off. "Will you be able to help--?"

"Whatever you need, financially, you know I've always got you. I know it'll short out your check a little, and I'm always willing to help. Just let me know what you need, okay?"

Can't ask for anymore more, right? "Thanks."

Right?

Gordon kissed my forehead. "I need to get to work. I'm running behind. Thank you so much for this, seriously. Everyone is going to be so excited that you're coming. Especially Billy's wife. She thinks you're amazing."

I wrinkled my nose. "She does?"

"Yes," he said before he kissed my forehead again, "but I need to run. See you around dinnertime?"

I nodded mindlessly as he released me. "Yeah, see you for dinner."

He pointed at me as he backtracked toward the door. "Don't worry about cooking. I'll bring something home. Surprise dinner?"

"You know what I like."

He winked at me. "Oh, I sure do. Love you. See you after work!"

I waved at him as he rushed out the front door. "Love you, too."

As I listened to him whistling as he rushed out to his pickup truck, I thought about the moment I had first laid eyes on him. We were in high school, and when he plucked that book out of my hands in the library only to sit down in front of me and hand me his favorite one he had gotten from the shelf, I had been hooked. I mean, who would've thought that the captain of the lacrosse team read books?

I had been his from the moment he introduced me to 'choose your own ending' books.

"What happened to us?" I whispered to myself.

As I turned around and stared into our massive kitchen that rarely ever got used, I recoiled at the marble countertops. Things I had once deemed important for us to have no longer held the flair of adventure and excitement they once did. The herbs growing out of control that hung in the kitchen window made me heave a heavy sigh before I looked down at my engagement ring, and as the diamond glistened against my finger, the weight felt heavier than ever before.

What happened to us?

"Oh, sweetheart?"

I perked up and whipped back around to find my fiancée poking his head through the front door. "You forget something, handsome?"

He grinned. "I love it when you call me that. I forgot to mention: I booked our venue for next summer. Our wedding is gonna be a blast."

I found it hard to breathe. "You—you what?"

He snorted, as if he were proud of himself. "I know you kept talking about how picking a venue was stressing you out, so I found one that you're going to love. So, take that off your plate, all right?"

"Wait, wait, wait, wait," I said as I rushed toward him. "You actually booked it?"

He beamed with pride. "Yeah, I actually did."

"Wh-wh—where? Where did—did you book it?"

The smile slowly faded from his face. "What now?"

I felt another fight coming on, but I didn't have the energy to stomach it. "Nothing. It's just—I'd like to go look at it. You know, get a sense of where everything's going t--."

He wagged his finger at me. "Oh, no you don't. I've known you for too long, Naomi. I know when you're pissed. You're actually upset with me, aren't you?"

I sighed heavily. "I just wish you would have involved me with--."

"Are you kidding me right now?"

"Gordon, please, I just--."

He threw his hands into the air. "You mean to tell me I have to listen to you bitch day in and day out about me not stepping up and me not making decisions and me not being spontaneous any longer, and then when I go and do that exact same thing—all the while solving an issue you've been having for damn near a year—and I'm somehow still the bad guy?"

My face melted into one of cold stone. "All I want is to be involved in your decision-making process. That's all I'm asking here. You make plans without ever consulting me, and then it's somehow my fault when I don't step up to the plate last minute!"

"Well, now you know how I've fucking felt these last few years!"

"Then why the fuck are we even engaged since you're obviously so damn miserable!?"

"I don't know, you tell me!" he bellowed.

I stood there, panting, in an effort to catch my breath. Did he really not understand? Did he really not get it?

Where did my Gordy go?

"The venue for a wedding is important to me. Our wedding is important," I said breathlessly, as my shoulders slumped a bit. "All I wanted was to be part of that process, that's all."

He shook his head. "The wedding isn't what's important, Naomi. What comes after it is. And for you to be so worked up and so focused on one day makes you selfish, in my opinion."

My back straightened at his words. "Is that really how you feel?"

"It's a day to be shared. It's a day to celebrate both of us. Our union, not just your magical fairytale whims. This is real life. What we have is real life, honey. And all I'm trying to do is take stuff off your plate so that you can actually enjoy this process. Why can't you just be okay with the help?"

I no longer had it in me to fight. I no longer had it in me to argue. So, I did what I always do.

I relented.

"I'm sure it'll be lovely," I said as I plastered on the best smile I could.

He smiled as he cupped my cheek. "There, was that so hard? Just to trust me, for once?"

"Don't push it," I murmured.

He chuckled as he kissed my cheek. "I'll see you for dinner. And I promise, you're going to love this venue."

I watched mindlessly as he backtracked toward his truck. I stood there, leaning tiredly against the doorframe as he whistled his way into his truck, cranked the engine, and headed on down the road. Is this what my life would be like? A series of arguments where I ended up relenting just to appease my husband.

Is that really all there was in the world?

I waited until his truck faded into nothingness in the distance. I waited until I knew without a shadow of a doubt that he wasn't turning around. Then, I walked back into the house and tugged my engagement ring off my finger. The tan line around my skin glared at me, as if it were angry that I could even fathom such an action. And as the front door fell closed behind me with the softest of clicks, I felt a weight lift from my chest.

As I slid my engagement ring into my pocket, it felt like I could breathe again.

And I worried about what that meant.

I mean, Gordon and I had been together since our high school days. Two days of dating through some of the worst years in a kid's life, and we somehow made it work after we graduated. He was mine, and I was his, and every time we got together with his old friends they hemmed and hawed about how they couldn't believe we had kept things together for so many years. They always asked us how we kept things fresh. How we changed it up. How we always looked like days' old lovesick puppies instead of war-torn adults battling one another day in and day out.

Gordon was a pro at answering those questions.

Mostly because I didn't have a clue as to what to tell them.

Give up every single fight, for starters.

Everyone expected us to get married. We were high school sweethearts, after all. Everyone wanted an invitation to the fairytale wedding the world was expecting of us. Two kids from opposite ends of the tracks, bringing their families and lives together purely based on love. It was the story everyone wanted.

And yet, it was the story that made me feel like a rat trapped in a cage.

Beep-beep-boop.   Beep-beep-boop.   Beep-beep-boop.

My weird ass ringer started going off, and it pulled me out of my trance. Thank fuck. I was tired of running myself in circles, only to dig my own grave with every step that I took. I raced back into the bedroom, scooping my phone off my bedside table, hoping it was the hospital calling to tell me that I could have a day off.

When I saw it was my father calling, however, I jumped into a different mode.

"Shit," I hissed as I answered the call. "Daddy? You okay?"

"Get off me! What the hell are you doing!?"

"Shut him up and get him outside."

My eyes widened. "Daddy? Dad. Dad, can you hear me?"

"Don't you dare put that—no! Stop! Someone, help me!" he cried out.

"Daddy!" I shrieked.

"You fucked up, old man."

My eyes widened as I slipped into my house shoes and raced for the front door.

"You cost us a lot," another voice said.

"Leave him alone!" I yelped as I searched around for my car keys. "Come on, come on. Where are my fucking keys!?"

"Get him in the truck," yet another voice said.

"No!" I cried out. "Leave him alone! He did nothing wrong!"

I snatched my keys up and raced out the door with my tits flopping around in my field of vision. I yanked my house robe off the coat rack as I flew toward my car, trying my hardest not to stumble over my own two fucking feet that were clad in nothing but slippers. I wrapped it around my body and shoved my arms into the fuzzy little holes. I cursed my flimsy tank top and ragged jeans as I slammed into my hatchback, cranking the engine without a second thought. And as I tore out of the driveway, I fumbled with my phone in my hand.

Gordon. I needed to call my fiancée. But calling him meant hanging up on Dad, and I sure as fuck wasn't doing that.

So, I sent Gordon a text.

Me: Dad's in trouble. Get to his house. Call 9-1-1. EMERGENCY!

Dad's voice cried out so badly that it grew hoarse. "Someone, help me! They're taking--!"

"Dad!?" I asked as I put the phone back to my ear. "Dad, can you hear me!? Please, dear God, tell me you can hear me. Daddy? I'm coming. Just hang on, I've--."

Everything fell silent. Just as quickly as I heard my father screaming, his voice completely disappeared. My gut gripped. My heart stopped in my chest. The worst of the worst dawned on me as I thought about what I might find once I got to his house. Was he dead? Bleeding out on the floor, with no one to help him? I checked my text messages and didn't find shit, so I shot off yet another one to Gordon.

Me: GORDON! 9-1-1! NOW!

Then, as I put the phone back to my ear, I heard what sounded like breathing.

Heavy, weighted breathing.

"I hear you, you know," I said as my voice grew curt.

The breathing stopped, but the silence persisted. So, I did the only thing I knew to do.

"I don't know what you want, but my father doesn't have it. If it's money you're looking for, he doesn't own it. If it's expensive items you're looking for, you've robbed the wrong house. And if something happens to my father? I won't stop hunting you down until all of you are rotting away in prison for the rest of your sorry, pathetic excuse of a life."

A chuckle emanated from the phone. A deep, reverberating, harnessed chuckle that spread goosebumps all over my body.

"Come and get it," the deep voice taunted.

Before the call dropped and left me sitting at a stoplight, waiting for the motherfucking thing to turn green.

2

NAOMI

Come and get it.

Come and get it.

Come and get it.

"9-1-1, what's your emergency?"

I pulled into the driveway of my father's ranch-style home and saw the front door hanging wide open, and Gordon wasn't anywhere in sight.

Had he even seen my texts?

"Hello?" the voice asked.

I cleared my throat. "Yes, I need to report a burglary in progress."

I heard typing on the other end of the line. "What's your name, ma'am?"

I got out of the car and started looking around. "Naomi Ryland. I'm at my father's house. His front door is wide open and there are--."

"Slow down and breathe for me. Is anyone hurt?"

I darted toward the right side of the building and picked up a shovel off the ground. "I don't know, but if you don't get here before I get inside, someone will be."

"Ma'am, if there's a burglary in progress, like you say, then it's best for you to stay put. I need an address. Do you know where you are?"

I rattled off my father's address as I rested the shovel on my shoulder. "I heard at least two other voices in there with my father, if not three."

"Ma'am, for your safety I need you to--."

"And what about my father's safety?" I hissed into the phone as I stood at the back door of my childhood home.

"I have dispatchers en route. They're ten minutes out. If you could just--."

"Thank you," I whispered before I hung up the call.

Then I slowly reached for the doorknob and jiggled it to see if it was open.

When the door popped loose, I winced. Shit, had someone heard that? My heart leapt into my throat as I looked back down at my phone, wondering if I should call Gordon instead of text. He was always so good at answering my texts, though. I opened them up and saw that he hadn't even read them, and I knew I was on my own.

At least for the next ten minutes.

"Fine," I murmured as I rolled my shoulders back. "I'll do this myself."

I tucked my cell phone into my back pocket before taking my first step into the unknown. I didn't hear a soul, and the fear that coursed through my veins ran thicker than the blood that pumped my heart furiously in my throat. I ran through all the techniques Gordon had taught me in order to keep me safe. I had grabbed a weapon, check. I cleared my corners, check. I stopped and listened for any sound that may be echoing across the room to try to identify the obstacles before me. Check.

It was hard to resist the urge to call out for my father, though.

Nothing looks out of place.

I had been with Gordon long enough to know what it was that police officers looked for at a crime scene. If someone had been taken, then usually many things were disturbed. Curtains pulled from their perched positions. A table knocked over. Possibly a glass that was broken in the fight. I heard my father struggling. He had been fighting against someone, even in his frail state. Yet, there was no evidence of a fight.

Save for the front door being opened, nothing was broken. Nothing was turned over. Nothing even looked like it had been stolen, including my father's wallet that he kept in a bowl on a small table right next to the front door, so he'd never forget his I.D. before leaving the house.

"Dad?" I called out against my better judgement as the shovel slid to the floor. "Are you here?"

The cardinal sin. I had given away my position. Even I heard Gordon's chastising voice in my head as something warm and tight wrapped around my throat. I gasped for air in order to cry out. In order to scream as much as I could in the hopes of alerting my father's neighbors that lived at least a mile down the road. But, just as I girded my stomach to pump the sound through my throat and up my mouth, a hand clapped around my lips.

Silencing my voice in an instant.

"No!" my muffled screams released.

I felt someone picking me up off my feet and I kicked my legs in the air, trying to throw them off balance. Adrenaline rushed through my system, sharpening my ears and harnessing my muscles. I bucked back, trying to get my feet back down to the ground so I could heave that motherfucker right over my back.

But as I tried to break free, a set of lips pressed against the shell of my ear.

"The more you struggle, the slower he'll die."

Where the fuck are they!?

I stopped struggling, but I knew I was in trouble. The voice in my ear wasn't the same voice on the phone, and that confirmed my worst fears. There had been multiple intruders.

And as far as I knew, they had already killed my father.

"What do you want?" I murmured against the man's palm.

My assailant snickered. "I'm going to slowly remove my hand. But, if you make a sound at all? I give the command."

Fuck, there was absolutely more than one of them, and I knew I was in trouble. Much more trouble than I knew how to handle. But he stayed true to his word. When I didn't make a sound, he released me, and I whipped around as quickly as I could to get a good look at the man who thought he could lay his hands on my family and get away with it. And, for the smallest of moments, I was struck by how...

Jesus, I thought criminals were supposed to look like shit for their mugshots.

"What do you want?" I managed to choke out.

The lean, chiseled man, with his blonde hair and icy blue eyes, gave me the most crooked smile I'd ever seen as his rolled-up leather jacket sleeves boasted of muscles bulging from his forearms.

Ah, there's the criminal.

"We want what is owed to us," he said as he clasped his hands behind his back.

I raked my gaze down his form. "I don't know who you guys are or what you want, but it's imperative that you let my father go. He's sick."

"A desperate plea. How quaint."

I pointed toward the kitchen. "See all of those orange bottles stacked up by the fridge?"

The man didn't even flinch. "I did when we first walked in."

His words turned my gut. "He needs those meds. I come over just about every morning to make sure he's taken them, so I know that he hasn't had them yet. He'll die if he doesn't get them, so where is he? Where did you take him? Because I'm telling you, I don't have the strength to bury another parent and-
-."

"I thought I told you to shut her up."

The gruff voice that had mocked me over the phone sounded behind me and I gasped. I whipped around, quick as lightning, and I watched as a behemoth shadow lumbered down the darkened hallway. My eyes widened as I took a few steps back. I had to crane my neck back to keep the man's shadowed head in view as he approached me. Where the hell had he been hiding?

I mean, I cleared all my corners just like Gordon had once taught me. So, where the fuck had he been hiding?

"I don't know who you are or what you want, but my father, he needs his--."

The sliver of light pouring through the kitchen window caught his shadowed body and my breath got ripped from my lungs. The behemoth's steel-gray eyes held me hostage as the weathered, jagged scar across his face weakened my knees. I felt my back fall against something hard. I slid my hands around, trying to find anything to help. A weapon, or a picture. A door-knob, or a window. Something to get me out.

Something to keep me alive.

"You," I glowered.

The man hovered over me with his gigantic shadow, shrouding me away from view. And as he lifted his hand into the air, he snapped his fingers.

Before the slender man with the oceanic eyes wrapped me back up.

"No! Please! Where have you taken m--."

He clapped his hand back over my mouth, but that didn't stop me from talking.

"My fiancée is on the way!" I shrieked. "I called 9-1-1! They'll be here before you know it, you son of a bitch!"

I kicked my legs up and slammed my heel into what I figured were his balls. But instead, I had slammed my heel into his thigh.

Causing the man with the metal eyes to grin. "Feisty."

He looked me up and down, devouring me with his hungry stare before he pinned me with his glare.

"Your father sinned, and he needs to pay."

I scoffed and started talking, but it was no use. The man's grip on my mouth was so tight that I barely got the words out.

"Hand," the man simply said.

And just like that, the man holding me hostage moved his hand from my mouth to my neck.

Before he gripped my throat so tightly that I gasped for air.

"What the hell could a 70-year-old man have possibly done to you guys?" I choked out.

The man behind me chuckled. "Can't fuck with our money and get away with it. We got bills, too."

I bucked against him, hoping that my cell phone in my back pocket whapped him right in his ball sack. But instead, his grip around my neck grew tighter.

Before his lips found their way to my ear once more. "Don't tease me, little girl. You might not like what happens after if you do."

I tried my best to focus. "Where is my father?"

Behemoth tilted his head. "Interesting."

I gnashed my teeth together. "If you don't give me the answers I want, or I don't like the answer I get, there will be hell to pay in ways you've never seen. Now, where in the fuck is my father, you worthless piece of shit?"

Behemoth grinned. "Promise?"

Hope drained through my tired ankles. "What exactly did my father do to fuck with your money, or whatever the hell it is you think he did?"

The man behind me snickered. "It's cute, you trying to get answers out of us."

I tried to rip away from his grasp, but he only wrapped himself tighter around me.

"Tell me what he did!" I yelled as loudly as I possibly could.

Which, quite frankly, wasn't very loud at all.

"Tie her up and toss her somewhere," Behemoth said. "I'm tired of her."

The man behind me chuckled. "You know, it's been a while since we made an example out of someone. We could take them both."

Fear gripped my throat as the mountain man in front of me devilishly smiled. "An example. That might pull the guys out of the woodworks for a bit of fun."

"Plus, we're very overdue for reminding our fellow towns-folk exactly who we are."

My voice grew hoarse. "I can't wait to see you bastards slapped in handcuffs. You're going to pay for this!"

The man behind me strengthened his grip on me so tightly that my arms fell asleep all the way up to my shoulders. Behemoth moved toward me, cloaking me in his shadow as his body heat raged against me. It grew harder to fight. Harder to see straight as my fear overwhelmed me.

But when I felt his fingertips dancing along my skin, I shoved myself so far back into the man behind me that I felt his stiffened dick against my clothed ass crack.

"Mm, mm, mm," the man behind me hummed. "Or we could take her for another reason."

"Over my dead fucking body," I glowered.

Behemoth licked his lips. "She'd be quite a ride."

"I would rather choke on my own denim jacket than get naked with you," I spat.

You know, before I gathered spit and snot into my mouth and hocked it out at his motherfucking face. The man didn't even flinch, though. He simply raked his leather-bound arm over his face as Hell itself settled behind his eyes.

"We'll make a prime example out of you and your father, and when we're done--."

"Just me," I said quickly.

The man behind me snickered. "Trust me, you aren't in a position to be making demands."

So, I said the only thing that I knew would keep my father out of harm's way. "Okay, you can do it."

Behemoth tilted his head. "Do what?"

Tears crested my gaze. "Take me for a ride, or whatever the hell kind of torture is waiting for me. You can have it. I'll freely give it. Just leave my father out of this. You leave him alone and let him go."

Where the fuck were the sirens? Why in the hell hadn't someone arrived yet? Why the fuck was it taking Gordon so long to check his motherfucking text messages!? I was doing everything right. Everything that he taught me. I was stalling. Passing by the time until someone could get to me. I threw them every left hook, every idea that I could think of that stood the chance of getting them to stop for a fucking second.

And yet, none of it worked, because as Behemoth turned and walked away, I begged.

"Please, take me instead," I said desperately. "You can do anything. I mean it, seriously. I won't run. I won't do anything you don't tell me to do. I'll stay out of your way, and—and I— I'll—."

The whimper in my voice agitated me, but I had no more

cards. No more tricks. No more lessons Gordon had taught me over the years in order to keep myself safe. All I had was myself and the only bargaining chip I had.

Which was also me.

"You, for your father's life?" Behemoth asked as he turned to face me.

I gasped for air as I tried to speak, but I couldn't. The man behind me had a grip much too tight. The pain mounted, choking off my hoarse voice's ability to produce any sort of sound.

And, without prompting, he had mercy on me.

"Let her go," the madman commanded.

The man behind me flinched. "Seriously?"

Behemoth glared at him. "You heard me. Now."

And just like that, I was free, albeit gasping for lungfuls of air.

"Take me instead," I said as I placed my hands on my knees and panted for air. "My father, whatever you're doing, he won't survive it. Not without his meds. How's that gonna look for your example-making, huh? Killing some old man who doesn't have two days to rub together for more time? I'm sure you'll look like badasses to every single teenager in the county."

Behemoth tilted his head, but I noticed the tick of his lips. Was that man... smiling?

"Is that so?" he asked.

I pointed toward the fridge. "Just look for yourself."

He peered over his shoulder and clocked the meds. "Huh."

I caught my breath and straightened my back. "Take me instead of my father. Please. He won't do anything. He's harmless. The most he'll do is call 9-1-1 and report what's happened, but something tells me you guys already know what to do about that."

As the gargantuan of a man pivoted his head back toward

me, he licked his lips. Those steel-gray eyes ignited with a fire behind them that unnerved me, and his gaze slipping down my body as if I were some prize to behold. I straightened my back. I gripped my fists at my side. I knew I had his attention, and if I could just keep it a little while longer, I knew someone would come bursting through that front door.

I simply had to stall for more time.

"You're really thinking about it, aren't you?" Slender man asked. "About running."

And as Behemoth's gaze came back to mine, I expected to hear sirens. I expected to see an ambulance. Possibly even a fire truck, just tearing into the driveway. I mean, how long had we been there? How long had it been since I messaged Gordon?

But there was nothing.

Not even my fiancée.

Alone, like I had felt for the last few years of my relationship with him.

"So?" I asked as I shrugged. "Do we have a deal? Me, for my father's life?"

"It'll be easy to get the old man to shut his mouth if his kid's life is at stake," the man behind me said.

"Yes," I said breathlessly, "listen to him. My Dad? I'm everything he's got. I'm all he's got at this point. Ever since my mother's death. You take me, and you can get that man to do anything."

Maybe then they'd keep me alive, just to keep my father under control.

I was shocked when the big man didn't even hesitate.

"Deal," Behemoth said with a wild smirk. "But we're going to make sure your father knows that if he calls the police or comes after you in any way? You're *both* dead."

"Perfect," the man behind me snickered.

"Wait, what? No! Leave him alone! Leave him out of this!" I shrieked. "You can kill me. Just leave him out of this!"

But the Behemoth simply gripped my cheeks and forced my gaze to his. "If you fight, you're both dead. If you upset me, you're both dead. If he calls the police, or sends someone after you, him and you are both dead. Those are my terms, you snide little girl, and if you don't like them? Then you should've thought twice before getting involved."

3

RANGER

"Come on," Dutch grunted as he dragged the girl toward me, "just a bit more. Yep. There you go. See, was that so hard?"

I noticed his fingers curling into the girl's skin, his lean muscles within his body fighting every cell inside to keep her at bay. Hell, even if I'd had my hands on her, she would have made me struggle. A small little thing, with tits flying about and hair waving in the wind she created with her own force. She had fire in her veins. I'd give her that. But Dutch handled more than his body made others assume. Fucking Christ, even as he held the girl at bay with her flailing legs and her blood-gathering finger-nails, he stood still as a stone, his voice harsh in my ear.

"Are you kidding?" he snarled. "Her for him? That wasn't the job."

I flickered my gaze toward him. "It's not like the guys are staying at the clubhouse right now. So, you tell me, then."

He blinked. "Tell you what? That the guys are gonna kill you when they get back and find some girl in our--?"

I turned my entire body to face him. "What the fuck we're gonna do with a sick man? Huh?"

Dutch glared at me. "He's not the one that ruined our job."

I tilted my head. "If his kid's in trouble, he'll be more willing to cooperate. Besides, it's not like the clubhouse is full. Remember? It's Hell Week. The guys never stay at the house during Hell Week."

He blinked. "Yeah, I can see that."

Trooper sighed. "We should be at Hell Week. I love Hell Week. It's my favorite week of the year. Crews gathering. Bonfires raging. Pissing off the police. Why aren't we at Hell Week again?"

Dante snickered. "Because we like getting paid more than we like getting laid."

"Sure about that?" Troop asked with a chuckle.

"Hey, at least Hell Week's in our area this week," I barked. "So, shut the fuck up and quit giving me guff. If we get into deep shit, the guys are right there, assholes."

Dutch rolled his eyes. "Sure, if that's what you wanna think. But I still think this is a shit idea."

I turned my back to him and headed for the front door. "Good thing I didn't ask your opinion."

I stuck my hand out the door, waving down Trooper. I needed that big old bastard to come back with that man. I watched as he pulled out of the shadows of a meadow of trees right across the road. As if the location were calling for the darkness to hide within it. The van eased onto the road before pulling into the driveway. Right behind the car, our little lick of fire had driven into our trap. And as he threw open the driver's side door, he hopped out.

Before shrugging his hands into the air. "The fuck, Ranger? We were supposed to be out of here three minutes ago."

I waved him in. "Get in here before someone sees you."

Three strides and a leap, and he soared through the front door only for his eyes to land on the girl. He didn't even have to speak for me to know what was rushing through his head, either.

"The other guys aren't gonna roll with something like this, Range."

I closed the front door and clapped his shoulder as I walked by. "Leave the plan to me, Trooper. You just get us out of here when the time comes."

"Yeah, yeah," he murmured as he slid off his leather driving gloves. "Always with the getaway. Got it."

Dutch snickered. "Not our fault you're the best driver of the group."

Trooper rolled his eyes. "So, I get stuck with the boring jobs. Fuck you."

"Fuck you!" Dutch exclaimed.

"Shut the hell up," I grumbled.

And they did exactly as their President asked.

"If we leave the old man out there for too long, he's gonna fry in this heat."

I watched the girl's eyes widen before she started fighting against Dutch. Again. As if the third time would be a charm, or something.

"Cut it out, or he's dead first," I spat.

Her emerald green gaze whipped over to me, and for the smallest of moments, I was jealous of Dutch. Jealous that he had her luscious curves pressed against him and not me.

God damn it, that girl was fuckable.

"I have to say, though," Trooper said as he walked up to the girl, fingering her brown hair, "it's nice to be trading up this time."

The girl practically growled at him, and the sound was so adorable that I almost smiled.

Almost.

"We might have lost our weapons," Dutch said as he yanked the girl closer to him, "but at least we'll get to relieve a bit of stress along the way."

I reveled in how her eyes widened. How her gyrating body, full of fire and frenzy, stopped at Dutch's statement. Now she understood. Now she'd obey.

And if she didn't, she died.

Just like her old man, if she wasn't careful.

"Trooper," I said.

"What's up?"

I nodded toward the front door. "Knock the old man out and put him in bed. It's time to get out of here."

"No!" the girl shrieked.

She kicked her legs into the air, and it gave Dutch the perfect opportunity to catch her body in his arms. I grinned as I turned around, listening to her feeble attempts to get away. Dutch wouldn't let her, though. His looks fooled everyone. Sure, lots of people thought he was a string bean with googly eyes or whatever, but that man lived for a good fight. But, beneath his carefully tailored, unassuming persona he painstakingly kept up for the public was a fluid sort of strength that even surprised himself sometimes. He had spilled more blood than any of us combined. He was the most dangerous out of all of us. Cold. Calculating. Intelligent beyond most of us in the crew, combined.

A truth that the girl would soon figure out if she wasn't careful.

"Let me go!" she exclaimed against Dutch's hand. "Don't you dare touch my father!"

Dutch scoffed. "You want him safe? We gotta touch him to get him inside. You just want him to come along with us?"

That stopped her sounds.

"Good," Dutch said, "then shut up before I make him watch you die."

As I stood in the living room, I kept an eye on Dutch in my peripheral as I watched Trooper bring in the old man. I had to admit, he looked like shit, but the second his gaze darted over to the girl, he bellowed with a voice that took even me by surprise.

"Naomi! No! What are you doing here!?"

"Daddy!?" she cried out.

"You let go of her. Whoever you are, get your fucking hands off my daughter!"

Trooper tossed the old man at my feet as Naomi kept throwing out those muffled screams. Her father looked up at me, staring me down with those same green eyes, and the fire behind them told me everything I needed to know about where his daughter had gotten her feisty little soul.

A soul I couldn't wait to tame with my cock.

"You let her go, you son of a bitch," her father hissed.

"Daddy, just stop. Please. Let me handle this."

I peered over my shoulder. "Get her in the van."

"No!" her father cried out.

I reached my boot out and pushed against his shoulder, knocking him to the ground. He was pathetic. Frail. Weak. He wouldn't withstand the plan I had for him anyway. But his daughter?

Naomi was the ticket to getting our money for those weapons.

"Shit, fuck!" Dutch hissed.

"You leave my father alone! If you touch him, I swear to hell on high I'll kill you myself!" Naomi shrieked.

My head whipped toward her, and I watched as Dutch nursed a wound on his hand. "You good? Or do you need a real man to do your job?"

He shot me a look. "Troop? A little help here?"

"Leave her alone. Please," the old man croaked out.

"Daddy, it's gonna be okay. Just do what they're telling you to do. I've got this. Gordon and I—ah!"

"My pleasure," Trooper said as he marched toward Dutch

and the girl, wrestling her away from him. I watched with glee as he stole that thick little princess from Dutch's grasp. How he wrapped her mouth shut with that ace bandage the way we did her father. How he threw her over his shoulder as if her ample body weighed nothing.

My skin felt jealous at the fact that both of them had already touched her.

"Knock her out if she won't shut up," I commanded.

Trooper chuckled as he carried her out the front door. "Can't wait to feel that yelp of hers around my dick. What do you think, boys?"

"No! Please! I-I-I'll do anything. Just leave my daughter alone. I beg of you. Please, she's been through enough," the old man said.

I looked down at him with a smirk on my face. "Trust me, you'll beg plenty before I'm done with you."

From the second that girl had dipped into her father's bedroom with those luscious tits entering first, I knew I had to have her. Feel her. Wrap her body around my cock until I filled her with my seed. But that was for later. For a different day.

First, we had to be concerned with getting our asses out of there.

"All right," Trooper said as he barged back through the front door. "What now?"

"Not for nothing, by the way," Dutch said as he came up behind Trooper, "but the street's getting a bit busier out here. We've overstayed our welcome by around..."

"Seven minutes," Trooper said.

My gaze flickered around. "Troop, knock the man out and get him in bed. Dutch, clean up around here a bit. We've got a few broken things and a picture off the wall."

"On it," he murmured.

"Come here, old man," Trooper said with a grunt as he wrenched the man off the ground.

And as he dragged that hoarse-voiced man down the hallway, Dutch started his furious cleaning while I pulled out my burner phone and called church with the rest of the guys.

They were not gonna like the fact that I was pulling them away from Hell Week, either.

"Help! Somebody, please help me!"

Naomi's screams followed us all the way back to the clubhouse, perched on a cliff side surrounded by sharp edges on all sides except the front porch. Motorcycles revved in the distance, signaling the onslaught of angry men that wanted their paychecks.

But god damn it, her screaming had to stop.

"Somebody! Please! Help--!"

I cocked my hand back and lunged at her, watching as she flinched. But it shut her up. "One more sound out of you, and I'll send Dutch back for Daddy Dearest. Got it?"

Tears streaked her cheeks, but she nodded quickly.

"Good," I glowered, "Troop?"

"Yeah?"

"Get her in the basement and lock the door."

The girl's eyes widened. "Please. No. I'll be good. I'll be good! Put me down! Please, put me down!"

I smirked. "You heard the girl, Troop. Put her down."

"Allow me," Dutch said as he slipped past me and opened the basement door.

"Down you go," Trooper said with a grunt.

The tumbling of her body satisfied me as Dutch slammed the door closed. He flipped the lock, then mockingly wiped his hands off in the air as if he had accomplished something. We had accomplished nothing, though. Not until we had our money.

Not until our client paid for the bullshit they had put us through.

"Come," I said as I headed upstairs, "the guys will be here any second."

"Heeeeelp!" Naomi shrieked from the basement as she pounded on something. "Somebody! Can anybody hear meeeeee!?"

Dutch growled as he flipped the lock and ripped the door open. "It won't take us but a motherfucking second to toss your dead body into the ocean before going and getting your father again. So, can it!"

And when silence fell across the house, I drew in a deep breath.

"Dinner's at eight, Naomi! If you aren't awake, you don't eat!"

Then I nodded my head at Dutch, signaling for him to close the door.

Which he did.

"I think she's crying," Trooper said as Dutch locked the door back.

"Good," I said as I turned and headed upstairs, "her father ruined our biggest transaction of the year. She can drown herself in her tears, for all I care. Come on. It's church time."

I headed into the gathering room on the top floor of the clubhouse. The sprawling mansion clinging to the hillside had been rundown and abandoned when we first found it. So, it became my mission as their newly appointed President to pull us all together by funneling our personal money, time, and energy into sprucing the place up. Everyone had a room, in case they needed it. The core group of guys had offices as well. Plus, we had our conference room that overlooked the ocean.

I enjoyed that view more than I let on most days.

"Well," Trooper said as he and Dutch came into the room behind me, "that didn't go as planned."

"Yeah, yeah," I mumbled beneath my breath.

"You know, we sell weapons, not bodies," Dutch said. "But even if we did, that girl's body downstairs won't fetch nearly the kind of price we were looking at this afternoon."

I closed my eyes. "Shut the fuck up so I can think."

As I stood there, gazing out toward the water with my hands clasped behind my back, I watched my reflection fill up the floor-to-ceiling window. I'd always been a big child. So big, in fact, that my own father blamed me for the death of my mother while she gave birth to me.

Guess him dying of a grief-stricken drug overdose was my fault, too.

"Range?" Trooper asked as he placed his hand on my shoulder.

I didn't bother looking down at him. "Everybody here?"

He nodded. "Did a headcount. We're all here."

I shrugged off his touch and turned to face my crew. "All right, everyone. Take a seat. We have a lot to discuss."

Bury, another one of our driving experts, scoffed. "Let me guess: the buyer backed out like we thought."

"No, actually," I said as I walked over to my seat at the head of the table. "So, let's sit and talk about it."

"I think I'll stand," Doc said.

I pinned him with a glare. "You sit, or you're out."

That got them to take their seats very quickly. Didn't give me a hell of a lot of time to piece my mind together, but then again, the guys never cared about that.

All they wanted was the truth, anyway.

"So, you gonna tell us why we're not getting paid right now?" Bury asked.

"Or why we no longer get to enjoy Hell Week?" Thor asked.

"Boo. Hoo. Hoo," Dutch said flatly.

I pulled out my chair and sat down, listening to it groan underneath me. "During our transaction, someone found us."

Thor pointed aimlessly and tilted his thumb toward the floor. "That why I heard crying coming up from the basement?"

"You heard that, too?" Bury asked. "Because I heard that."

I held up my hand and silenced the guys. "Yes, that's why you hear crying. An old man stumbled across us on his daily fucking walk, of all things."

Dutch growled to himself. "Fuck these clients."

"We knew they were gonna be trouble from the start," Bury said.

I drew in a deep breath to settle my anger. "Just like we assumed would happen, we got caught. And when we followed the old man back to his house, we had every intention of bringing him back here to punish him for the money he took from our pockets because he was so damn nosey."

Thor tilted his head. "I take it you've got a plan, then? On how to get us our money?"

I leaned back in my chair. "As far as I'm concerned, this is the client's fucking fault. They're the ones that didn't feel comfortable meeting up with us in one of our specified locations."

Thor leaned forward, planting his scarred and tattooed forearms onto the wooden table. "That isn't what I asked, Range."

Dutch leaned over and whispered in my ear. "Now's the time where you've usually got a plan to let us in on."

I slowly turned my gaze toward him. "And when I've got a plan, I'll fill you in."

Trooper stuck his hand into the air, and it made me roll my eyes. "This isn't grade school, Troop. Just talk."

His hand fell back down into his lap. "We all know this is the client's fault. Had they met us where we originally intended, this would've all been fine. So, I say we use that."

A sly smirk spread across my face. "Tell them that we're willing to still do the transaction, but now it'll require a ten percent--."

"Twenty percent," Thor growled.

I pointed at him. "—twenty percent surcharge for being an absolute asshole, and they'll still have to meet us where we want before the trail on us gets any hotter than it already is."

Bury scoffed. "And if they don't agree?"

Dutch grinned. "Then we'll blacklist them with every weapons dealer on the West Coast. You know, since they wanted to act all high and mighty instead of playing it smart."

"Actions, meet consequences," Trooper said.

"All in favor of guilting these assholes into more money, raise your hands," I said.

And as every single hand from every single one of my men shot into the air, I stood to my feet.

"One thing," Bury said as he wiggled his fingers in the air.

Troop groaned. "No, you guys don't have to give up your fucking hotel rooms for the week. Unless they're more than ten minutes away."

"Fuck," Bury groaned.

"You can bunk with me. My hotel's got room service," Thor said as he slapped his hand against the man's chest.

"Everyone done belly-aching about how they're not gonna get laid at Hell Week?" I snarled.

"We'll all be within ten minutes of this place in case shit pops off," Doc said.

I didn't like how disagreeable they were being. In fact, I

wanted to wring their fucking necks. But they had a point. We'd all been looking forward to Hell Week ever since it was announced that it would be in our neck of the woods. A whole ass week of rubbing elbows with family, friends, and good fucks. I, myself, was disappointed that I had to miss it, but this deal came with too much money to justify a week off. That's why the three of us tackled the job. Dutch, Troop, and I. We were the core of the crew, which meant we had a duty to our brothers to see money like this through. It's how we took care of our own, even if it meant giving up our first vacation in years together. The guys, however? We'd all run our asses so ragged these past couple of years that they deserved a week off. And I sure as hell didn't want to take it away from them for something as trivial as this shit.

So, I settled my gut on the compromise and clapped my hands three times in succession.

"Plan agreed upon. Church is dismissed."

After all, I had a very important phone call to make.

4

NAOMI

"Hello? Can anyone hear me!?"

I had no more tears to cry. I had no more life left in me to fight. Even my voice started giving out, cracking and fraying out with every other exclamation that fell from my lips. I heard so many footsteps above my head. So many lumbering, echoing, heavy steps. How many people were in the house? Where the hell was I?

Were they going to kill me?

I flopped down onto the edge of the bed, one of the few pieces of furniture that kept me company in that basement. The lights above my head were bright, illuminating every single corner that seemed impeccably clean for a prison. There was a wall that cornered off a bathroom that sat diagonally from the bed, and outside of the dresser and bedside tables that were afforded to me. There wasn't anything else in the room.

"Gordon, god damn it, where are you!?" I yelped.

I hung my head and placed it in the palms of my hands. No one had come for me. Not my fiancée. Not his partner from work. Not 9-1-1. No one. Did I really matter so little to the world? Is that why things between me and Gordon had been going downhill? Because I simply didn't matter?

"At least Daddy's safe," I croaked out.

Can I really trust those guys, though?

I leapt up from the bed with a renewed sense of vigor and rushed up the stairs to the basement door. I banged on it with my fists, slamming them as hard as I could stand as my voice girded itself from a place deep within my gut.

And when I bellowed, I knew those bastards could hear me.

"If I figure out that you assholes took me and still hurt my father, I'm gonna sic my motherfucking fiancée on you, and he's a damn cop! I won't stop until each and every one of you is--!"

The door slammed open, crashing into me before I went tumbling down the steps. I rolled head over heels on myself, slamming into the carpet at the bottom of the steps. I groaned in pain as I rolled over onto all fours. It took every ounce of strength I had to gather myself back to my feet. And the entire time, heavy footfalls echoed down the steps.

Tum. Tum. Tum.

Tum. Tum. Tum.

Tum. Tum. Tum.

I stumbled back toward the bed, trying to put distance between me and the beast lumbering down the steps. I panted for air as my head throbbed in pain. My entire body ached in places I didn't even know to exist, and I watched, waiting for his shadow to emerge.

Tum. Tum. Tum.

Tum. Tum. Tum.

Tum. Tum. Tum.

"Who are you, and what do you want?" I asked.

But when the man emerged, I found the one named

'Trooper' staring at me from across the room. Coming slowly toward me, his gaze locked and his grin wide.

Carrying what looked like a tray of food.

"Dinner time," he said as he set the tray on the bed.

I scooted behind it, pressing my back to the wall. He held his arms out, as if to present something I was supposed to compliment him for. I didn't care, though. I wasn't hungry. All I wanted was for Gordon to show up and whisk me away so that I could go back to my life.

Do I really want to go back to my life, though?

"My, my," he said as he raked his hungry gaze up and down my body, "scared looks good on you."

I swallowed hard. "How can I trust that my father is okay?"

He held up his finger, telling me to wait, of all things. Where the hell was I going? Where in the fuck did he think I'd dart off to, anyway? I watched as his hand slid into his pocket. His fingers dawdled around in his jeans, and as I watched those dexterous fingers slid against his thigh, I wondered who in the hell had the task of painting on those jeans he wore?

And why couldn't I stop staring at them?

"There we are," he said as he pulled out a cell phone. "Let's see... ah. There it is. Hold on a second."

He pressed a button before the room ignited with the sounds of a phone ringing. But I damn near came out of my skin when my father's voice flooded the room.

"Naomi? Is that you?" he asked quickly.

I vaulted over the fucking king-sized bed and snatched the phone out of Trooper's hand. "Daddy! Oh, Daddy. Are you all right? Are you safe? Is anyone with you right now?"

"I'm fine. I'm okay, Princess. Are you okay? Where did they take you? Have they hurt you?"

"Watch your questions, old man," Trooper warned.

I spun around and practically spat at the man. "Shut the fuck up or I'll make you shut the fuck up."

Trooper snickered. "Promises, promises."

"Princess, you have to listen to me. Those guys, they were-
-."

I shook my head. "Have you taken your meds? I know it's dinnertime. Have you taken them?"

Dad paused. "At a time like this? Stop worrying about me and start worrying about yourself. You've always been terrible at that, you know."

I groaned as I rolled my eyes. "Just answer my question. Have you taken your meds? Are you hurt? Has Gordon come to see you at all?"

I felt something bury its way into the tendrils of my hair before a force stronger than my own willpower yanked my head back.

"Watch it," Trooper warned.

I nodded my head quickly as Daddy kept rattling things off. "I haven't seen Gordon, Princess, but this isn't over. He's going to get you back. You know he is."

Trooper reached for the phone. "That's enough. Give it here."

I turned my back to him, trying to steal a few more seconds as my voice weakened with another set of tears. "You—haven't heard from him at all today? He didn't even come by?"

"No, Princess. Why?"

"Aaaaand, that's enough of that," Trooper said as he plucked the phone from my hand.

"Daddy! No! Give me that back! He still hasn't answered me! Have you taken your meds!?"

"Princess? What are they doing to you? Take your hands off my daughter!"

"I love you, Daddy! Take your god damn medication!" I cried out in desperation as tears streaked my cheeks.

"I love you, Princess. Stay safe! Gordon will handle this, I promise!"

And as Trooper hung up the call, I watched him take the battery out of the back. My eyes widened as he kept taking the damn cell phone apart, piece by piece, dropping it to the ground at his feet. With every piece that fell, I realized just how much trouble I was in. They used burner phones. They sold weapons and used motherfucking burner phones. And as he stomped his boots into each and every piece, shattering them into unusable slivers, I felt the breath being ripped from my lungs.

"Guess that fiancée doesn't really care about you after all," Trooper said as he kicked the pieces of the phone at me.

I moved my hand mindlessly toward my back pocket. Maybe I'd get lucky. Maybe my cell phone was still on me. But, as my hand slid along the back pocket of my jeans, the smoothness of its form stole my breath away. I dropped to my knees and picked the small chunks of the burner phone into my hands, studying their lifeless form.

I was fucked.

And for the first time in my life, I wished for Death to take me quick.

5

TROOPER

"Jesus, does she ever fucking stop?" I hissed as I dropped my fork onto my plate.

Ranger shrugged as he continued shoveling dinner into his face. "Stop what?"

I rolled my eyes. "Don't even play like you don't hear that shit. Dutch?"

He sipped his soup with his free hand in his lap like the proper little lady he was. "I think it's actually kind of nice."

I blinked. "Nice?"

He didn't bother looking at me as he took another slurp. "Yeah. Like Christmas music, or something."

Ranger chuckled. "Only you would think a bitch crying is background music."

"Christmas music," Dutch said as he took a bite of his sandwich. "There's a difference."

I groaned as I leaned back in my seat. "Well, I can't fucking stand it. When the hell is she gonna run out of energy and pass out?"

As her wailing grew louder, I found my hands pulsing for the heat of her neck. I hated that noise. The noise of a woman aimlessly drowning herself in her own fucking snot. It reminded me of how badly my mother used to cry at night before I killed that useless son of a bitch she wanted me to call a father.

Asshole had it coming, too.

No one hits my mom and gets away with it.

Ranger stretched out, his hand patting his protruding gut. "Who's turn is it to do the dishes?"

I stood quickly. "I'll do it."

Dutch picked up his bowl. "You did them last time."

I snatched the bowl out of his hand. "And I'll do them this time. Now, scram."

As the guys made their way out of the kitchen and back upstairs, I tried to busy myself with washing the dishes. Well, rinsing them off, anyway. I scrubbed them down, feeling the bubbles of the soap popping against my sun-toasted skin. The sun started setting over the water, casting shades of purple and pink throughout the sky.

And still, that woman downstairs couldn't put a fucking lid on it.

"Enough," I growled as I slammed the last dish into the washer. "If she won't shut up, I'll make her shut up."

She didn't have a reason to cry, anyway! She's the one that gave herself to us. If anything, she should've been thanking us that she wasn't already dead. I kicked the dishwasher closed with my foot and started the cycle, listening as the water pipes all kicked into gear.

Then I stormed into the basement, kicking the fucking door open with my foot.

"Jesus Christ, are you ever going to shut up!?" I bellowed as I emerged downstairs.

She scrambled to get behind the bed before she tucked that quivering lower lip of hers over her teeth.

Effectively shutting her up.

"See? Was that so hard?" I asked as I threw my arms out to either side.

Naomi wiped at her tears, and the motion of her arms alone drew my gaze back down her body. Christ, what I wouldn't give to see those curves jiggling for me as I stuffed her full of my dick. I licked my lips as her breathing grew ragged. As if she were spent from a night of carnal pleasures. But, as my gaze kept traveling downward, I found the food tray I had brought down to her.

Untouched.

"Ranger won't like that, you know," I said as I motioned to her untouched tray.

She sniffled. "Not hungry."

I walked over to the tray, and she yipped like a stray dog. She scurried out from behind the bed as I picked up the food, listening as she scampered over into the small L-shaped part of the basement that dumped itself into a decent-sized closet.

I pointed to the door. "Open it."

She looked over at the doorknob. "Why?"

I flinched toward her quickly and she jumped before doing as I asked. Dear God, why the hell did women ask so many fucking questions all the damn time? They were asinine, and unnecessary, and as I watched her quickly open the door, she paused.

"There's a table back here?" she asked.

I shrugged. "Where else were we going to put it? Go sit down."

Shockingly, she did as I asked without hesitation. Maybe she was finally coming to her senses. While she rubbernecked around at the closet-kitchen-infusion Dutch insisted on having down there, I sat the tray of cold food in front of her.

Before I sat in the chair off to her left.

"Look at it this way," I said as I picked up a piece of Hawaiian bread. "Free vacation. Am I right?"

I held it up to her lips, but she simply scoffed. "Yeah, sure. If you call captivity a walk in the park."

I shrugged. "Hey, you're the one that did this to yourself."

That's when she whipped her glittering gaze toward me, staring me down with a glare that could have killed me, given the chance. "No, you're the one that did this to *us*. So, are you going to tell me what the hell my father did that was so bad? Or, are you going to keep acting like--."

I shoved the bread into her open mouth. "He interrupted a very important transaction with a client."

She bit down into the bread and chewed. And chewed. And chewed some more before she took the rest of the bread from my hand and picked at it with her fingers. Plopping small bites between her lips like some dainty little thing.

She was far from dainty, though.

I couldn't wait to throw her around that basement a bit.

"You know, selling drugs is pretty stereotypical," she said as she kept picking at her bread. "I figured you guys would've at least been involved in something with a bit more... oomph to it."

I flashed her my best smile. "Do my teeth look rotted out to you? Because if they do, I'll have to contact my dentist. He's got some explaining to do."

She snickered as she shook her head, and I saw the shadow of a smile attempting to streak across her face. She did a good job with keeping it at bay, though.

Maybe too good of a job.

"Really, though," I said as I pushed the cup of soup toward her, "you need to eat. Range won't be happy that you haven't eaten yet."

She shrugged. "Tough shit. For all I know, that soup is poisoned."

I picked up her spoon, dipped it into the tomato soup, and took a sip of it. I placed it down and watched her while she watched me, her gaze searching for any sign of demise. I leaned back. I crossed my ankle over my knee. I relished her dutiful gaze, and I sure as hell clocked the way her eyes lingered upon the bulge beneath my jeans.

I tugged at it with my hand, and she quickly looked away, causing my grin to grow.

"So?" I asked as my head tilted off to the side. "You gonna eat? Or do I need to get the big guy again?"

She rolled her eyes before dipping the bread into the soup and tearing a hunk of it off with her teeth.

"You know, I like a more traditional girl myself," I said as I stood, "but Ranger would love how you just dug right in there with your hands."

She slowly looked up at me, her stare blank and vacant. "I don't give a shit what any of you think."

She held my gaze as she dipped the rest of the slab of bread into the tomato soup, damn near soaking it to the brim. Her narrowed stare held me captive as she unhinged her jaw like a fucking serpent and stuffed the entire thing into her cheeks. She looked like a goddamn hamster, with her cheeks jutting out the way they did. And every time she chewed, her mouth opened just a tad.

Right up Ranger's alley.

"You know," I said as I bent down into her face, "you should be careful showing us that pretty little mouth of yours. Never know what you might find stuffed in it."

She stopped chewing, and her face paled. Good. She needed to be afraid. She had no fucking clue who she was messing with, and if she wasn't careful, her blood would spill into the ocean along with her father's.

"Good girl," I said as I tapped her cheek.

She jerked away and damn near choked on her food in the process.

"Try not to kill yourself on the food while I'm gone," I said as I backtracked out of the closet. "I still have plans for you."

Hearing her speed up that chewing of hers made me damn near cackle. I knew she had something she wanted to say. A quip that so desperately wanted to fall from those plump lips of hers. But, as I turned around, I found her still chewing on the fucking loaf of bread she damn near choked herself with.

"Oh, and one more thing," I said as I grabbed the closet door, "Ranger wanted me to let you know that you can walk around this place as you please."

That jaw of hers worked overtime hours before she finally swallowed, chasing it down with the lukewarm soda that had likely lost all of its bite because it had sat open for far too long. Still, she washed down her Ranger-sized mouth full of food before standing to her feet.

"I can even go outside?" she asked.

It was cute, the hope in her voice. "You can certainly try. Though I don't think you'll like what you find when you do."

"What do you mean?"

I turned my back to her. "Enjoy your dinner."

"Seriously, what does that mean?"

"Eat it up before Ranger gets down here."

"Trooper!"

God damn it, I loved it when she said my name. "Have a nice evening!"

Even though she called out after me, I kept my pace. I propelled myself up the steps, quaintly leaving the door unlocked to see what she might do. Did I have Ranger's permission for any of it? Nah. But I was curious to see how badly she wanted to test us.

I was itching for a reason to punish her, anyway.

I leapt up the steps, two at a time, until I charged into my room on the second floor. It didn't take long for me to hear those scurrying little footsteps of hers rushing around downstairs, and oh, the smile it brought to my face. I perched at the bay window in my room, waiting for her to figure it out. Waiting for her to step outside, so I could prove to her just how fucked she was and how she needed to listen before Ranger decided he'd had enough.

Though a part of me enjoyed watching her struggle.

Or anyone else, for that matter.

Her footsteps grew furious as my door crashed open. Ranger's angry face stared me down, but all I did was crook my finger toward him. I nodded at the window. I patted the seat beside me as he walked into the room. And as Dutch joined us, his face was equally confused. We all peered out my window toward the northern side of the clubhouse.

Watching as Naomi found her way out onto the wrap-around porch.

"Noooooooooo!" she cried out.

"Now, she knows she's going nowhere," I said with pride.

Ranger patted my shoulder. "Good job. Maybe now she'll shut up."

6

———

NAOMI

I don't know how long I stood there, staring out at the water. I don't know how long I gazed up and down the road, watching and waiting for any sort of car to come by. The road was deserted. The land in front of us, deserted. The ocean, more deserted than I had ever seen it.

I was surrounded by nothingness.

And my hopes of Gordon finding me quickly dwindled.

At least Daddy's safe.

It was the only solace that kept me company as I watched the rest of the sun set over the water. I would have thought it beautiful, had it not been for the circumstances surrounding it. I found myself thanking my stars that I didn't have windows in the prison they had tossed me into, because if I had to stare at something so beautiful night after night while cooped up in that hellhole, I may have actually killed myself.

At least Daddy's safe.

As darkness draped over the world, I made my way back inside. If they had enough confidence to allow me to come outside, then I knew I was outnumbered. I couldn't see anyone, but that didn't mean they were there. Just like inside my father's house.

At least Daddy's safe.

I didn't know that for certain, though. As I laid down in bed, somehow making it back inside without someone harassing me in the process, I didn't sleep a wink. I kept thinking about all the things they were doing to my father. Beating him. Spitting on him. Mocking him. Starving him of his meds. For all I knew, they had gone back to my house the second they knew I was back inside just to dispose of him.

The thought made me so sick that I darted to the corner bathroom just in time to heave dinner into the sink.

"Oh—mmph—my God—blrgh."

Please Daddy, just be safe.

Chunks of bread threatened to choke the life out of me as red spewed from my throat. I gripped the sink, hanging on for dear life as my stomach doubled over onto itself. My knees gave out, crashing my clothed tits into the mess the sink had caught for me. And as I scrambled to get my legs back beneath me, a second round started.

A second round of dry heaving that rid me of whatever strength I had left.

"A hot shower helps me after a good puke."

The familiar voice behind me made me groan as I found the strength to pick my head up. My feet still slid around beneath me, but I managed to clock the thin stature of the man everyone called 'Dutch.'

Though, I was getting the feeling those weren't actually their names.

"If I wanted your opinion, I would have—mmph."

I puked into the sink again before catching my breath.

"I would have asked for it," I said breathlessly.

The man moved without a sound, his long legs carrying him

to my side. He pulled a water bottle seemingly from out of nowhere, and I heard the beautiful sound of him cracking the plastic top open.

"Rinse your mouth out," he said plainly.

I snatched it out of his hand before I straightened my back. My legs screamed at me to stop. They cried out for mercy and rest as I twisted the cap off and dropped it into the sink. I held the bottle up to his lips, mustering the rest of the strength I had within me.

And as my stare found those icy blue eyes of his, I rolled my shoulders back.

"You drink first."

He folded his hands together in front of him. "Poisoning isn't our thing."

"No, just kidnapping people off the street who piss you off. Now, drink it."

He snatched the bottle back out of my hand and raised it into the air, pouring it down the back of his throat. I watched that Adam's apple of his bob up and down, and for the smallest of moments, his figure entranced me. He was long and slender, like a ballerina, but with muscles that were etched against his bones.

It wasn't until he picked up my hand and placed the bottle against my skin that I came back to reality.

"Your turn," he said plainly.

I had to admit, the liquid tasted divine. After swishing some around in my mouth and spitting it out into the wretched-smelling sink, I guzzled the rest of it. Chug after chug, filling my empty stomach and sloshing around. I drained the bottle of every last drop before I handed it back to him, then I set my sights on cleaning out the sink.

Which basically just meant turning on the water and splashing it around a bit.

"So, do I even get to know the names of my captors?" I asked.

I watched his reflection in the mirror as he leaned against the wall. Again, making no noise as he moved. "I'm Dutch. The big one is Ranger, and the one who thinks he's funny is Trooper."

I blinked. "I meant your actual names."

He didn't hesitate. "Those were our given names after we pledged our crew."

I groaned as I finished washing out the sink. "Great, I've been taken by a gang."

In what felt like mere milliseconds, my arm twisted around behind me before my entire body whipped around. I would have yelped, had it not been for the fact that Dutch had a grip on the back of my neck. And as he shoved my cheek hard against the wall he had been leaning on, I stood on my tiptoes to try and get my arm free.

"Are you fucking nuts?" I choked out.

His mouth fell to the shell of my ear. "We're nothing like those pathetic street gangs that roam this sorry excuse for a coastline."

It was the first time I had riled up any of them, and it made me giggle. "Oh, I'm sorry, did I upset you? Poor thing."

He dropped my arm almost immediately, and I turned to face him. But that was a mistake, because the second I did, he wrapped that large hand with those dexterous, thin fingers of his around my throat and lifted me clear up off my feet.

Causing me to grip his forearm just to keep from choking to death.

"Dutch, I—I didn't--."

"Put her down," a gruff voice said.

Not just any voice, though.

Ranger.

The Behemoth.

Dutch dropped me without a second thought before he maneuvered around me, and as I forced myself to my feet, I looked up to find Ranger towering over me. Cloaking the whole of me in his shadow.

Before, he wrapped his hand around my arm and yanked me toward him.

"Ah!" I yelped.

He got right into my face. "The harder you make this for us, the harder we'll make it for you."

I heard a chuckle from behind the wall that separated the bathroom from the rest of the basement before Trooper's voice sounded. "My kinda play style."

"Shut up," Ranger growled.

The stench of my puke-covered tits didn't seem to phase them one bit, which only served to terrify me even more. "What do you want with me?"

Ranger tilted his head, but didn't release his grip. "You're going to help us get the money your father stole from us. Come with me."

"What? I don't know how—ah!"

He dragged me, literally dragged me, away from the bathroom and toward the basement stairs. The more I struggled against him, the tighter his grip became, until my entire hand went numb just from his grasp. I dug my heels into the floor, only for someone to kick them out from beneath me. Whether it was Dutch or Trooper, I couldn't say. But when they stumbled out from beneath me, my skin squeaked across the tiled floor of the main floor.

Before, Ranger tossed me into a chair.

"Tie her up," he commanded.

"What? No!" I exclaimed.

No matter how much I fought, Trooper and Dutch made

quick work. Before I could fucking blink, the tightness of the rope against the skin of my wrists and ankles shocked me into reality. I didn't have a choice. I had no options. Gordon hadn't come for me. Emergency had been too slow in our lazy fucking town. And I was in the claws of the Devil's Spawn.

Or whatever the hell they wanted to call themselves.

Sounds blurred together as the stench of my own vomit overwhelmed me. As if my body were willing to dehydrate itself on tears alone, they started streaking my cheeks again, and my mouth begged for more water. The slimy, foul taste of dinner stained the back of my throat. My clothes were torn and ragged from being tossed around by a bunch of men who I knew were going to kill me once they were done with me. After all, I knew their names. I'd seen their faces. There was no way in hell I had a life after they collected whatever measly sum of cash they were going after.

Tears dripped onto my chest, finding their death between my cleavage as they slipped beneath the collar of my shirt.

Before a phone got shoved into my face.

"You meet us as the exact coordinates, at the exact time, with the *exact* amount of money you owe us for the botched transaction, plus twenty percent for our heartache." Ranger demanded, "Or, she dies, and I put your god damn fingerprints all over her corpse. Your choice."

"What? No!" I cried out.

"Okay, okay, okay, okay! Fine! We can do it your way! We're sorry, all right. Just—can you just let her go? Or get her out of there? I'm telling you, we still want the guns, and our boss is more than willing t—."

I didn't even have the energy to cry out for help any longer. It wasn't as if I were surrounded by anyone with any decency.

Or heart, for that matter.

"Good," Ranger glowered, "see you soon."

And when he hung up the phone, I watched with watery eyes as he disassembled the phone. Piece by piece, just like Trooper had.

Before dropping them to the tiled floor and crushing them beneath his boot.

7

———

NAOMI

"Dutch!" Ranger barked. "With me. Trooper."

I heard the **thwip** of a blade being exposed before I felt the binds around my wrists and ankles fall away.

"Jesus, thank you," I said breathlessly.

"Take her back downstairs," Ranger commanded.

I whipped my head up. "No, please. I-I-I'll be good."

Trooper chuckled as he gripped my hair. "I bet you will be."

"No, no, no, no, no! Please!" I exclaimed as I fought against his grasp. "You said I could roam around the house! You said so! Trooper told me!"

The shadow of a grin ticked Ranger's cheeks. "Enjoy your evening, Naomi."

My skin crawled at the way he said my name. Trooper dragged me back to the basement door, and I flailed as hard as I could. I slammed myself into walls and kicked my legs out at him, trying to throw him off balance enough to get his hand out of my fucking hair. But the harder I fought him, the tighter his grip grew.

Until I felt strands of hair popping away from the top of my scalp.

"Let. Me. Go," I grunted as I struggled down the steps.

"You're a little tease, aren't ya?" Trooper growled.

"Ah!"

He tossed me toward the bed, and I slammed onto the mattress, face first. My trembling hands attempted to push me up, but before I caught my bearings, someone grabbed my ankles. Head over heels I went, my body being tossed around as if I weighed nothing. As if I were nothing but a hacky sack ball bouncing off the sides of people's feet.

Then, I heard the clinking of chains.

"What are you doing?" I glowered as I sat up.

Trooper stood to his feet, holding what looked like a chain with something red attached to the end of it. I squinted my eyes, my body frozen as he knelt on the mattress at the foot of the bed.

Before he snatched my ankle right out from beneath me.

"Fucking hell!" I exclaimed.

"The first one is always the...ugh... hardest," he grunted as I flailed around.

I kicked so hard that I damn near caught his jawline. He wrapped what I thought was a red piece of fabric around my ankle, but as he went to attach it, I felt the rough sensation of leather against my skin. And as he reached below the bed, brandishing yet another chain, I knew what was happening.

"Oh, hell no, you don't," I hissed.

I scurried along the bed, giving chase to the man attempting to chain me to it. I clamored off the bed and took off, wondering how far the chain would get me. But, as it halted me dead in my tracks, I fell to the ground and slammed my nose right into the carpet.

Sending tears toward my eyes as pain ricocheted through my skull.

"Please, don't do this," I said with a soft whimper.

"My, my," Trooper said as he yanked me up by my hair,

which seemed to be a signature move for him at that point. "You really are a fighter. What ever did I do to deserve such a prize?"

"I am no one's prize. You will never--."

"Whoopsie-daisy," he said as he scooped his arms beneath my body and tossed me back toward the bed, "must've slipped."

As I crashed back down onto the bed, the pain my nose kept sending throughout my entire body rooted me to my place. The jangling of chains and the feeling of leather tightening against my skin infiltrated my ankles and knees as I gazed up at a waving ceiling. It undulated side to side, as if water were penetrating its surface. And even though tears kept rising to my eyes —tears of pain, and fear, and anger—I refused to cry them any longer.

Not in front of cowards like Trooper.

"Leave some for the rest of us, will you?" Dutch called down the stairs.

Trooper chuckled before he called back. "Can't promise anything, Dee!"

My lower lip quivered slightly before I tucked it over my teeth. No weakness. No mercy. No fear.

I wouldn't give them a damn bit of what they wanted.

"Just kill me already, if that's what the endgame is," I spat.

I tugged at the restraints as my tears grew hotter, but I forced myself to stop moving. Trooper stood at the foot of the bed, his shadow moving around and up my right side before he stood over me, his gaze playful and foreboding.

Any man who got some sort of sick joy out of what was happening wasn't a man to be fucked with.

I watched him unsheathe his knife before the ***thwip*** of the blade made me swallow hard.

"Oh, don't stop on my account," he said as he ran his knife alongside his smooth jawline. "I love a good struggle."

I hocked the biggest motherfucking loogie on the face of the planet, just like Gordon hated, and spat it right at his face. I watched it cling to his nose, splattering across his cheeks so much that he had to close his eyes. And as he closed his gaze to wipe his face, I started tugging furiously at the restraints. Jiggling around, and tossing my arms and legs, hoping to find a weak joint that snapped those motherfuckers right out from beneath the bed.

But, as he wiped his face off and his eyes opened, I stopped my fight.

I wouldn't give him a damn bit of what he wished.

"It really is cute, you know, how you try your best to show us how strong you are," Trooper said with a grin on his face.

I snarled up at him. "I hope you choke on your own shit one of these days."

He walked down to my hips before placing his knife along the underside of my jeans. "I'm more of a knife play kind of guy, to be honest."

I gasped when he slipped the knife underneath the fabric of my jeans. Right at my ankle, where the cool touch of the metal graced the angry heat of my skin. My jaw clacked together, my teeth chattering as if a cold spell had just dawned upon us, and as he ran the knife along the inside of my leg, my jeans gave way as if they were nothing but butter.

He carved those pants off me until one single rip from his hands exposed my entire lower body.

I knew what was coming, and I knew I was helpless to stop it.

"I'll never consent," I said, my voice frogging out from the effort to keep from crying out in sheer fear.

He moved like lightning, swift and agile, holding his knife up to my throat. I lifted my head, extending my neck as far as I could in the hopes that he wouldn't gut me where I laid. I squeezed my eyes closed. I curled my toes, waiting for the inevitable.

Then, I felt his hand cup my clothed pussy.

"You don't have to, Naomi," Trooper purred as he traced my neck with the flat side of his knife. "Your body already has. I mean, just look at how eager your hips are."

I shook my head softly. "Mm-mm."

"Go on," he urged with a snakelike temptation, "just take a quick peek. I promise, the view it worth it."

I drew in a deep breath before I peeked an eye open, and I saw the confused cacophony my body had given away. My nipples puckered so tightly that they shone through my bra and tank top. My skin flushed slowly from head to toe, and the burning of my cheeks matched the burning of my thighs. Even I smelled my pussy, desperately wanting to unfurl for someone's dexterous touch.

It had been so long since Gordon and I had indulged in anything close to sex, and as my hips pressed harder against Trooper's hand, a shocking thought crossed my mind.

Might as well get something out of this whole situation.

"Mmm, such a delightful scent, too," Trooper said softly as he knelt on the side of the bed. "I wonder if that fiancée of yours enjoys that smell."

I yanked at my binds, and that caused him to slide the knife back up to my throat. I lifted my chin and closed my eyes, waiting for the small slice that would spill my blood all over the bed. It didn't come, though. Even though I anticipated it— expected it—it never came.

Instead, I felt him dip his fingers beneath my panties as his knife stayed put against my pulse point.

"Ooooh, so wet," Trooper growled.

My breathing grew ragged as he parted my stubbled pussy lips.

"You know, if you were mine," he said as he devoured me with his gaze, "I wouldn't let you shave. Such a waste. There's nothing better than the texture of a woman's hair tickling my cock just before I plunge into her depths."

"Oh," I moaned softly, a sound that crept through my lips no matter how hard I tried to keep it at bay.

And Trooper's chuckle washed over me like a goddamn flood of lava, warming me from head to toe in places Gordon had never once touched.

"Such a good girl for me," Trooper murmured as he leaned down into my ear. "Does Gordon think you're a good girl?"

I swallowed hard as his fingertips found my bulging clit. "I-I-I—I don't know."

He nipped at the shell of my ear, and I damn near blew through the roof. "Well, he should, if you spread this easily for him."

I shook my head quickly. "I-I-I—oh, fuck!"

The second he slid a finger into my pulsing entrance, my back arched. It came clear off the bed, and with it a bombastic laugh fell from Trooper's lips. It blanketed me, weighing me back down to the bed, as if he were mocking me all the while proving his point.

But fucking hell, he did have some lovely fingers.

"Now, where's that lovely little... spot?" he asked.

I groaned the second his fingers rumbled over that pebbled little place. "Shit."

"Mm, mm, mm. Do you kiss your father with that mouth?"

As the pad of his thumb touched down against my throbbing clit, I wondered how in the hell he felt this good. Long forgotten was the knife at my throat as my hips bucked with pleasure. Long forgotten was the anger I felt toward him for binding me to the bed after just being freed moments before. Long forgotten was my circumstance, and in its place came euphoric ecstasy in the form of none other than Trooper's hands. And as I ground against him, my heels digging into the bed itself, I sought my end.

After all, I practically deserved it, at that point.

"I love a girl who takes what she wants," Trooper growled.

"Fuck, fuck, fuck. So good. So good," I choked out.

Trooper hissed in my ear. "You're lucky I'm not talking to all of you right now, because you'd never hang on well enough for that ride."

I flickered my half-hooded gaze toward him. "I see someone thinks highly of themselves."

His gaze met mine, and the sincerity behind them filled my gut with more heat than I would have wished. "One day, pretty girl, I'll fill you with my dick. And then, you'll get the picture."

I found myself hoping he was right.

Fire coursed through my veins as my body continued to cave to him. My toes curled, arching my back as my head tilted onto the pillow. His fingers teased me. His thumb tickled my clit. It traced along its outline, sending shockwaves of electricity surging through my body. My mind fell blank. My eyes rolled into the back of my head. All I knew was my impending orgasm. All I wanted was for it to crash over me so that I could release some of the fucking stress I'd been carrying around for much too long.

"So close. So close. So close," I panted softly.

"There it is," Trooper purred as he raised up. "Come for me, Naomi. Be the good little girl I know you so desperately wish to be."

"Oh, fuck!" I cried out.

Everything came to a grinding halt. The prickling cold of his knife pressed heavily into my neck as my hips bucked ravenously for his touch. My eyes rolled back, with fireworks bursting in the darkness. My hands twisted into the bedsheet beneath my body. My juices dripped down my ass crack, flooding his hand as my pussy pulsed around his digits. His thumb stayed put, allowing me to use it at will as my hips darted around like a hummingbird drinking from a flower.

"Troop—er," I choked out.

And as I reached up for him, trying to hold on to something other than the bed, the restraints stopped me.

Halting my orgasm in its tracks.

"Ah," Trooper said as he eased his hand out from between my legs, "coming back down to reality, I see?"

I closed my eyes before he could see the tears rising in them once more. "Yeah, I guess you could say that."

"Open your eyes."

"No," I said plainly.

He quickly pivoted the knife, and I felt its sharp fangs seated against my soaking wet panties. "Open your eyes, little Naomi."

I slowly opened them, which allowed silent tears to spill down my cheeks. The guilt that overwhelmed me choked off my ability to breathe. I struggled to contain myself. To contain the hurt and betrayal that fell against my tired body. That wasn't cheating, right? I mean, I could have consented and enjoyed myself, sparing my mind the trauma, or I could have continued to fight and endured the pain that came with it. The trauma that came with it. Gordon would understand. He'd know that I'd never cheat on him in a million years. Not willingly. Not unless under complete duress.

Right?

"Naooooomi?" Trooper singsonged playfully.

"What?" I choked out before licking my dried-out lips.

I watched him hold his glistening fingers up to his mouth.

My eyebrows rise as he stuck his fingers into his cheek, lapping off every droplet I had afforded him. He hummed in ecstasy, as if he were face-first in a slice of warm chocolate pie. And I had to admit, it was entrancing.

"You really do taste as good as you look, pretty girl," Trooper's gravelly voice proclaimed.

My gaze dropped to the bulge against his pants, and the thickness alone made my jaw drop open.

"Oh, don't you worry your pretty little self over that," he said as he gripped my chin, forcing my gaze to cling to his. "If you're a good girl, you'll get it in due time."

I hated how much I wanted to feel him. How much I wanted him to do that to me, over and over again, until I passed out from sheer exhaustion. It had been so long since a body-shattering orgasm had torn through me like that, and the guilt alone pushed tears to the edges of my eyes. Guilt cut off my ability to breathe, and I had to switch to my nose. I wasn't a cheat. I would have never consented had I thought any other choice was possible.

He'll understand. Gordon will understand once he finds me in this shithole.

But I whimpered as he traced his thumb along my lower lip. A thumb that smelled of me. That smelled of my womanhood. And as he left small traces of my scent along my own skin, the chanting in my head grew louder.

He'll understand. He'll understand. He'll understand and be proud of what you did to survive.

Jesus Christ, though, how lovely it would have been to have come twice.

"Now, clean yourself up," Trooper's hardened voice said as he sheathed his knife. "The restraints are a simple latch mechanism. You'll be able to free yourself just fine. Give me your hand."

I held my right wrist up to him and watched as he undid the damn thing like you would a fucking dog collar.

Then he turned his back to me and left me in my own juices.

Leaving me breathless as my body finally readied itself to slip into what was surprisingly a decent night's sleep.

8

———

DUTCH

BOOM! BOOM! BOOM! "Dutch! Get the hell up! Church time!"

I groaned as I rolled over in bed. "What time?"

BOOM! BOOM! "Twenty minutes!"

"Jesus fucking--," I hissed as I tossed my arm over my face, "yeah, yeah. I'm up."

BOOM! "One more for good measure!"

"Fuck you, too," I groaned.

The sound of motorcycles rumbling up the street rattled my ribcage. It sounded like the damn apocalypse descending upon us, but it shouldn't have surprised me. The big day was upon us. After scouting out our meet-up area yesterday, it didn't shock me that Ranger wanted to be in everyone's ear one last time before we cleaned up the mess Naomi's father had made.

And yet, I was pissed that I didn't have time to shower.

"Gross," I murmured as I threw the covers off me.

Lumbering into the bathroom always gave me a shock to my system. The tiled floors were always piercingly cold, so I splashed some hot water onto my face. I stared at the bags beneath my eyes. Jesus Christ, when did I get so old?

"When Ranger started waking me up in the mornings," I murmured.

I cleaned myself up as much as I could. Well, as much as I could stand, anyway. I hated the feeling of being unclean. Dirt had no place in my world, and neither did smell. I practically took a whore's bath at the sink, scrubbing my armpits and groin with a soapy washcloth. And after doing the best that I could under the circumstances, I dried off before slipping into some clothes.

I arrived in the conference room on the third floor just in time to slip into my seat before Ranger turned to face us like the dramatic bitch he always had been.

"Today's the day we get paid, everyone," our President said as he placed his hands on top of the table. "Dutch and I scouted out the place yesterday, and it's primed for the exchange."

Bury, one of our newest prospects, cleared his throat. "Y'all need a lookout for the exchange?"

I shook my head. "Nowhere to perch you."

Ranger pointed at me. "Dutch has this one under control. This isn't a learning transaction for anyone. We need this done, and we needed this done yesterday."

Trooper kicked his feet up onto the table before he started playing with one of his smaller sets of knives. "What time is everything taking place?"

"Me and Dutch leave in an hour."

Bury tilted his head. "You're doing this in the middle of the day? Is that smart?"

Ranger shot him a look. "The area where we'll be is concealed in darkness. No point in waiting any longer than necessary."

"Don't worry," I said as I peered over at Bury's worried face, "we'll get your money in time for your mother's payment to the hospital."

I felt bad for the man. I really did. His mother had been diagnosed with cancer for the third time in her life, and this time was the most aggressive. They were buried under mounds of medical debt, hence why Trooper practically dragged him to us, kicking and screaming.

If anything, we owed it to the members of this crew that needed this money to simply survive.

"So," Trooper said as he kicked his feet back off the table, "want to walk us through how this is going to happen?"

Ranger finally took a seat as all eyes turned to face him. "We're meeting at--."

"Is someone going to bring me breakfast!?"

My brow furrowed. "Is that--?"

Thump, thump, thump. "Hello? Can anybody hear me!?"

Trooper chuckled. "Such a riotous one, she is."

Ranger shot him a look. "You haven't fucking fed her yet?"

Trooper shrugged as he walked his fingertips over the blade of his knife. "Didn't know she was awake, quite honestly."

"I'm starving down here!" Naomi's muffled voice exclaimed as it pierced the hardwood floor beneath our feet.

And that's when Lancer started to laugh. "Maybe one of us should take her for a ride. You know, show that girl her place."

My hand moved so quickly toward that motherfucker's throat that someone actually gasped.

"What did you say?" I asked calmly, my fingers curling into Lancer's pulse points along either side of his neck.

He opened his mouth and choked for air. "I just—Dutch—I can't—."

"Dee," Trooper said curtly.

I released the pathetic excuse for a man and eased myself back into my chair. "You leave her to us. Got it?"

Lancer rubbed his neck as he stared at me with widened eyes. "Jesus, Dutch. What gives?"

I crossed my leg over my knee and settled my hands into my lap as I felt Ranger's inquisitive look boring a hole into my forehead.

"So, you were saying?" I asked, locking my tired gaze with his.

Ranger's nose wrinkled softly before he cleared his throat. "The transaction is taking place at our throwaway warehouse. Dutch and I plan on making examples out of these buyers. They come ready to screw us over? We come ready to lock them inside and torch the place."

"Did they agree to the twenty percent surcharge?" Bury asked.

Ranger nodded. "Without hesitation. Dutch is lookout while I solidify the transaction, and if everything goes according to plan this time around, every single one of you will see payment for your part in this by the end of the day."

Lancer cleared his throat. "Anything else you need from us, you know all you gotta do is say so."

Ranger grinned. "Maybe work on keeping that mouth in check for now."

The guys chuckled as I looked down at my hands. There was something about all of this that didn't sit right with me. Not the transaction, mind you. But, Naomi. Her fiancée was a cop. So, why hadn't we had a run-in with the police yet? Unless she had been bluffing about that part in an attempt to—.

"Dutch!" Trooper called out.

Something knocked against my forehead before it fell in my lap, and the guys started holding back their laughter as I gazed at the triangular piece of paper that had flopped into my lap.

"Real mature, Troop," I said as I picked it up between my fingertips.

"Says the guy daydreaming about the girl downstairs," he said with a grin.

I put the triangular-shaped object between my fingers and flicked it at him, sending it soaring for his neck. It sliced against his skin, causing him to hiss as he clapped his hand over his neck.

"Seriously? A paper cut, at a time like this?" Trooper asked.

I turned my attention back to Ranger. "We don't have much time."

Ranger nodded as he stood. "Everyone stays here until I radio in with the all clear. Then, you're dismissed. Dutch? You're with me. Trooper?"

He stood to his feet. "Keep an eye on the guys, I know. I know."

And as Ranger clapped his hands three times before dismissing church with the flick of his wrists, I headed straight for the kitchen.

The very least someone could do was put together a goddamn meal for the poor girl before we turned our sights to more important things.

My earpiece crackled to life as I sat there in my camouflage, perched on the roof of the warehouse.

"See anything?" Ranger asked.

I peered through the scope of my rifle. "Dust kicking up in the distance. They're finally here."

"Good. If they come ready to transact, maybe I won't charge them for the six minutes they've made us wait."

I caught their SUV coming down the road. "Nice vehicle they're in. Maybe ask for the pink slips."

Ranger barked with laughter. "You and those pink slips."

I shifted a bit with the wind, listening as it rustled through the trees. "Can't ever have enough pink slips. That's practically my side hustle."

"You mean the half-a-mil you make every year isn't enough?"

I clocked the SUV as it came to a halt in the middle of the warehouse's abandoned gravel parking lot. "Not for these rifles, it isn't. Also, heads up. They've parked."

"Thanks, I'll take it from here."

Watching those two men scramble to get out of the vehicle brought a smile to my face. Good. At least they knew they were fucked. The two men threw the back doors of the SUV open, carrying two duffle bags a piece, no doubt stacked with the money they owed us.

I heard that TrackingPoint XS1 rifle calling my name as the two men disappeared inside.

"They're in," I murmured as I recalibrated my position.

"Got eyes on them. Hang tight," Ranger murmured before he cleared his throat. "Gentlemen. You got what I need?"

I loved being the lookout. There was no better spot in the world than sitting in a place that made people feel as if they were alone. The fear in men's eyes before they encountered us fueled some of the best dreams I'd ever had in my life. Watching them scramble like two little kids in trouble with Mommy Dear filled me with an unmistakable amount of pride. My rifle glistened in the rays of sun allowed through the heavy treetop canopies that had overgrown around the warehouse. A relic from another time, completely forgotten by society.

It was still my most impressive donation to the crew, to this day.

I heard the unzipping of the duffle bags while Ranger murmured to himself. No doubt, counting the money right in front of them in order to make sure it was all there. Every time he surpassed another million, my skin prickled. Goosebumps of satisfaction flushed its way across my skin, and I couldn't wait for that money to hit my account.

I had so many plans for this particular stack of funds.

"Good," Ranger said, "follow me."

That was my cue, and I silenced my footsteps as I scrambled along the roof of the warehouse. Silence was my friend, and darkness, my shroud. I moved nimbly over the concavities of the caved-in roof, leaping toward safety before I perched my rifle on my shoulder.

I peered over the edge of the rooftop and watched as Ranger led the two men toward the navy-blue hatchback car the two of us had jumped in to get to our final destination.

"No bikes?" one of the guys joked as he started chuckling.

I didn't have to be down there to witness the look Ranger shot the man, and it shut him up right in his tracks.

"Here," Ranger said as he popped the trunk, "take it and go. You've got five minutes before my partner starts blowing out your tires."

"Partner?" one of the guys asked.

And when Ranger pointed up at me, I aimed down my sights at both of the men.

Before popping off a bullet in between their bodies.

"Holy shit," one of the guys hissed.

"Come on, let's get out of here," the other guy said, as he started scrambling.

Ranger's chuckle spread a smirk across my face. Watching them run was the highlight of my day. I followed them along the outside of the building, keeping my sights trained on them at all times. They tripped over themselves, dropping bags while Ranger hauled a goddamn wooden box filled with ammunition with his own two hands.

I swear, I couldn't pay any streaming service for that kind of entertainment.

"Now," Ranger said as he loaded the ammunitions box into their trunk, "get the fuck out of here before I change my mind. And tell your boss that if he ever wants to do business again? He better get it right the first fucking time."

The second he closed their trunk door, the two men scampered like little baby deer toward the front of the vehicle. They slammed themselves inside, practically toppling over themselves as the one behind the wheel struggled to get the damn key into the ignition. Ranger stood there, his arms crossed over his chest, looming over them with that etched look of murder on his face.

I kept my sights trained on their wheels until they were out of sight, out of mind.

Then Ranger turned to face me on the roof. "You wanna get down here and come stick your face in this money?"

I disengaged my rifle and tossed it over my shoulder. "How about we get out of here first? Just in case."

He nodded. "Good point. Let's go."

With my rifle slotted into a holster across my back, I leapt off the edge of the roof. With my hand clinging to the side, I tossed my feet over until I felt them tiptoe along a window's ledge. I released my hand, dropping myself before my fingers caught me on the ledge, scaling one level after another, using nothing but my hands until I dropped down to my feet.

"You really are a spider monkey, you know that?" Ranger asked as he pulled an apple out of his pocket.

I furrowed my brow. "Has that been there this whole time?"

He shrugged. "A man's gotta eat."

I rolled my eyes as I brushed past him. "Come on. I'll drive."

With our money stowed away in the trunk, we blazed a trail back to the clubhouse. Dirt kicked up beneath the fresh tires of our crew's group form of transport when we needed to keep a low profile while riding together. Vans were too conspicuous, and our bikes were way too fucking loud, so whenever we could wiggle a vehicle out of one of our buyers, we did.

Plus, the constant exchanging of vehicles helped us to keep a low profile within city limits.

Yet another idea the crew could thank me for.

"A hundred bucks says Trooper's already fucked her," Ranger said as he hit the highway.

I chuckled to myself. "You know how that bastard is. He's probably teasing her right now."

"You got any plans for her yet?"

I crossed my leg over my knee. "I'll let you two go first before I hit her with the grand finale."

"What if she doesn't like cocky assholes?"

I started picking at the dirt beneath my scrawny finger-nails. "Every girl likes a cocky asshole. What they don't like is an actual asshole, and you wear that role better than any of us."

Ranger snickered. "And don't you forget it."

The ride back to the clubhouse was always longer than the journey there, mostly to shake a tail and avoid any risks of expo-sure in the process. But, once we pulled into the parking lot of the clubhouse, I saw Trooper hanging out on the porch with those big-ass feet of his just chilling on the porch railing. He had a beer in his hand and a smile on his face, which only meant one of two things.

He had either dove headfirst into Naomi's luscious body, or he had already allocated his funds to something stupid.

Like those damn knives of his.

He had, like, twenty-two sets of them just hanging out all over the walls of his room.

"Weirdo," I murmured.

"Hey, Troop!" Ranger exclaimed as he threw his car door open. "Wanna give me a hand with the grocery bags?"

I slipped my door open and stood to my feet. "So, Ranger and I have a bet going."

Trooper stood to his feet and threw back the rest of his beer. "Oh? What kind of bet? Is it one I can participate in?"

"It's about you, actually," I said as I walked toward the trunk of the car.

Trooper leapt over the railing and came soaring toward us. "I knew I felt my hears burning. What's the bet?"

Ranger pulled out a duffle bag and tossed it to him. "You fucked her yet? Or no?"

Trooper didn't even have to answer for me to pinpoint. "Ha-HAH! Just a tease, right? You're way too cocky with those fingers—Ranger? Ante up," I said as I held my hand out toward him.

Ranger grumbled beneath his breath as he pulled out his wallet and slapped a hundred-dollar bill into my hand. "Fucking waste, if you ask me."

I folded my hand over the money before tucking it into my hip pocket. "So, how was she?"

Trooper shoved his fingers into my face. "Smell 'em, and weep."

Ranger barked with laughter as I shoved his hand out of my face. "Yeah, no thanks."

Trooper shrugged as he hauled his duffle bag toward the porch. "Suit yourself. But you're the one missing out."

"You got another one of those beers?" Ranger asked as he tossed me a duffle bag.

I caught it and headed toward the porch. "Make that two."

Trooper tossed the bag into the house before pointing toward the cooler. "Help yourself."

Ranger tossed his two bags in before I set mine on the floor near the coat rack. "Don't mind if I do."

"You fed the girl lunch yet?" Ranger asked.

I walked over to the cooler and dug out drinks for both myself and him. "Yeah, she's kind of no good to us if you starve her."

Trooper grinned as he closed the front door. "I should've fed her something else, honestly. Lesson learned, I guess."

I handed Ranger his beer, and he snatched it out of my hand. "Gotta go place some calls. Get this money allocated. Don't sit out here too long. We need to keep a low profile for the next forty-eight hours."

"We know, we know," Trooper said as he flopped back down into his chair. "Just give us enough time for a beer and we'll come inside."

"You better," Ranger murmured as he cracked open his glass bottle.

And as he headed inside, I eased myself into the rocking chair next to Trooper.

"We really need to make sure we feed her on time," I said as I opened my own beer. "A girl can't live on dick alone."

Trooper snickered as he clinked his fresh beer with mine. "She likes it more than she realizes. I don't think that fiancée of hers has dicked her down for a while."

"Shame," I said before I took a long pull from my drink. "What a waste."

He patted my shoulder. "You're telling me."

I had to admit, the sun on my face felt nice. "Got any plans for this one?"

Trooper knew what I meant. "I've got my eyes on a nice, shiny new prize."

I rolled my eyes. "Pretty soon, you won't have room on those walls of yours to store anything else."

"And that's half the fun, Dee. Half the fun."

I sat there, gazing out over the deserted flatlands of the plot of land the crew had purchased scores before I had ever pledged myself to the Twisted Metal crew. Had anyone told me that one day, I'd be the lead Enforcer for one of the liveliest crews on the West Coast, I would have punched their fucking lights out. After all, the U.S. Army didn't take too kindly to their men working for the other side.

And yet, when I found myself no longer re-upping my contract as a young twenty-something, that's exactly what happened.

More money in it, too, which was nice.

"What about you?" Trooper asked after finishing his drink. "Got any plans for this one?"

I grinned at the idea. "You'll see when the time comes."

"You know I love a good surprise."

CRASH!

THUD!

"Ah!"

"God damn it," I groaned as I downed the rest of my beer.

Trooper chuckled. "You want to check, or should I?"

I pushed myself onto my feet. "I'll do it. Better go make sure Ranger doesn't break the poor girl."

"I expect details," Trooper called out after me as I headed inside.

Making my way to the basement in the hopes that the girl wasn't fucking dead after pissing off our in-house Mountain Man.

9

RANGER

"Son of a fucking nut sack, stupid goddamn—come on," I grumbled.

I tossed some soup into a bowl and thrusted it into the microwave. Why the hell Trooper didn't give a shit about feeding the girl was beyond me. Everyone needed food, and we sure as fuck weren't in the business of starving people to death. So, while the scent of tomato soup permeated the kitchen, I set my sights on making my favorite sandwich for our very noisy guest.

Bologna and mayonnaise, with a hint of Dijon mustard.

"Hey, Troop!" I bellowed.

I heard the front door crack open. "What?"

I reached for some produce in the fridge. "You think the girl downstairs likes tomato on her sandwiches?"

The pause told me everything I needed to know. "Why the fuck would I care?"

"Why the fuck would I care?" I mocked beneath my breath. "Thanks for nothing, asshole!"

The front door slammed closed, and I set my sights on slicing the tomato as thin as possible. No use in putting chunks of tomato on a sandwich if she was only going to pick them off. Me? I loved a good sandwich. A bit of salt, some pepper, lots of meat piled high with lettuce, tomato, and onion.

If she didn't like it, it was her problem.

"Dinner time," I murmured.

I carried the tray downstairs, with the staircase creaking beneath my footsteps. Even as a new construction almost four years ago, the damned floors sounded like they'd cave any second whenever I was around. The basement door hung wide open behind me as I turned myself to the side, making room for my fucking shoulders.

"You hungry?" I asked as I touched down on the carpeted floor of the basement.

Not hearing her answer agitated me, but when I looked up to find her, I saw why she was pissed.

"Jesus, he tied you down again?" I asked as I set the tray at the foot of her bed. "Come here. Jesus fucking Christ, Troop."

She laid there, still as stone, with her gaze locked on the ceiling. If I didn't know any better, I would have thought she died, were it not for the way her thick tits slowly rose and fell with her breathing. It was hard not to stare. She was an angel wrapped in a coat of thickness that called to my fingertips. But the second I untied her appendages, she scrambled to the headboard.

Before she curled her knees as close to her chest as possible.

"You good?" I asked.

She glared at me, but didn't speak. So, I simply pointed to the food at the opposite end of the bed.

"Eat."

She tilted her head. "No."

I rolled my eyes. "You're gonna need your strength, so eat."

She scoffed. "Why? So you can fuck me, too?"

"You're not my type."

She held her head high with pride. "Good, because I don't like small dicks anyway."

Why the hell did women always go for the small dick jokes? It was trite and overdone. And yet, it did exactly what it always did.

It pissed me off enough for my forearm to jut out and slam against her neck.

CRASH!

THUD!

"Ah!" she cried out.

I heard the food clatter to the floor as I gnashed my teeth together. "You can be smart, or you can be alive. But you can't be both. Got it?"

"Fuck you," she choked out.

Before she spat a throat full of snot right into my eyes.

"Stupid bitch!" I bellowed.

I felt her scrambling. I heard the bed groaning beneath her movements. But she underestimated me. With a swipe of my hand in midair, I felt the tendrils of her hair grace my palm. Not quite how I had imagined it, but then again, we couldn't have everything we wanted in life. And as I yanked her off the bed, her spit dripping down my face, I slammed her back against the wall.

Before pinning her there with my knee between her quivering thighs.

"Let me go, you Beast!"

I held her throat against the wall with my bare hand as I used the other one to wipe at my eyes. "I can still feel your whore juices, little one."

She snarled like a feral animal. "Takes one to feel o—help!"

I gripped the locks of her hair and tossed her back to the bed, watching her bounce on top of the mattress. "Maybe a good fuck will shut you up."

My hands didn't even get migrated to my belt buckle well enough before she thrusted her foot out, jamming her heel straight into my balls. The pain was blinding, but I'd be a fucker in hell if she'd ever see me buckle to her. My toes curled inside of my steel-toed boots. I ground my teeth together, damn near biting through my motherfucking tongue as I kept my gaze hot on her face.

And as she slowly withdrew her foot, she giggled tritely. "Heh heh. Well, isn't that... interesting."

I licked my lips as a growl fell from my tongue. "Come here, bitch."

"No!" she yelped.

I reached for her across the bed, ready to pull her to its edge before pinning her beneath me and showing her exactly who owned her. But she pushed herself off the edge of the bed, tumbling to the floor before scrambling across the food.

"You'll never catch me, you son of a bitch!" she exclaimed as she bolted for the door.

And as she left a trail of tomato soup in her wake, Dutch appeared out of the darkness.

Stopping her dead in her tracks as she ran straight into his chest.

"Now," Dutch said as he gazed down at her body sprawled out at his feet, "where are you going at this time of the day?"

She launched herself back to her feet, and I had to admit, she was agile for a woman of her girth.

"None of you are touching me," she said as she pivoted her pointed finger between the two of us. "Do you hear me? None of you!"

Dutch took a step into the basement. Then another, and another still. Backing her up with every movement of his impossibly long stride.

"Pretty sure you already broke that promise to yourself the

moment you let Trooper touch you," he said, as he sniffed the air around her. "And I have to admit, I'm a bit jealous."

The pain finally subsided between my legs enough for me to move, and I made way for her movements. With every step Dutch took forward, she had to take two backward, and before we knew it, she fell to the edge of the bed, her curves bouncing with the shivering of her body.

I smelled the fear dripping from her skin.

Along with the scent of her womanhood wafting from that pussy of hers.

"So," Dutch said as he gripped her chin, forcing her to look up at him, "what are we going to do about your punishment?"

Tears crested her eyes as her lower lip started quivering. "Pu-pun-punishment?"

He snickered as he knelt one knee on the bed between her glorious thighs. "Don't act like you don't know exactly what I'm talking about. Trying to escape? Fighting us every step of the way? You're a regular--."

"It's no fun when they don't want it," I said curtly.

Dutch paused before his gaze dropped to her trembling lip. "She smells divine, though."

I reached out my hand and gripped the collar of his leather jacket before yanking him away. "Your last warning."

Dutch shrugged off my touch before turning to face me with that deathly cold stare of his. "You have a soft spot for her, too. Don't you?"

I wrapped my hands in his shirt and pulled him so close that I felt his uneven breath on my face. He should have been worried, too.

We didn't hurt what was in our possession.

"It's no fun. When they don't. Want it."

He held up his hands in mock surrender. "Whatever you say, Range."

He shoved me away from him before sliding his hands down his shirt. I kept my attention clung to him as he tossed Naomi a playful wink. I knew he'd be back. I knew he'd have her before we figured out what in the hell to do with her. But betraying the ideals of our crew was never an option.

And we never hurt what we owned.

"Thank you."

Naomi's soft voice barely met my ears as Dutch disappeared into the darkness of the staircase. I walked toward it, stopping midway between her perched position on the bed and the door I needed to lock her behind. She didn't deserve the freedom we had given her. And yet, as I raked my gaze up and down her body, something about her told me she wouldn't run.

Which struck me as odd.

"Cause anymore fuss, and we'll throw you to the dogs," I spat.

She nodded quickly. "Understood."

I turned my back to her. "And trust me, they don't like women as much as we do."

She snickered. "Could've fooled me."

I closed the gap between me and the basement stairs. "Clean up the mess you made, and if you do a good job, I'll bring you some more."

"And if I don't want to be your personal slave?"

I peered over my shoulder. "You don't play nice, you don't eat."

She sprang to her feet. "Now, wait a second. I thought you just said--."

I turned my entire body toward her, my fists clenched at my sides. Every single muscle in my body pulled taut as frustration overwhelmed my sense of realism. I had always prided myself on keeping a cool head. On being the voice of reason whenever we had a victim at our disposal. But somehow, this girl had crept beneath my skin and pissed me the fuck off.

Causing my voice to bellow across the entirety of the basement.

"Shape up, or STARVE!!"

And as she crashed back down to the mattress, her curves dancing for my eyes to behold, I turned around and made my way back up the steps with the sound of her soft crying following me around. I didn't care, though. I couldn't. I had more important things to take care of than to babysit some self-entitled, spoiled little brat.

Things like getting my men paid.

10

TROOPER

"Morning," I said as I traipsed into the kitchen.

Dutch simply waved his hand from behind the newspaper while Ranger stood gazing out the kitchen window.

"You fed the girl yet?" I asked.

Ranger simply shrugged, though. "Does it matter?"

My eyebrows rose as I looked over at Dutch, and even he had come out from behind his morning reading.

"You, uh," I said with a grin, "you done with her or something?"

He sipped his coffee. "Or something."

I stole another glance at Dutch and practically saw light volleying around in his eyes. We knew what that meant for us, and we were ready for it.

It had been a long time since we'd had any kind of fun in our clubhouse.

"Well," I said as I walked over to the kitchen cabinets, "guess I'll take her breakfast, then."

"I'm sure you will," Dutch said with a chuckle.

And when Ranger didn't interject, I knew she had done a number on him.

"How's your dick?" I asked as I started stacking the plate with breakfast.

Ranger shot me a look. "You'll find out in a few seconds if you don't shut up."

I patted his shoulder as I made my way to the refrigerator. "Just drink your coffee, Big Man. We know you need at least three before you can talk."

He grumbled beneath his breath, but I didn't bother catching what he had said. After all, I had an impromptu breakfast date to keep. So, with a plate of food and a cold glass of apple juice, I made my way into the basement to greet the woman of the hour.

Only to find her bed completely empty.

"Oh, boy," I said breathlessly as I sat the food and drink on the dresser beside the bed.

"Naomi?" I asked. "You in here?"

I didn't want to say her name too loudly because I knew what would happen if Ranger found this room empty. He'd kill her. Despite all the rules we followed and the code we pledged ourselves to, Ranger was a fucking monster in the mornings without his caffeine.

He'd kill her if I didn't find her.

"Naomi," I said curtly, "this isn't funny. You're gambling with your life. Now, come out and have breakfast. I know you didn't eat last night, so you've gotta be hungry."

When her voice didn't echo back at me, I rushed over to the closet. I threw the door open and checked every single corner before lunging toward the shower. I threw the curtain back, ashamed to admit that she wasn't there. And after getting down onto my hands and knees to check beneath the bed, I sprinted back up the steps.

"Everything okay?" Dutch called out.

"Yep!" I exclaimed.

I skipped the main floor. If she had been there, we would have already found her. Heard her, or smelled her, or generally come across her. So, I bolted up the steps to the second floor. Door after door, I threw open, checking closets and underneath beds.

She had to be somewhere.

We were screwed if she wasn't.

"Naomi," I hissed, "where the fuck are you? This isn't funny any longer."

I knew there was no reason for her to be on the third floor. After all, the only thing that was up there—other than a bath-room—was the conference room and the--.

"The balcony," I murmured.

Fucking hell, she was going to jump.

I'd never moved so quickly in all my life. Panic gripped my throat in ways I simply couldn't explain as I hoofed it up the steps. I crashed through the door into the conference room, finding the chairs cockeyed from the last church meeting Ranger had called.

And there, out on the third-floor balcony, overlooking the cliff side that fell straight into the ocean, was Naomi.

With her legs dangling off the ocean side.

"It's a long way down if you jump," I said as I held my hand out in front of me.

She shrugged. "Pretty much the point, don't you think?"

Her words hit a bit too close to home, and I knew I had to find a way to talk her out of it. "Any reason why you want to jump?"

Her gaze slowly pivoted over her shoulder, and the shocked stare that dripped over her features made me regret my question.

"You honestly can't figure out one single reason just by looking around you?"

I slowly held out my other hand, but didn't dare approach her without warning. "I know an unhappy soul when I see it, Naomi. And you were far from happy when we found you in that house."

She turned her gaze back toward the unending horizon, and my soul sympathized with her. Had my heart been able to reach out and comfort her, it would have. I knew how she felt, not being happy with her life, but not seeing a way out of that unhappiness. It was a dark place. A place of hopelessness and failure. Like you tried your best, over and over again, yet nothing ever comes of it except more darkness.

More hopelessness.

More failure.

"You know," I said as I slowly lowered my hands, "my father loved snorting lines off the scars he gave Mom during his drunken fits of rage."

Her head tilted to the side, but she didn't speak. So, I continued.

"He sold everything he could get his hands on for his next high. And when we had nothing else to sell, he sold Mom."

I took a step toward her, and she didn't move.

"If he wasn't beating on her with something, he was selling her body to his drug dealers for his next fix. And there wasn't a thing I could do about it. Everything Mom ever bought me to try to distract me from my life, he stole. Everything she ever tried to get me out of that situation. He thwarted. He wanted me there. He wanted me to see his power over us."

She cracked her neck. "Sounds like someone deserves to die."

I grinned to myself. "Don't worry, I took care of that some time ago."

That whipped her gaze back over her shoulder. "You killed your own father?"

I shrugged. "If you found your father raping your mother, wouldn't you kill him, too?"

She licked her lips as those gears turned behind her eyes, and I swear to hell on high the movement of her tongue alone arrested my attention.

"Good on you," she said as she turned back toward the balcony view. "Some people don't deserve the life they've been given."

Not many people shocked me in my life. I expected the worst and welcomed the best. But, as those words fell from her plump little lips, I found myself impressed. I never thought she'd have it in her, quite honestly. She did such a good job of making herself seem so prim and proper. Down to earth, but with an honest moral code.

In another life...

"Are you still close with your mother?" she asked.

I took that as an invitation to go stand beside her, but I made sure to keep a hand close in case she thrusted herself off the balcony. And as I stood next to her, I drew in a deep breath of ocean-salted air.

"Not after she kicked me out and called me a murderous traitor, no," I said plainly.

She nodded mindlessly, and I knew she was no longer on the same planet as me.

"Penny for your thoughts?" I asked, as I nudged her.

"Huh?"

I grinned as she looked over at me. "Or, another orgasm. I'm up for that, too."

She smiled and shook her head. And I swear to hell on high that the heavens opened up a bit more. The sun shone a bit brighter.

It was amazing, the way her smile lit up her emerald green gaze.

"Naomi, right?"

She furrowed her brow. "What?"

"That's your name?"

She nodded. "Yeah, it is."

I held my hand out to her. "Pretty name for a pretty girl. I'm Trooper."

She looked down at my hand before she placed her palm against mine. "It's nice to meet you, Trooper."

I shook her hand, and her warmth sizzled up the expanse of my arm. "It's lovely to meet you, too."

She quickly pulled her hand away and retreated back into her mind, her gaze unfocused and locked.

"What's on your mind, pretty girl?" I asked.

And much to my surprise, she answered me. "When I got to the house and saw my father's front door open, I texted my fiancée. Told him there was a problem. And I guess I'm just... wondering why he never showed up. He always shows up. He should've showed up."

I leaned against the railing and faced her. "Sounds like a shit fiancée, if you ask me."

She didn't fight me on it, either.

Guess she'd been doing a lot of thinking in that basement.

"I mean, does he at least dick you down well?" I asked.

She barked with laughter, her entire body coming to life with the chorus of a thousand singing angels. She teetered back along the railing, her legs outstretched as the wind kicked up. I wrapped one of my arms beneath her back, catching her as she released bubbles of laughter she simply couldn't hold back. But when the wind caught her body, it rocked her the other way.

Damn near sending her over the edge.

"Trooper!" she exclaimed.

She clung to me, holding onto my clothing for dear life. The happiness in her gaze quickly gave way to fear, and as she clutched my t-shirt, I wrapped my arms around her.

Preventing her from falling over an edge she had wanted to plunge herself into mere minutes ago.

"I gotcha," I said as I cradled her close. "I'm not letting you go."

She looked up at me from beneath those long eyelashes of hers. "You're not?"

I shook my head. "No. Not ever."

Her eyes danced between mine. "Outside of the other night, the last time I'd ever orgasmed like that was months ago."

I shook my head. "That man shouldn't be allowed to get married with those kinds of sins under his belt."

She leaned her forehead into my chest. "Yeah, especially when he wakes me up with it."

My grasp tightened around her. "Wakes you up with what?"

"Can you help me off this thing? My ass is going numb."

I scooped her into my arms without a second thought and placed her on her feet. "Wakes you up with what, Naomi?"

She refused to look at me, so I gripped her chin and forced her to stare at me.

"I won't ask again," I said, my voice lowering with very syllable.

She cleared her throat. "It doesn't matter, anyway. Not like I'm ever going to see him again."

I pulled her face so close to mine that her breath pulsed against my mouth. "What does he wake you up with, pretty girl?"

And as a whimper bypassed her parted lips, she said the two words that sealed his fucking fate.

"His dick," she whispered.

Because those two little words told me everything I needed to know regarding how she felt about it.

"Enjoy the view," I said as I released her.

"Where are you going?" she asked quickly.

I walked back inside. "Help yourself to the kitchen as well. Whatever you find, you can have."

"Trooper!"

"And Naomi?" I asked as I spun around.

"Yeah?" she asked breathlessly.

"Don't jump. From someone who understands," I said as I turned my wrists over to show her the long, dexterous scars, "it isn't worth it."

"Oh, Trooper," she whispered.

"Help yourself to the house," I said as I turned around, heading for the stairs. "I'll see you tonight. I've got things to take care of."

Like figuring out every single shred of fucking information I could find on her pathetic excuse for a fiancée.

Which meant I had to talk to Dutch.

11

———

DUTCH

Zzzt.

Zzzt.

Zzzt.

SHING!

I loved sharpening my knives. The way they glistened afterward rivaled the most beautiful of sunsets. That twinkling sound when optimal sharpness had been achieved rang in my eardrums, and as I held the knife to the light, a smile overtook my face.

"There we go, sweet girl," I whispered. "Just like ne--."

SKADOOSH! "Naomi's fiancée is a cop."

I tilted my head toward my door that had crashed into the wall of my bedroom as Troop's voice slammed into me.

"Didn't we already know that?"

He scoffed as he stepped into my room. "The girl, Naomi, has a fiancée that's a cop."

I set my knife down and picked up another one. "Don't tell me you didn't know her name. Even I knew her name before now."

And as I gripped my sharpening stone, I went back to those soothing, repetitive movements.

"You panicking because Range doesn't know this?" I asked.

There was something in his voice that didn't sound quite right when he answered me. "Her name, or about her fiancée?"

"Both? Either?"

The sigh that escaped him stopped my movements. "Haven't gone to talk with him yet."

"But you're here because he thinks he's a threat and you want him gone. Right?"

Troop nodded. "Something like that."

I turned my attention back to my knife.

"I don't kill men blindly," I said as I focused on the shimmer finally emerging against the blade. "That's Range's territory."

That's when Trooper started spitting it out. "I don't want him dead... yet."

"Then what is it you *do* want?"

His voice vibrated as he spoke. "She just admitted to me that her fiancée borderline rapes her."

My movements froze. "What do you mean, borderline?"

He rushed toward me and perched on the edge of my bed in front of me. "She was just upstairs on the balcony. About the jump. The whole nine."

My eyes narrowed as I studied his face. "But, she's all right?"

He waved his hand in the air as his voice grew hoarse.

It always grew hoarse when he was pissed.

"Yeah, yeah, she's all right," he said before he raked his hands through his hair. "But she did admit to me that he wakes her up with his cock in the mornings and doesn't even have the decency to give her a fucking orgasm in the process."

I turned my attention back to my knife. "It's a shame, but it doesn't sound like--."

"She also said he doesn't ask permission first."

My knuckles turned white as I clutched the hilt of my knife. "He what now?"

Troop stood. "See!?"

It took every single ounce of energy I had to control my breathing. "That's—it's--."

"It's not right, is what it is."

I forced myself to pick up my sharpening stone and kept smoothing it against the blade in my hand.

"It's savage is what it is," I said through gritted teeth. And as I held my shimmering blade up to the light, I thought about what it might look like with that bastard's blood dripping down it.

"So? Will you get us some information about him? Anything other than what we already know?" Troop asked.

I stood to my feet and grabbed both of my knives, one for each hip. And as I tucked them into the holsters on my belt, I cleared my throat.

"Give me a day and I'll have a file on him."

Troop sighed with relief as he stood. "Thank fuck. Okay, one down, one to go."

I ran down a brief plan for my day in my head. "You going to talk to Range?"

He rushed toward my bedroom door. "I have to talk with him about her fiancee's profession. Make sure he knows. I feel like he knows, but--."

"Trooper."

He peeked over at me. "What?"

I nodded. "Deep breaths. Get your voice back first."

His nostrils flared with what I knew was anger. "Yeah. Yeah, yeah. You're right."

I walked up to him and patted his shoulder. "In the meantime, do you know where Naomi is?"

"You're going to tell her?"

"No, but I am going to get her perspective on something. Now, do you know where she is?"

He shook his head. "Your guess is as good as mine."

I reached down and opened the door. "Don't wait up. I'll be back when I'm satisfied."

With my two best friends holstered on my person, I charged through the hallway. I didn't know where Ranger had gotten off to, and I honestly didn't care. I had a question I wanted to ask Naomi. I needed to read her face. Hear her voice. See her reaction in order for me to make my decision.

She was just upstairs on the balcony. About to jump. The whole nine.

"Let's see if someone still likes the view," I murmured to myself.

I pivoted on my heels and started in toward the kitchen. The wrap-around porch had been Troop's idea. He was always a sucker for a pretty sunset. However, I enjoyed gazing out at the water for a slightly different purpose.

And something told me Naomi felt the same way.

As I slipped through the cracked side door that sat just off to the left of the kitchen, I heard sniffles coming from the back deck. I silenced my footsteps, my hands clasped behind my back as I formatted the conversation in my head. Did I ask her outright? Would she like a conversation first?

Jesus, I'm shit at conversation.

As I turned the corner and found her leaning against the deck railing, a gust of wind kicked up. Her brown hair seemed to sparkle with little bits of shining colors that reminded me of the honey my foster mother used to gather out back. I tilted my head, watching as the soft blanket she had wrapped around her shoulders fluttered about helplessly, revealing the soft and subtle curves she possessed beneath.

It almost made me want to reach out and--.

"Ah! Dutch!"

Her exclamation jerked me out of my trance as her hand gripped her heart.

"Jesus Christ, do you ever make any noise when you walk? I didn't even know you were there!"

I nodded. "That's usually the point."

Naomi scoffed as her gaze fell to the knives on my belt. "Are you here to kill me or something?"

I shook my head. "That's not the point of this encounter, no."

"What's the point, then, Your Highness?"

I furrowed my brow, but I didn't hesitate to walk up to her. The heat of her body reached out to me. Even as she pressed herself against the railing, I locked my gaze with her wide green stare as I searched her soul for the answer I sought.

She was a locked vault, though. So, I cleared my throat.

"Troop is under the impression that your fiancée rapes you."

Naomi blinked. "Oh."

"Is that the case?"

She balked. "What!? No. I never said that to him, and I don't know where he's getting it from."

I tilted my head as the grip I had on my own hands behind my back grew tighter. "So, it isn't true that your fiancée likes to wake you up with sex in the mornings without your permission."

She paused. "Well, I--."

"Do you enjoy it when he does this?"

Her gaze sank in defeat. "Not necessarily. Though, sometimes it isn't the greatest."

"Do you guys ever have a conversation about it beforehand?"

She blinked. "A conversation about what?"

"Sex. Waking you up with it. Has he ever talked about it with you?"

She shrugged. "Doesn't there come a point in a relationship where you really don't have to have that conversation?"

Anger bubbled beneath my skin. "So, let me make sure I have this right: he doesn't ask for your permission, you don't always like it, and he doesn't have a conversation with you about it beforehand. But he still has sex with you when you're unconscious."

Her brow furrowed and her gaze grew unfocused. "I mean, I guess if you wanted to boil it down--."

"That's rape, Naomi."

And as she slowly turned her back to me, the shaky breath she drew in sealed my afternoon plans.

"I can take care of him," I said as I stared out over the ocean waters above her head, "if that's something you want."

She shook her head softly. "I don't even know what that means anymore."

"It means whatever you'd like it to mean."

"I don't know what you're asking, Dutch," she said as her voice grew hardened. "But I don't want him dead, if that's what you're trying to ask. I'm not a shithead, like you guys."

A smirk crawled across my face before I forced it back down into the pit of my gut. "So, your fiancée's a cop?"

"Good to know Trooper's got a big mouth," she murmured.

"In your opinion, Naomi, is he a threat?"

She peered at me from over her shoulder, and even with the anger and sadness that swirled behind her pristine peridot eyes, she was the most beautiful woman I'd ever seen.

"I don't know what you mean," she said breathlessly.

I locked her stare with my own. "Is he going to cause us trouble? Is he going to come after you?"

I had my answer when she refused to give hers. But a movement caught the corner of my eye, dragging my attention down to her hands. They were perched on the wooden deck railing, her fingers softly playing with the engagement ring still seated on her plump little left hand ring finger.

What a pathetically small diamond.

That told me everything I needed to know right there. No man ever cheaped out on an engagement ring unless he didn't care for the woman he was proposing to. What purpose any man would have to propose without actually loving someone was beyond me. But something told me it had to do with his career advancement.

Because while I'd never met her fiancée, he struck me as the kind of douchebag that would do whatever it took to get ahead.

"Are you done with your questions now?" Naomi asked.

I turned around and started inside. "If you need somewhere quiet to think, there's a hidden door in the hallway off the living room. Third panel on the left. Press in and push up."

"What?"

I paused at the door and drew in a deep breath. "You deserve better."

I slowly turned my head toward her and found her staring at me with those watery eyes of hers.

A woman like her shouldn't cry so much.

"You deserve better than him," I said.

She swallowed hard. "Tha—thank you."

"Remember," I said as I stepped inside, "third panel on the left. Press in. Push up."

"W-w-wait a second," she said as the pitter patter of her little footsteps rushed up behind me. "Where are you going?"

I tore through the kitchen as I focused on my first goal of the day. "I have a cop to see."

"Please, don't kill him!"

I stormed down the hallway toward the front door. "I make no promises."

"Dutch, please!"

As I ripped open the front door, I ran the plan in my head one last time. First, I had to find what station he worked at. Then, I had to figure out where she lived. After that, I needed to pinpoint hobbies. What that asshole did for fun when he wasn't torturing a woman he has promised to love with the measly dollar-store ring he had purchased. I needed to know what he was doing to find Naomi. Whether he had put together a task force, or even reached out to other, less ideal people in the area. We all needed to know if he was hot on our trail, or completely ignoring the issue.

And if that meant the man died today, then so be it.

One less shithead in the world ruining all the good women.

"Here we go," I said as I slung my leg over my bike, "time to prep my file."

12

NAOMI

The revving of a bike engine pulled me out of my trance, and I took off for the kitchen door. I threw it open, not bothering to close it as I dashed down the hallway. What in the hell was Dutch about to do? Why had he kept asking me all of those questions about Gordon?

"Dutch!" I exclaimed as I ripped the front door open.

I was too late, though. Much too late. All I heard was the bike engine revving off in the distance as a cloud of dust came soaring in my direction. I sputtered with my coughing as I shut the front door. The wind kicked up again, slamming the dust against the window as the sound of little rocks tinked against the glass.

Shit, the kitchen door.

My ears locked with the sound of his motorcycle. It fell quickly off in the distance, revving and roaring until the sound was nothing but a distant hum, swallowed up by the sounds of the ocean. Dust coated the kitchen floor as I raced toward it. I managed to fight against the air current long enough to latch the door in place, but as I looked down at the dusty footprints I had left in my wake, my ears lost all contact with Dutch's bike.

For all I knew, they'd bring me Gordon's head as a threat to keep me compliant.

You know they're not gonna do that.

I pushed the voice in my head off to the side. I didn't like that voice. As I frantically searched for a broom, I tried my best not to acknowledge the fact that I was warming up to the guys. I mean, I didn't hate them, and that wasn't something I thought I'd ever feel. Three men who tried to abduct my father, and I didn't hate them?

"What the hell is wrong with me?" I hissed.

After finally locating a broom in the pantry, of all places, I started the arduous task of sweeping up dust. It gave me time to think. Time to consider the position I had been put in. They had given me free-roaming privileges, after all. Hell, I damn near jumped into the ocean itself, had it not been for Trooper tracking me down.

Maybe if I simply... walked out the front door, they wouldn't notice.

You know, until one of their dicks needed a bit of attention.

He didn't fuck you.

That was the most confusing thing of all. Trooper had me right there. He had me strapped down to the nines, flailing beneath him. He could have easily taken what he wanted. And yet, he didn't.

"Jesus, I need to get out of here," I whispered to myself.

After sweeping the dust up into a pile, I took a chance and cracked the door open. The wind was still coming, but not as great as it had been, and it enabled me to sweep the dust outside before it got caught up in the dust. It swirled about like a miniature tornado ripping through our world. And as it spiraled off the edge of the deck, I wondered what it would be like to be swept up with it.

Carried away to a place where life didn't seem so... impossible.

Remember, third panel on the left. Press in. Push up.

"Couldn't hurt, I guess," I said through my heavy sigh.

I didn't know what to think any longer. Nothing made sense. It was as if my own personal nightmare had come to life, complete with Gordon abandoning me and everything. It made me sick with frustration simply to think about him. Shouldn't he have already found me by now? What the hell was taking him so long?

Maybe he doesn't want to find you.

"Shut up," I glowered as I found the hallway Dutch had been talking about.

"One. Two. Three."

As I rumbled my fingertips over the wall panels to my left, I stopped in front of the third one. I shook my head as I stared at it, running my fingertips along what Dutch said was a door. It didn't look like a door, though. No handle. No hinges. Hell, even when I knocked on the wall, it wasn't as if it sounded hollow or anything. Still, I leaned against it until I heard the tell-tale latching sound before pushing up, just like Dutch said.

And as the wall caught onto something, it began rolling up.

Only to reveal the beast within.

"Guess you talked to Dutch," Ranger said.

I stood there, frozen in my spot.

"Well?" he asked as he stood from the couch.

I nodded, but I found myself unable to speak.

Ranger scoffed as he shook his head. "Damn man's got a big mouth."

"At least he's not a big asshole."

He stalked toward me, his shadow already cloaking the whole of me, even though there was still at least fifteen feet of room between us.

"You keep that shit up," he said as he finally closed the distance between us, "and I'll lock you in that basement for good."

I shrugged. "Try your best."

He took another step forward, right in between my legs, and I stumbled to try to get away from him. I backed up, hoping to give him enough room to simply skirt on by with no other words exchanged between us. Trooper and Dutch didn't scare me one damn bit. But, Behemoth over here? He scared the shit out of me.

My plan didn't work, though, because the second my back sank against the wall across the hallway, he placed his hands against it.

On either side of my head.

"Troop and Dutch seem to be seduced by you," he said as a grin worked its way across his scarred cheeks, "but I see right through you. They may feel you've earned privileges to roam around, but don't think for one fucking second that I don't always have my eye on you."

I snickered. "Kinky. Do you treat all your girlfriends this way?"

The growl that fell from his lips had nothing on the searing heat that bombarded my skin when he wrapped his hand around my neck.

And in that moment, part of me hoped he might snap it.

"Go ahead," I said as my voice fell flat. "See if I care."

I closed my eyes, waiting for the permanent darkness to overtake me. I didn't care any longer. You know, whether I lived or died. I had hit rock bottom, and I had no strength to climb back out of the grave I had somehow dug for myself. I deserved it, anyway. I had stuck with a man I'd been questioning for years. I allowed him to control my schedule and use up my sick days for his stupid last-minute plans. I allowed him unfettered access to my body if it kept him happy. After all, I couldn't cook, and I was never home long enough to clean. The least I could do was give him sex whenever he wanted it.

God, what a miserable life I had carved out for myself.

"Turn off the lights when you're done," Ranger said.

His hand slid away from my neck as my eyes slowly opened. "What?"

He started down the hallway. "And close the door. Troop's terrible about closing that door. It lets out all the good air."

I furrowed my brow. "What?"

"And for fuck's sake," he said as he turned to face me, "don't--."

I cleared my throat. "Do you hate everyone all the time? Or, just those that aren't afraid of you?"

He held out his arms as if he were a god. "Does an ant fear a boot before it's too late?"

"You're monsters," I said as I shook my head. "All of you."

He turned his back to me once more and turned the corner. "Well, judging by the sound of your fiancée, he's more of a monster than we'll ever be."

His words ripped the air from my lungs, and I found it hard to breathe.

"And for fuck's sake," he said as he poked his head back around the corner, "don't leave the fucking television running. Runs up the damn bills."

To this day, I'm still not sure how long I stood there. A minute. An hour. An entire day. It all felt the same. But once my legs started moving, they didn't stop until I crossed the threshold of the hidden room. The door leapt to life, hissing and griping in its own little way as it slid down the wall and back into place. The door latched, and the lights dimmed, illuminating the space with such a romance that it almost felt like heaven. The sconces along the wall flickered with a warm white light. Almost as if they were candles and not lightbulbs. The warm light beneath the couch caught my eye, lighting up the plush carpet beneath my bare feet. I curled my toes into its warmth. I lugged my tired body toward the oversized couch and flopped down, allowing the cushions to swallow me whole. And as I gazed up at the ceiling, I found myself surrounded by books.

Floor to ceiling shelving, with books. And DVDs. And games.

Video games. Board games. Card games.

It made me wonder who decorated the room in the first place.

Though, something told me it had been Dutch.

"God," I groaned as I rolled over, "maybe I can get some--."

Kshhh! "Get down! Get down! Get down!"

"Aaaaahhhh!"

KABOOM!

I jerked up at the sounds, making myself dizzy as something hard beneath my thigh clicked. Light poured from the wall to my left, and as I shielded my eyes, I tried to reach for the protrusion beneath me.

Only for the light to keep flickering, with all sorts of voices coming through.

"The Galapagos Islands are home to--."

Kshhh!

"Run! Run! Run for your life!"

Kshhh!

"You can't handle the--!"

Kshhh!

"God damn it!" I yelped as I finally yanked the remote control out from beneath my leg. "Shut up!"

I pressed the red power button and the box of doom powered down. Silence filled the room once more with nothing but the sounds of the gusting wind outside creaking the bones of the house every once in a while. I flopped down, tossing the remote off to the side. I'd never been one for television. That had always been Gordon's avenue. I preferred a good book, or a nice walk, or maybe even a bit of an impromptu afternoon swim.

Gordon didn't like to swim, though.

Not after he almost drowned as a child.

Do you have anything in common with him at all?

I groaned. "You shut up, too."

I pulled a couch pillow over my head and stuffed it as close to my ears as I could stand. I wanted the voice in my head to shut up. That little narrative voice that had pissed me off over the years with all sorts of nonsense and fuckery. That voice had gotten me into a lot of trouble as a child. Sneaking out with Gordon. Riding to school with him on his bike and getting my skirt caught in the chain. Changing my nursing school of choice because he wanted me to stay closer to him after we graduated.

Accepting his half-assed proposal.

"Can it," I grumbled.

I curled my legs as close to my chest as I could stand and closed my eyes. My head pounded with an ache so deeply embedded into my system that I wasn't sure I'd be able to make it go away. Maybe if I slept long enough, I'd wake up feeling better.

Maybe if I slept long enough, I'd wake up from this hellish nightmare.

Maybe if I slept long enough, I'd wake up and find myself back in bed with Gordon calling after me and Dad coming over with breakfast.

And as I laid there, thinking about being back home, happiness didn't overcome me as much as I thought it would. It didn't bring me peace or serenity. It didn't give me something to look forward to, or work toward. It was just... another memory. Another world. Another lifetime, or so it felt.

Which pulled silent tears down my cheeks as I succumbed to the darkness around me.

Hoping and praying that when I woke up, I was anywhere else but there.

Anywhere else but home.

Anywhere else but inside of the nightmare I had created for myself.

13

DUTCH

"Hahaha! That's some bullshit, Dogma. You know you fucked up."

The man with the bald spot scoffed. "Are you ever gonna shut the hell up with that nickname?"

Gordon, the man with the beady eyes and wry smile, slapped the man's shoulder. "When you stop pissing me off with that Saran Wrap bullshit. I damn near pissed all over my shoes this morning!"

It made me sick to watch, and that was a first for me. As I sat there, perched on an abandoned rooftop a quarter of a mile away from the downtown police precinct, I pointed my cone of communication—as I so aptly called it—right toward that motherfucker as he stood underneath the awning of the front door of his place of work.

While shooting the shit with a friend as if his fiancée hadn't gone missing.

Does he even know she's missing?

My knives pulsed against my hip bones. What I wouldn't give to plunge them directly into his chest. Men like him made me sick. Every single laugh that fell from his fish-thin lips made me want to yank his testicles up through his throat. Sure, we peddled weapons. But, he was on another level of disgusting we never broached.

We gave a shit about the women around us.

"Hey, hey, hey," the man named 'Dogma' said as he slapped Gordon's gut, "you, uh, workin' out there?"

Gordon snickered. "The only workout I get nowadays is convincing my girl I deserve a blowie."

Dogma barked with laughter. "I told ya not to propose. That's when shit goes south."

Gordon tossed his cigarette to the ground and stomped it out. "Bah. Sex has been shit for years now. Yanking it in the shower is nothing new for me."

I ought to shoot you in the dick.

What good-for-nothing bullshit little boy laughed with his co-worker about his goddamn sex like while his woman was missing? If my woman had been missing, I'd be out there mowing motherfuckers down with my knives across their throats until I had her back in my arms.

That man didn't deserve her.

And Naomi deserved to know who she was really engaged to.

"Time for some pictures, asshole," I murmured to myself.

I gathered some worn-down bricks together and created a small perch to sit. With headphones on my ears recording everything I heard, I reached around behind me and slid my backpack off. The asinine conversation I had to torture myself with grew tiresome quickly. The men talked about everything from their lack of sex lives to how disgusting the Reuben sandwich was at the deli up north all the way down to court dates where they had to appear and give testimony.

And not one single time did Naomi's disappearance come up.

"She really knows how to pick them," I murmured as I screwed the lens onto my camera.

Snapping pictures of that asshole throwing his head back in laughter brought me a great deal of pride. That man didn't love her. Hell, for all we knew, he didn't have a fucking clue as to the fact that she had gone missing in the first place. I zoomed in and snapped as many pictures as possible. Pictures of him and the guys that shook hands with him as they came out of the precinct. Pictures of this 'Dogma' asshole and the cigarettes they traded back and forth, chain-smoking like a bunch of backwoods shitheads.

Maybe once Naomi saw that no one was coming for her at all, she'd change her tune with us.

"Hey! Lockwood! Traeger! Get your asses inside and get to work!"

Dogma and Gordon looked at one another before Gordon grinned. "Sure thing, Cap."

The man, decorated in all sorts of patches and medals, pointed to Dogma's hand. "Got an extra for me?"

Dogma smiled as he brandished a cigarette for his boss. "Of course. Here ya go."

Cap nodded toward the doors. "Now, get your asses inside. The mayor's on his way."

As Dogma hightailed it inside, I watched Gordon step off the sidewalk. I followed him with the lens of my camera, watching him dig around in his pocket before he pulled out a set of keys. I kept him in my sights. I watched him unlock a Navy blue Subaru Forester before he reached inside for something, and a grin as wild as Ranger's booming voice peeled across my cheeks.

Now, I knew what vehicle he drove.

I packed up my gear as quickly as possible while I listened through my headphones to their captain sucking that damn stogey down in three or four puffs. It made me shake my head as I packed everything away and clamored down off the side of that building. The worn-out brick gave me some great footholds for my toes, which made scaling the outside of the building as easy as slicing a hot knife through ice cream.

Then, I dug around in my pocket until I pulled out the GPS tracker that had been burning a hole in my thigh.

I got you now, you son of a bitch.

"All right, asshole. Let's see what you're really up to."

As Gordon finally came out the front door of the police precinct, it was damn near dinner time. I had waited outside for nearly five fucking hours, waiting for that man to reappear. There was something about all of this that didn't sit right with me. A piece of the puzzle I was missing that might help me translate exactly what I was looking at. I mean, Gordon didn't even look to be grieving! And that meant only one of two things:

Either he didn't know Naomi was missing, or he didn't have to worry about her retrieval.

And it was the latter that made me follow him all the way home.

Tailing someone is an art. It takes precision, attention, and prompt execution in order to work correctly. I hadn't chosen the best vehicle for the day, either. My bike made too much noise, which meant that the GPS tracker was my only saving grace. I couldn't be revving around town while trying to keep a low profile three car lengths behind the man. So, as I watched the GPS screen on the tablet I held in my hands, I watched as he pulled his car out of the parking lot.

Then turned left to head toward Main Street.

Let's see what you get up to tonight.

I kept a good distance behind him. At least ten different car lengths. And with my bike engine being swallowed up by after-work traffic, I felt comfortable pulling out my camera and snapping pictures of each and every store he dipped into after leaving his office. First stop? The grocery store. What every man thinks of when the love of his life goes missing.

"Maybe he'll make a good Reuben for dinner just to stick it to them," I said as a smirk spread across my face.

After groceries, it was a drive-thru. A greasy burger with a double order of fries after spending $102.34 in the store picking up food. Yes, I knew how much his bill had been. After all, what good were stealth movements if you couldn't put them to practice every once in a while?

I loved tailing that asshole.

He had it coming to him, anyway.

Then he pulled back out onto the main road. I waited for two traffic light sequences before pulling out as well, then relied on my tablet to tell me where in the hell he was going. I cut through a couple of alleyways, only to see him dart down a back road instead of staying on the main road. And as I waited for an opening so I could follow him into the darkness, that little voice in my head came to life.

Go up and around. Box him in.

I turned on my left-hand turn signal and blazed a trail into traffic. Horns honked as I cut off cars, and I did exactly what my gut told me I needed to do. Instead of following behind him, I kept one eye on my mounted tablet and the other on the road in front of me. I went up two entire blocks before taking a right, and something inside of me screamed to stop.

So, not only did I stop, but I scrambled to get my bike hidden behind an abandoned dumpster before I searched for some sort of rooftop fire escape.

"Come on," I grumbled, "there has to be one somewhere."

Every time I checked my tablet, the GPS tracker hadn't moved. Instead of going home, he had parked himself in the middle of a stack of buildings that had been under construction for almost two damn years. For all I knew, he had found the tracker and ditched it. Or, hell, maybe he had abandoned his entire vehicle in the process!

Gordon didn't strike me as intelligent, though.

In fact, Gordon didn't strike me as anything other than some ordinary police officer.

So, why were the hairs on the nape of my neck standing on end?

I have to get up onto a rooftop.

After circling the buildings and assessing my best vantage points, I found a rusted-out fire escape. It wasn't the sturdiest thing on the planet, but I was light on my feet. I leapt up, catching the last rung of the ladder against my palms. And as I hoisted myself up, the entire structure started to creak.

"Come on," I murmured as I pulled myself up to the second story, "just get me to the roof."

In a specialty where speed and accuracy needed an even blend, I didn't like how long it took me to get up to that roof. I wasted damn near six minutes of good surveillance time just trying to get myself up the rusty fire escape. Luckily, the building was ten stories high and had a pretty decent brick retaining wall around the outside of the roof.

Meaning it wouldn't take much to hide me from prying eyes.

"There you are," I hissed as I dropped my backpack. "What the fuck are you doing out here at this time of the evening?"

Gordon was just... waiting there. His car, running. His hand hanging out the driver's side window. Just sitting there, in the middle of an alleyway, listening to music. The notes wafted in my general direction, causing my head to bob to the beat. Freddie Mercury, an absolute legend in my book.

At least he's got decent taste in music.

I took my time getting set up. I placed my tablet down before sliding the headphones over my ears, and I tucked the cone into a worn-out groove in the retaining wall. I pointed it directly at Gordon, using the shadows the other taller buildings cast in order to conceal me. I chewed on the inside of my cheek as I screwed the lens back onto my camera, ready to take pictures and listen to any and all incoming communications.

Because those damned hairs on the nape of my neck were giving themselves a fucking workout.

"All right," I said as I got down onto my knees and used the wall to conceal my position, "let's see what you're really up to."

Minutes turned into hours, and all I heard was Gordon butchering some of my favorite Freddie Mercury songs while chomping his jowls. He ate his dinner, and then busted out chips, and then opened up a jar of pickles, then dove into some jerky.

I was shocked the man's heart still agreed to pump after listening to him stuff his face for damn near two hours.

Tick, tick, tick, tick, tick.

"Shit," Gordon hissed.

That perked up my ears, and I peered over the retaining wall. The ticking noise that had come out of nowhere seemed to distress the man, and I moved as slowly as possible to not attract attention. I held my breath, listening as the ticking sound grew closer. And as I watched Gordon step out of his SUV, he started wiping his hands off on his pants.

Nasty.

I started snapping pictures the second those blacked-out SUVs came into view. The ticking came from the front vehicle as they eased down the alleyway. I furrowed my brow as my senses started to heighten. My hearing sharpened, becoming sensitive to each and every sound that happened around me. I followed the SUVs with my camera and wasn't the least bit shocked that their license plates had those tinted covers on them.

Still, I snapped pictures in the hopes that Lancer, our tech guy, might still be able to pull something from them.

"Gordon," a deep voice said.

I watched a broad man in a pristine suit lumber out of the back of the first SUV, and my stomach sank.

"There's no fucking way," I whispered.

"Hey, hey!" Gordon said as he lifted his hands into the air. "I was wondering when you guys were going to show up."

I started snapping pictures as quickly as possible. Everything I could take a picture of, I captured. I watched bodyguards easily the size of Ranger pour out of the second SUV, and the look on Gordon's face shifted from one of friendliness to one of fear.

He needed to be scared, too.

That man was meeting with none other than Tommy Gun Griggs.

The mafioso that had the entire West Coast underground criminal syndicate beneath his motherfucking boot.

"What the hell have you done?" I whispered.

"So," Tommy said as he held out his chubby arms, "how were the mountains?"

Gordon nodded as he slid his hands into his pockets. "The mountains weren't as beautiful as I figured they would be, but at least there was a nice lake to jump into every once in a while."

"A lake, huh? No river to go fishing in?"

I double checked things in order to make sure their conversation was being recorded. It didn't take a genius like me to know that they were talking in code. But, the fact that some police officer needed a reason to talk in code with the biggest mafioso on the West Coast gave me the missing piece that had been bugging me all damn day.

Gordon was a dirty fucking cop.

"You slimy little snake," I murmured as a smile spread across my face.

Honestly? I didn't think the man had it in him. The rumors I'd heard about Tommy Gun Griggs would chill even the deadest of corpses out of its grave. He was ruthless and took pride in the torture he brought down upon those who betrayed him. I heard through the grapevine that at one point in time, the feds almost had him. That is, until the witness testifying against him turned up with no head, no teeth, no prints of any kind, and his skin burned through and through.

Rumor has it that his head had been delivered to the man's fucking wife.

Not good. This is very not good.

"What about the campfire?" Gordon asked.

Tommy's head tilted off to the side. "I ain't done with my questions yet."

Gordon held up his hands. "Ask away, then. I'm an open book."

Tommy snapped his fingers and two of the bodyguards lunged at Gordon. He started grunting and groaning, struggling aimlessly against the two men who kicked his feet out from beneath him. I continued to snap pictures and record everything I could as I watched things unfold with my own eyes. Gordon dropped to his knees as three bodyguards lined Tommy's backside. With their guns drawn and aimed at the man, Tommy fisted the man's hair and yanked his head up to meet his gaze.

I held my breath as I listened to his voice come alive in my headphones.

"Find the river and don't you fucking call me until you do."

Tommy balled up his fist and socked it against Gordon's jaw, forcing him to the ground. Then, with a snap of his fingers, he twirled his hand in the air, rounding up his bodyguards just like that. With Gordon groaning on the ground, blood dripping from his lip, those mountain men treated Tommy as if he were a precious woman. Opening the door for him, offering their hand to help him into the car.

"So, the mafioso is a pretty little princess," I whispered.

I had no idea what to make of anything. As the SUVs backed down the alleyway, with that ticking sound following behind them, Gordon moaned and groaned on the ground as he struggled to get up. Part of me wanted to put a bullet in his damn brain and get things over with. It wasn't as if the man deserved to live, after having his fiancée stolen from beneath him and not giving a rat's ass in the world about it.

Then again, what if he had commissioned Tommy and his goons to help find Naomi?

Is she part of the code they're speaking?

It all felt so far-fetched, but I couldn't deny what I had just seen. Gordon was wrapped up in the mafia, and I had to tell the guys. So, I waited for that pathetic excuse for a man to gather himself. He pulled himself up off the ground, tumbled back into his Subaru, and eased on down the alleyway, not stopping until he turned back onto the main road.

Which gave me the opening I needed to get off that damn building.

I had to get back to the guys.

I had to tell them what I had seen.

And I had to figure out if Naomi knew any of this about her fiancée before I pursued it further.

14

TROOPER

"Ranger!?"

I cupped my hands over my mouth before I drew in a deep breath.

"Range! The hell are you, man!?"

I groaned as I slid down the banister of the stairs. I don't know where in the world that man had gotten off to, but I needed his geese-poop-scooping expertise. Those assholes were back, and I'd be damned if I was going to scrape that shit off the deck when it was his turn to do so.

"Range!" I exclaimed as I turned down the hallway. "Range, you down here!?"

Soft snores came from behind the panel to my left, and I grinned as I raised my hand. I pressed it against the panel, hearing it click and snap into place. I shoved my hand up, watching it roll up into the wall itself before I turned, figuring I'd find Range spread out along the couch, snoring his balls off.

But instead, I found Naomi curled up into a ball, sleeping soundly with a blanket tucked around her body.

"Well, then," I said with a chuckle, "at least someone took my advice."

Still, I couldn't leave her there. Well, I could, but if Ranger found her, he'd roll her ass off the couch before kicking her out into the hallway. He was really possessive over that fucking couch. So, I walked over and scooped her luscious body into my arms.

"So soft for me," I said as I cradled her close.

She nestled her head against my shoulder and the shiver that worked its way down my spine held my dick hostage. I focused my sights on the basement, easing on down the steps until I came to the edge of her bed. Laying her down turned into my lips gracing her forehead, and I swear to hell on high I wanted nothing more than to crawl into bed with her and whisper all of the nasty things I wanted to do to her in her ear.

But, just as I reached for the blanket to tuck her in, I found Ranger.

Or, rather, Ranger found me.

"Hey, Troop."

I tossed the blanket over Naomi and spun around to find him sticking his head into the doorway. "You know I was calling for you earlier, right?"

"Yeah, I didn't want to talk to you. Anyway, Dutch is back. Says it's urgent."

I scoffed. "Seriously? You ignored me the entire time?"

He disappeared up the stairs. "Now, Trooper."

I rolled my eyes and peeked over my shoulder at Naomi one last time. She looked so peaceful, with her lips softly puckered and her cheek smashed into the pillow. She looked so inviting, and I had to shove my hand into my pants to rearrange my dick.

After all, an erection pressed against a zipper isn't the most comfortable thing in the entire world.

Bet her pussy is, though.

"Troop!" Ranger bellowed.

I smirked as I started for the steps. "Now you know how it feels to be ignored, asshole."

I heard him grumble something, but it was lost on me. I turned off the lights and closed the basement door behind me, but I didn't go so far as to lock anything. Ranger probably would have, but she had given me no sign that she'd be bolting for any doors.

Not after the cliff sides she had witnessed firsthand, that would catch her fall if she dared.

"Finally," Dutch said as I emerged from the stairs, "get over here. We need to talk."

I held out my arms and smiled. "So? How did it go?"

Ranger's face fell into one of stone. "Tell him what you just told me."

My smile faltered. "Tell me what."

Dutch thrusted his tablet toward me. "See anyone you recognize?"

I walked toward him and snatched the tablet out of his hand. My gaze dropped to the screen, and the second that chubby little dickweed stepped out of the SUV, my jaw hit the floor.

"Tommy Gun Griggs? Where the fuck did you--?"

Dutch pointed to the screen. "See that cop?"

My eyes widened. "You're fucking kidding me."

Ranger folded his arms across his chest. "Her fiancée is as dirty as they come, apparently."

I watched the scene unfold as my heart stopped in my chest. "Do you know what they're talking about?"

Dutch thumbed over his shoulder toward his backpack that he still wore. "I got the audio on a separate recording. They're obviously speaking in code, though. Talking about mountains and lakes and finding a river, or some shit."

I wrinkled my nose. "They've been working together long enough to have a code?"

Dutch shrugged. "That was my initial thought, though. Who the hell talks in code with someone they're just starting to work with?"

"A code has to be developed," Ranger said.

I shoved the tablet into Dutch's chest. "Do we think Naomi knows anything?"

He turned the tablet off. "That's what I need to find out. I need to know if she knows, and if she does, I need to know *what* she knows."

Ranger turned on his feet and started into the kitchen. "Let's put everything out on the table and see what we're looking at."

I walked over to Dutch and leaned into his ear. "Does he know Naomi's gone?"

Dutch shot me a look. "You can answer that question for yourself here in a second."

I had no idea what in the fuck he meant by that, but when he started laying things out on the kitchen table, I understood why he said what he did. There were pictures of that man smiling. Pictures of him at work, making jokes with friends. Hell, even taking orders from his boss as if nothing had happened. Even the audio with Tommy Gun himself didn't seem panicked. Not after they kicked him to his knees. Not after Tommy punched that fucker in the face—which I was completely jealous of, by the way—and certainly not after Tommy and his men had left him there in that alleyway by himself.

"He never once mentioned Naomi?" Ranger asked.

Dutch shrugged. "Unless she's somewhere in all that code they were slinging around, no. He's not acting like a man whose fiancée's been abducted."

Ranger clapped his hands together as a rare smile spread

across his cheeks. "Well, if he's dirty as fuck, then chances are he doesn't wanna blow his cover with his own damn boss. But, either way, we've got a fuckton of very damning evidence on our hands. We could work this to our advantage."

Dutch shook his head. "Why the fuck isn't he concerned? Shouldn't he be concerned that his woman is missing?"

Ranger scoffed. "Who the fuck cares? We've got the damn police precinct on their knees with this one. You think he's the only dirty cop? Hell, no. Because if there's one thing I know about dirty cops, it's that when there's one you see—."

"—there's two you don't," Dutch murmured.

"So, neither of you care about what this is going to do to Naomi?" I asked.

Ranger snickered. "Got yourself a little crush there, do you?"

Dutch shook his head, though. "He's got a point. We have to figure out if she knows anything about this. She may be just as in the dark as we were before I tailed the man."

"And this could really backfire on us, too," I said as my head came out of the clouds. "I mean, if he's in bed with someone like Tommy Gun, and they've been working together long enough to sling around code, who knows? Maybe the mafia is looking for her, and that's why he's not panicked about anything."

Ranger's head fell back. "Ah, shit."

I raked my hand down my face. "She deserves better than that piece of shit."

Dutch scoffed. "I'm likely to agree with you."

"Oh, great," Ranger said as he tossed his hands into the air. "Now you're both pussy-whipped."

"So," Dutch said as he heaved a heavy, tired sigh, "what's our next move? This could potentially blow up in our faces, especially if her fiancée is working with the mafia in order to get her back."

"Plus, her father may end up growing a pair," I added.

Ranger's gaze hardened. "Make sure he doesn't, then."

That's when we heard the pitter patter of soft footsteps before her voice sounded.

"If you go after my father, I'll find a way to kill all of you."

I whipped around at the sound of Naomi's voice, but Ranger was the one that barked with laughter.

"I'd love to see you try," he glowered.

The poor girl looked fucking exhausted, with those heavy bags beneath her eyes.

"You need sleep," I said as I took a step forward.

She clenched her fists at her sides and straightened her back. "The deal was me for my father. That deal stands. And if it doesn't? I've got no issues finding a way to kill all three of you without batting an eye."

Dutch stepped up to my side. "Naomi, there's something you need to--."

I held my hand up. "Yes, you're right. That was the deal."

Naomi's gaze danced between the two of us. "If you're concerned about my fiancée being a cop? Not my fault. You should've done your research before you decided to charge into my father's home and take him hostage. That's on you, not me. You don't like it? Well, here I am. You're more than welcome to kill me. Anything would be better than spending another day listening to the three of you bicker like a bunch of women."

"Hey!" Ranger barked.

"No! You, hey!" she exclaimed as she pointed her finger at him. "I don't give a shit who you are! I've reconciled the fact that you'll kill me sooner rather than later. You won't hang on to dead weight like me. I'm good with that. I made my choice. But I swear to hell on fucking high, if I catch even a whiff of you idiots backing out on your end of the deal, your blood spills before mine."

I grinned. "You've got a lot of gumption in those curves, pretty girl."

She practically spat her words at me. "And that's all you'll get to see for yourself, you shithead."

Ranger stepped in front of me and Dutch. "You need to understand that you have no control right now. You're in no position to be making demands with anyone, much less us."

That only made her grin. "A woman always has more control than men think. It's why men are always toppled by a strong woman. It's why men drive this world into the ground when women have the capability of making it better. More prosperous. Men do nothing but destroy. It's the women that are tasked with building things back up."

She stalked toward Ranger, standing on her tiptoes just to get closer to his stone cold face.

"So, tell me," she said as she pointed her finger directly against his chest, "do you really think I have absolutely no control?"

Ranger chuckled darkly. "Good. I'm glad you think that."

She blinked. "And why's that?"

He slapped her hand away before getting into her face. "Because the only sense of control you feel you have is because I've allowed you to have it."

Naomi didn't waver. "Then, prove it. If you think you're so tough and so in control, then prove it."

He tilted his head. "Says the woman who gets to roam around freely, yet hasn't made one single move to leave."

I looked over at Dutch, and even he had a blank stare on his face. It was like watching a goddamn train wreck, and we wondered who would get hit first.

Her, with her hand across his cheek. Or him, with his hand wrapped around her throat.

"Ranger?" I asked.

He straightened his back. "Now, go back downstairs to your little den of sin and--."

Naomi took a step back and cleared her throat. "Your guards do three rotation changes every single day. One at ten. One at four. One at nine. They circle around the building counter-clockwise before coming inside and doing rotations around each and every level twice, going in the opposite direction. Clockwise."

"And?" Ranger asked.

That's when Naomi smiled. "During the three changes, two things occur: one, the side door all the way at the end of the living room hallway that you guys think you have concealed is completely free from prying eyes for six minutes; and two, no one locks the front door."

"What?" Ranger hissed.

"Not only that," Naomi said as he held her finger in the air, "but no one comes down these basement steps. They check the door, but they never come down to check on me. That leaves me very vulnerable to the attic access in the closet-slash-kitchen down there that leads into the ductwork of the house. Did you know that the ductwork in this place is large enough to fit my hips? Interesting how that works."

Dutch grinned, and I had to admit I wanted to chuckle. She was smart as a fucking whip, and it was clear that her fiancée had taught her, in some ways, how to help herself.

But Ranger was furious. "Go on, since you seem to want to show us all how smart you are."

And Naomi took the bait. "Your evening crew doesn't like keeping that kind of routine schedule, though. The two men that park their lazy asses on the porch don't move for at least two hours at a time, which I don't think is part of their hourly rota-tion. Plus, they never check the third floor. I don't know how many times I've snuck up to the conference room and planned my escape by getting onto the roof that I know isn't guarded and distracting those porch dwellers long enough to steal the car they keep unlocked in the driveway."

I'd never seen that kind of anger on Ranger's face. "Well, thank you for telling me exactly who I need to fire and what needs to be fixed."

It was then that she turned her attention to Dutch. To the long, angular, dead-faced knife-thrower that stood as still as a statue at my side. My gaze dropped to her fingers, watching her wiggle her engagement ring off her hand. And as she held it out for Dutch, he opened his palm.

Before all three of us watched her drop it against his skin.

"Thanks for doing my dirty work for me. At least now I have answers," Naomi said flatly.

Then, she turned her back to us, stumbled her tired ass back toward the basement, and slammed the door behind her.

Leaving the three of us shocked and rooted in our places.

"Guess she didn't know after all," Dutch murmured as he closed his hand around the ring.

Ranger stormed down the hallway toward the front door. "I'll be back. Got some holes to shore up around this fucking place."

But all I thought about was Naomi downstairs. Alone. In that dark, cold basement.

With nothing but her broken heart to keep her company.

15

NAOMI

The darkness swallowed me whole as I eased myself down onto the edge of the bed. No windows meant no extraneous light, and as the night pulsed around me, I realized something very important.

I had no more tears to cry.

As much as I wanted to, as much as my body yearned for the release, I had no more for my body to use. I felt numb, like someone had injected me with anesthetics but forced me to stay awake. My heart rhythmically pumped against my chest. My shoulders rose and fell with my automatic breaths. They didn't even hiccup. Not once.

I had no more energy left in me to fight.

As I stared at the wall—at least, I thought it was the wall— my mind came to a grinding halt. In through my nose was drawn the deepest breath I had ever taken, and it felt like my lungs were opening up for the first time. I had no more options. I was out of ideas. Gordon wasn't coming for me, and Dad knew where his place was in all of this.

I was stuck.

And as far as I knew, this was my life.

"At least I don't have to go back to that shitty ass hospital," I whispered to myself.

We have to figure out if she knows anything about this.

A code has to be developed.

Tommy Gun Griggs?

My mind felt louder than ever, screaming my thoughts back at me as I replayed the conversation I had just overheard. I wasn't stupid, even though the idiotic men upstairs thought I was. And the second they had all been gathered, I snuck upstairs without them being any the wiser. They were terrible at that, by the way. If they thought they were keeping tabs on me, then they were shit at it. I had roamed more of their place than my own, most days, and while I had found multiple moments where I could have escaped, something always stopped me.

Now, I knew what it was.

"My fiancée is working for the mob," I said out loud.

"My *fiancée* is working for the mob," I said, with a different enunciation.

Then I cleared my throat. "My fiancée is working for the *fucking mob.*"

No matter how much I said it, or how I said it, none of it felt real. And yet, it explained so much. Like, where we happened to get the chunk of change we needed for the house we had purchased together. Sure, my salary paid the mortgage, but it wasn't as if we had the fifty grand to use as the down payment. I played the memory back in my mind. The last memory I had of ever being happy with Gordon, to be honest.

I allowed it to sweep me away as I continued staring off into the darkness.

"Sweetheart!? I got good news!"

I heard the apartment door slam closed as Gordon rushed into the bedroom. "What in the--?"

He looked my half-naked body up and down before he wiggled his eyebrows. "Already prepared to celebrate, I see."

I blushed as I pulled my robe closed. "What in the world? Aren't you supposed to be at work?"

He walked over to me and gripped my upper arms. "That's what I wanted to tell you. You remember all of those bonuses that work keeps backing out on?"

"Yeeeeah...?"

He drew me into his arms as a smile broke out across his face. "Well, they finally anted up. And it's exactly how much we need for the rest of the down payment."

My jaw hit the floor. "Your bonus was twelve grand!?"

He crashed his lips against mine, weakening my knees beneath me. "That's right, gorgeous. Let's call the realtor. Let's buy our dream house."

There were so many things about his schedule that changed after we purchased that house a few years back. His schedule became more erratic. Some nights, he didn't get home until well past midnight. We went from never once having established any sort of savings account to having scores of money dumped into one at the drop of a hat. I tried not to question things. I tried to see the good in what was happening. After all, Gordon had been a lifelong police officer, third generation. I figured all of those long nights and weekend work schedules when we were younger had finally paid off.

Or maybe I had taught myself to stay ignorant for fear of what the truth might have been.

"God damn it, Gordon," I whispered as my shoulders slumped.

"Penny for your thoughts."

Trooper's voice didn't even make me jump. Normally, I

hated the dark. But the way it shrouded me—the way it covered me in its grasp and blocked out the world—had started to rub off.

"Hey, Troop," I said breathlessly.

I heard the sly fall of his footsteps. The heavy canter on his left leg followed by the light pat of his right.

"Did you get shot or something?" I asked.

He paused. "You'll have to be a bit more specific."

"In the leg you're favoring. I think it's your left one?" I asked.

He chuckled, and the sound made me shiver. "You're very perceptive, you know."

I shrugged. "Comes with being a dirty cop's girlfriend, I guess."

The bed beneath me gave way a bit. "That's the first time I've heard you say something other than 'fiancée.'"

"Right now, I'm not sure he is my fiancée any longer."

"I'm sorry, Naomi."

I scoffed. "Are you really, though?"

I felt something warm slip around my knee. "Yeah. I really am. No one should have to endure that kind of betrayal."

I placed my hand mindlessly on top of his. "Thanks."

His body heat came closer as the bed depressed beneath my right thigh. "You know you're safe here with us, right?"

I barked with laughter. "Jesus Christ, that's rich. I'm safe with three bike-riding criminals, but not with my own—whatever the hell he is."

"I'm serious. You're safe here. No one from Gordon's spineless organization is going to be able to get to you here. We'll make sure they don't hurt you."

I slowly looked over at him and found his honey-colored eyes staring at me, piercing the surrounding darkness.

"Aren't you guys supposed to be the ones hurting me, while

they're supposed to be out there getting me home? Isn't that how this is supposed to work?"

"I know it seems--."

My voice grew a bit louder. "Isn't the man that I thought I was going to marry one day supposed to be the one busting down the doors, and not the other way around? Don't I have to have protection from you guys? Not from the people who are supposed to be the good guys!?"

He turned his hand over, allowing his palm to cradle mine. "I'm not going to sit here and assume to know what you're going through. I can't imagine, honestly. One of the things we hold dear around here is never stabbing our brothers in the back. That gets you killed around here."

"It should get him killed out there," I grumbled.

He snickered. "Spoken like Ranger, honestly. He would've enjoyed that statement."

I rolled my eyes. "I don't think he enjoys anything but protein shakes and red meat."

Troop's laugh made me smile. "You're a spitfire. I love that about you."

Wait, what did he just say?

"Sorry to interrupt," Dutch said as his voice came from out of nowhere, "but I need her time."

That, I flinched at. "Jesus Chr—do you ever make noise when you walk?"

Troop brought the back of my hand to his lips to kiss before standing. "She's all yours, String Bean."

I paused. "String Bean?"

Dutch's voice sounded without his presence in my field of vision. "A loving nickname the guys gave me because they're jealous of my legs."

I grinned as I shook my head. "Hey, Troop?"

"Yeah?"

"Thank you."

I felt his lips press into the top of my head. "No problem, pretty girl."

His nickname warmed me to my core before a soft, warm light illuminated my right side. I peered over my shoulder, watching Dutch's ocean blue eyes sparkle like the blond tendrils of his disheveled hair. His high cheekbones always made him look like he was smirking, even with his thin lips down turned into the heavy frown that sat upon his face.

He held up the oil lamp he carried and came to take up Troop's position beside me on the edge of the bed.

"An oil lamp, huh? Pretty old school, if you ask me," I said as I turned my stare back to the wall.

He sat it at his feet. "Not everything that's old is useless."

I snickered. "My father would put that on a wall somewhere if he ever heard you say it."

"He's fiery. I don't doubt it one bit."

I heaved a heavy sigh. "So, you need me for something?"

He slid a backpack off his shoulders that I hadn't even clocked. Man, I was getting rough at that.

"How are you doing?" Dutch asked.

I rolled my eyes. "I'm fine, for someone whose world has been flipped upside down."

He unzipped the top part of the bag. "I figured you'd want to see the pictures. Or maybe look at the videos that I took."

"Do I really, though?"

He pulled out a camera. "I don't know. You tell me. I've got it all right here. Should you wish to see it."

As he held the camera over my lap, I couldn't help but look down. His long, dexterous fingers clicked mindlessly through the snapshots, and the more I saw, the more my stomach turned itself into knots. There were photos of him and Dog turd—at least, that's what I called him—laughing outside of his place of work like nothing was wrong.

Like I hadn't gone missing.

Like I hadn't dropped off the face of the planet.

"I hate that man," I murmured.

"Dogma?" Dutch asked.

I groaned. "You know why they call him that?"

"They didn't go over the story, from what I heard."

I pinched the bridge of my nose. "Because he's a stubborn fucking white man who never progressed in his career because he felt he had to sell out in order to do it. And anything that goes against his incontrovertible ways is somehow a lesser truth than the way he's lived his life for its entirety."

"Wow."

I shrugged. "It's their way of making fun of the man, but he wears it like a badge of honor. It's so strange."

"Do you want me to keep going?"

I waved my hand in the air. "Sure, I guess. Can't hurt, right? Knowing who I was actually engaged to for a spell?"

The second the words fell from my lips, they felt more like the truth than anything else in my life. I wasn't engaged. Not any longer, at least. Even if I found my way home, even if the guys had mercy on me and took me back home, I'd never be able to go back to the way things were. I'd have to move out. Find my own place again. Block him from everywhere and pass the word around that Gordon and I were no longer together.

At least the guys hadn't ever tried to be something they weren't.

While my fiancée pulled the wool over my eyes for fucking years.

"Jesus," I whispered, "that's really him, isn't it?"

As Dutch started scrolling through pictures of Gordon

sitting in an alleyway, I watched as picture after picture brought two blacked-out SUVs into the picture. Out came a man whose face I had seen plastered all over the news multiple times throughout my childhood. Tommy Gun Griggs was one of the most feared men on the West Coast. A common-day bogeyman parents told their children about at night to scare them onto the straight and narrow.

And there he was, having a conversation with Gordon.

A man I almost married.

"I can't look at it any longer," I said as I turned my head away.

"Fair enough," Dutch said. "So, does that mean you don't?--."

"I don't want any of it," I said curtly. "Just... do what you need to do with it and leave me out of it."

I heard him shuffling around before he tapped me on the shoulder.

"What?" I asked as I looked over at him.

He nodded down into his lap, and when I dropped my gaze, I found my engagement ring sitting in the palm of his hand.

"Do you want this back?" he asked plainly.

I didn't even hesitate when answering. "I don't care what you do with it. Just get it away from me."

He nodded as he tucked it back into his pocket.

"You know, when I was--."

I closed my eyes. "I don't mean to be the rudest bitch on the planet, but if this is your way of trying to tell me that you understand how I feel, then save it. I promise you, you don't."

He clicked his tongue. "When I was in *foster care* growing up..."

I groaned. "Jesus, sorry. I'm just--."

He placed his hand on my shoulder. "You have no reason to be sorry. Okay?"

I peeked over at him. "Yeah, I guess I don't."

He reached his fingers up and tucked a stray strand of hair behind my ear. "When I was growing up in foster care, I kept to myself a lot. Tried my best to stay out of trouble. My first set of foster parents practically beat the statistics into my head. How many of us end up on the street when we age out of the system. How few of us made it to college. How even fewer of us go on to become something. You know, make something of ourselves."

I swallowed hard. "Did they practically beat it into you? Or literally beat it into you?"

His eye twitched. "The point is, I never knew what a family felt like until I found the crew. Until I pledged myself to doing what was best for these guys that had taken me in. And now, as their Enforcer, it's my job to make sure everyone under our rooftop is safe."

"Yeah?"

He slid his knuckles down my cheek, almost as if to stroke it. "Including you, Naomi."

His words warmed me in a way I simply couldn't explain. "Thank you, Dutch."

He pulled his hand away as his back straightened. "So, I'm only going to ask you this question once. Are you listening?"

I turned to face him. "Of course. You have my attention."

Those ocean eyes of his grew cold as ice. "If this man were to roll up on us. Gordon with the mafia, or even just Gordon with a couple of friends. Do you think you're safe with him? With them, I mean?"

I blinked. "Are you asking me if I'm safe with Gordon now, understanding who he really is?"

"Yes."

For the first time since high school, I had no clue how to answer that question.

"I don't know, Dutch," I said as my body finally found more tears to shed. "I have no idea if I am, or not."

And as my back gave way, almost as if my spine had given up on life itself, my head fell to Dutch's shoulder.

While he sat there, allowing my tears to soak his black t-shirt.

16

DUTCH

"I'm so sorry," Naomi choked out as wetness poured over my shoulder. "I-I-I—I just need a second."

I nodded. "Take your time."

My hands balled into fists as my thin, spindly little fingernails raked against my own skin. The crescent moons glared at me, begging me to stop as I sat there. Stiff as stone. My blood boiled with a need for vengeance. Never in my life had I experienced the rage that poured over me the way it did, but with every sniffle that fell from Naomi's precious little nose, I wanted to shear the skin off that spineless pig and use it as a rug.

Before I fucked his ex-fiancée on it.

"Oh, my God," she said breathlessly. "How is this happening?"

I shook my head as I sat there, feeling her body sink into me. Her softness blanketed me, like a protective weight charged with blocking out the world. My hands trembled in my lap. My toes curled in their boots. The smell of metal and the sound of cracking bone filled my ears as my fingers contorted in ways they had never stretched before.

I wanted to strangle that pathetic motherfucker with my hands for making such a beautiful creature cry.

How dare he.

"Fuck, come on. I'm so—s-s-s—so tired of—of crying."

I nodded. "I would be, too. It's been a lot for you lately."

She scoffed as she picked up her head. "Yeah, something like that."

I slowly pivoted my head to take her all in, even if it was just her flickering outline lent to me by none other than the oil lamp at my feet.

"I can't listen to you cry any longer," I finally said.

She wiped at her tears. "I know, I know. I'm so sor—."

But, the second her face wrinkled up again, I knew I couldn't leave her.

Not until she was all right.

"It's okay," I said as I started rubbing her back. "You're going to get through this."

She shook her head quickly as her gaze dropped into her lap. "I don't know if I want to get through it anymore. I don't— God, when the hell did it become such a burden to go home? Isn't home supposed to be what comforts you? It's just... it feels like it's ruined. Like I have—have no home, Dutch."

I scooted a bit closer to her. "Now, I quite understand how that feels."

She closed her eyes. "I'm sorry. That was insensitive."

I gripped her chin with my free hand and pulled her soaking wet gaze to mine. "Not if it's true. And in your case, unfortunately, it's true."

Her gaze fluttered open. "Why is he doing this?"

I shook my head. "I don't know yet. But I'll find out, if you wish."

Her stare searched mine. "Is that even something I can ask of you?"

I scooted so close that our thighs touched. "You can ask anything of me, Naomi. I'm at your disposal."

Her lower lip quivered. "Then, tell me something."

"Anything," I murmured as my stare dropped to those pillowy lips of hers.

"What do I do now? If I have no home, and no fiancée. No future to speak of. What—what do I do next?"

I couldn't help myself as my thumb smoothed over the softness of her lower lip. "Anything and everything, I suppose."

It was supposed to be a comforting answer. One that brought a smile to her face instead of the deepening ache that grew behind her darkened green eyes. But, as the words filled the space between us, her eyes watered over again. And I couldn't listen her to cry. Not any longer.

Not over some dumbass, sorry excuse for a man that didn't deserve it.

"I'm sorry," I whispered.

As she parted her lips to speak, I captured them with my own. I tasted her for the first time, and fireworks shot off in my brain. My arm tightened around the small of her back. My palm slid across her cheek, catching the back of her head as she gasped down my throat. And as our tongues melded together, I felt overwhelmed by her.

Intoxicated with her warmth, and her softness, and the scent pouring from between her thighs.

"Goddamn it, Naomi," I growled. "What the hell have you done to me?"

She whimpered as her arms came up, and the minute they draped around my neck, I snapped. I picked her up with nothing but my arm and slid her up the bed, blanketing her with my body. My leg slid up her thighs until it sat right against her clothed pussy. Her tongue fought me for dominance as her hands roamed throughout any part of my body she wanted to touch. She yanked at my clothes. Begged for my shirt to come off. And as I sat back on my haunches, watching the soft fire-light flicker along her delicious curves, I knew one thing for certain.

I'd never be able to give her up without a fight.

"Dutch, please," she said breathlessly.

I didn't even get my fucking jacket off before I slammed my lips back against hers. I sucked on that lower lip, turning her quivering into swelling as she bucked her hips wildly against my body. I threaded our fingers together before pinning her hands to the mattress. I wanted to feel her. Taste her. Drink her in before she came to her senses.

After all, who the hell would want to waste their time on a bastard child like me?

"Fuck," I grunted.

Seams ripped and buttons popped as I dug her out of her clothes. Her curves deserved more than the curtain drapery she had chosen for her body, but it didn't matter. No amount of linens or curtains could hide what my tongue wanted to taste. And the second I had her pussy bared for me, I wiggled myself between her juicy thighs.

Before sliding her legs over my shoulders.

"Fuck," she hissed as she threaded her fingers through my hair.

I growled as I lapped my tongue up her slit. "Better hold on tight, lucky girl."

She twitched with every movement of my tongue. With each circle around the base of her clit, she bucked. With every lap of my tongue along the sides of her dripping wet pussy, she rolled those pillowy hips of hers. What I wouldn't give to bury myself inside of her, only to ride her off into the sunset.

There were no sunsets where I came from, though.

Just darkness and desire.

And lust.

"Dutch," she gasped.

I inserted my thumb into her soaking wet entrance as my tongue flattened against her clit. Her hips rose clear off the bed, rocking and seeking what she so desperately wanted. What she so desperately deserved. I was more than willing to be her vehicle. To be the man who made her cum so hard that she forgot all about the spineless jellyfish she almost hitched her ride to.

And as her walls clamped around my thumb, I growled into that delicious cunt of hers.

"Fuck, fuck, fuck, fuck. Dutch. Oh, my God," she squeaked.

I hummed against her swollen mound as I held it between my teeth. Her hips were clear off the bed, and I watched as her skin flushed the most beautiful shade of red I'd ever seen in my life. I'd never once been a fan of the color. It was much too harsh, and it stood out in a crowd.

But on her, it was a delicacy to behold.

"That's it," I murmured as her hips dropped back down to the bed.

She tossed her arm over her eyes. "Jesus. You guys are just—you're—I—."

I teased her ass crack with my middle finger. "Having fun?"

She sucked air through her teeth. "Mmm, yeah."

I grinned. "Good. Because I'm not done with you yet."

Her juices followed my touch, dripping along her skin as it poured from her entrance. She drenched my hand, filling the room with her scent as she twisted her hands into the sheets beneath us. My cock bulged against the zipper of my jeans. I wanted nothing more than to fill that throat of hers until I poured my mark into her stomach.

But, I wanted to watch her cum for me one last time.

"Dutch, I-I-I—I've never—."

"Don't worry," I coaxed, as my middle finger breached her asshole. "I'll go slowly."

"Oooooh, fuuuuuck," she groaned as her hips arched into the air. "So full. So full. So full."

I chuckled as I nuzzled her pussy lips back open for me. "Hang on, lucky girl."

Her hands darted their way back into my hair as I dove in for seconds. I lapped her up, drinking every drop of arousal she offered me as the bed bucked with our movements. She clamped her thick thighs around my face, damn near drowning me in her center. And fucking hell, had that been the way the world ushered me out, I would have died a happy man.

"Dutch! Yes!" she cried out.

Her asshole opened for me like a morning rosebud, sucking the rest of my finger down. I filled her, both of her holes, as I ground my clothed dick against the mattress beneath us. She lost all control of her body. All sense of direction as my tongue sought out that swollen nub of hers. And the second I found it, I sucked it between my lips and refused to let go.

"Dutch. Dutch. Dutch. Ooooh, my God. Please. I need to cum. I wanna cum. Please, let me cum."

Her words swirled around my head, holding me captive as the zipper of my pants slowly worked itself downward. Her walls collapsed around my thumb. Her asshole clenched around my middle finger. Her juices dripped down my chin, soaking my neck as she marked me as her own.

I would have gladly taken up position next to her, too.

She was a vibrant woman, full of mystery and intelligence.

"Mmm, you taste outstanding," I growled.

"Dut—ch."

She choked out my name, and that was all it took. I flattened my tongue against her clit as I buried my face between her thickness and her body unleashed. Juices flooded my face. She soaked my mouth, pouring down the back of my throat as I swallowed as much as I could. I pumped my fingers, working her through the orgasm that crashed so hard over her body she damn near choked off my airspace.

I didn't care, though.

All I cared about was the fact that she was no longer crying.

"Oh, fuck," she said breathlessly as her body collapsed to the bed.

Her legs fell away from my face, freeing me as I came up for air. I eased my fingers out of her precious little holes, wiping them aimlessly on the sheet beneath us. And as I sat up on my haunches, still perched between her legs, I watched her reddened face pop up from her downed position.

Before a smirk spread across her face. "Looks like someone wants some attention."

I furrowed my brow. "What?"

She giggled. "You haven't noticed?"

Her gaze dropped to my crotch and when I looked down, I found my bulging erection poking out from between the zipper of my jeans. It pounded to life, throbbing and aching for release as pre-cum dripped from its tip.

"Ah. That," I said.

The bed shifted with the weight of her movement. "I guess I have a favor to repay."

"No," I said curtly.

She paused. "No?"

I sat back on my heels. "It wasn't a favor. You owe me nothing."

She got down onto all fours and crawled to me, her tits dragging across the bed in a way that made me lick my lips.

"And yet, I can't think about anything else except what you taste like."

She reached out for my rock-hard dick and wrapped her

hand around its base. Her gaze crept along my body, stopping to ogle at my abs.

"Never would've assumed those existed," she murmured as she softly stroked my leaking dick.

My head fell back as I tried to contain myself, because I knew if I put my hands on her, I wouldn't stop until I had filled every orifice of her languid, swollen body.

"Most people—ugh—don't."

She reached her tongue up and lapped at the deep lines carving out my muscles. Her warmth followed their divots, and I couldn't help but to lay back. Her softness molded to me. Her thumb swiped over the tip of my cock, lubing her palm with my pre-cum as she kissed and nibbled her way up to my chest. Her fingertips traced the outline of my pelvic muscles that disappeared between my legs, forcing my toes to curl.

Which only made my veins bulge more as her tongue crept back down to my throbbing girth.

"Mmmm," she said as she darted her tongue out, lapping at the pre-cum soaking my tip, "I guess I'm not the only one that tastes outstanding."

I looked up at the ceiling, trying to control the monster within. "You have no idea what you're unleashing."

She stroked my cock slowly. "What if I want to know?"

My gaze darkened as I looked back down at her. "Take the risk and find out, then, if you're so eager."

She didn't even hesitate. As she sank her warm, wet mouth around my cock, my head exploded into the clouds. My hand dropped to her disheveled tendrils, and I felt them wrap around my fingers. Almost as if that's where they had always wanted to be. Her tongue wrapped around me, licking the base of my dick as she hollowed out her cheeks, and I swear to hell on high it was a slice of heaven meant only for me.

I sank to the bed, my back against the sheets as she slid me down the back of her throat.

And as my hands buried themselves into her hair, I pumped my hips against her face.

"God fucking damn it, Naomi. Holy hell."

"Mmmmm," she hummed.

I kicked my boots off just so my toes could curl tightly without something in the way. I pumped my hips against her lips, feeling her spit dribbling onto my skin. It slid down my balls, tickling me in ways I'd never once experienced. And as my head got lost in the clouds, she slid her arms beneath my legs.

Before tossing mine over *her* shoulders.

"God, I've always wanted to do this," she whispered as she came up for air.

I grabbed the back of her head and slammed her throat back down the length of my shaft. "Don't you dare stop until I've filled your stomach. Got it?"

I felt her nod before her cheeks hollowed out once more and my abs tightened. Her warmth encompassed me so completely that I was almost jealous she had already been with Trooper. Not completely, though. It wouldn't have been the first time the three of us had shared someone.

It was just the first time I wanted to keep it that way.

"Fucking Christ," I hissed. "That mouth of yours. You'll be lucky if you go a day without sucking my dick ever again."

She came up for air and panted. "Bring it on, then."

I chuckled before another hiss fell from my lips. The way she had moaned my name only minutes before echoed off the caverns of my mind as my balls pulled up into my body. My toes curled. My back arched. My teeth ground together as growls and groans bubbled up the back of my throat. Every muscle in my body locked out, readying for blast-off as her throat closed around my cock.

Before my eyes rolled into the back of my head.

"Naomi," I growled. "Naomi, goddamn it, just like that."

The effervescent ecstasy that flooded my veins darkened my gaze. My body collapsed in a fit of sweat and juices as our intermingled scent swirled all around us. Her name fell from my lips, over and over, like a chanted prayer to a God I finally believed in. I only knew her. I only understood her. And as my back crashed back down to the bed, all I believed in... was her.

Naomi.

My lucky girl.

"Jesus Christ," I choked out.

She giggled as she placed her chin against my abs. "It's Naomi, but I guess I'll take it."

I snickered as a smile spread across my face. A genuine smile.

The kind of smile that only my knives pulled from me.

"Sharp as a blade, you are," I murmured.

She kissed just beneath my belly button. "Like one of your knives?"

I chuckled. "My knives can't suck my soul through my dickhole, lucky girl."

She barked with laughter, and the sound made me smile even more. "Will you stay here for a bit?"

I reached down and slid my fingers into her hair. "I'll stay here as long as you'd like."

She climbed up my body, like an ant on the side of a tree, and when her head fell against my raging heartbeat, I blanketed her in my arms. With her legs parted, her knees on either side of my hips, my cock stood there, ready for yet another round as the heat of her naked pussy teased my belly button. I kept my cool, though.

There would be plenty of time for him to get what he wanted.

"I'm right here," I whispered as I stroked my fingers through her hair.

She buried her face into the crook of my neck and nodded, but the only sound that poured from between her lips was a yawn. I rolled us over, placing her onto her side, and all she did was slip that soft, sensuous leg of hers between my own. With my dick finally getting the picture, I scooted closer to her. Close enough that I felt her heart beating against my own.

And as I laid there, softly stroking the knots out of her hair that I had created myself, silence gave way to her soft snoring.

Before her body completely went limp.

"There we go," I whispered.

I couldn't help myself. I kissed the top of her head before scooting away, and I did my best to cover her up with the comforter that had gotten trapped beneath her ass.

"Never thought I'd be jealous of a comforter," I groaned as I stuffed my dick back into my jeans, "but here we are."

I stood there, watching her shoulders rise and fall with her even breaths. No tears. No hiccups. No sadness of any sort. Just the heated bliss of her orgasms still peppering her cheeks as her tired body laid there, recuperating from an aerobics class I wanted to attend every damn day for the rest of my life.

What has this woman done to me?

I wanted to watch her all night. I wanted to keep her in my purview so that I knew she was safe. But a woman needed her privacy, and I wasn't going to rob her of that. I walked over and picked up the oil lamp, which was damn near about to go out. And as I made my way to the basement door, I took one last look at her over my shoulder.

Before the door opened for me instead of at my behest.

"What the--?"

Trooper stood on the other side, grinning from ear to ear. "Well, then."

My face fell. "What the fuck are you doing?"

He pulled a bottle of water out from behind him. "Figured you could use this."

I snatched it out of his hand before shoving him away from the door. I reached for the knob and eased it closed behind me, watching as Trooper's smile grew on his face.

"Shut up," I grumbled as I cracked open the bottle.

He held up his hands in mock surrender. "Hey, I didn't say shit."

I chugged some of the water back before cracking my neck. "So, what gives? You got a reason for being here? Or are you just being a perv?"

"He's not the one playing with his food," Ranger said as his shoulders blocked out the light filtering through from the top of the steps.

I looked up at him. "I don't like the sound of her voice. What's going on?"

Ranger tilted his head. "We've got work to do. Come on."

Trooper held out his arm. "After you, *lucky boy*."

I gnashed my teeth at him. "If you ever so much as utter that to anyone—including her—I will jam my fist down your throat and--."

Ranger cleared his throat. "We have to shore up the security issues you allowed to infiltrate our system. Think you can focus on something else other than your dick while we get it done?"

My nostrils flared as Trooper flashed me the most mockingly stupid smile I'd ever seen in my life. I shoved his face with my hand, pushing him into the wall before I scaled the steps two at a time. Ranger followed my every move, turning with me as I got to the top of the steps. And as I slid between him and the doorframe, I took another swig of water.

"You have to admit," I said as I shoved the bottle into

Ranger's chest, "her being attentive enough to figure out our patterns is pretty impressive."

"Says the man who allowed the vulnerabilities in the first place."

"The last thing I recall," I said as my gaze hardened on his, "you had to approve each and every move these men make. Did you see the vulnerabilities then?"

Trooper whistled low as Ranger's face darkened. "Are you trying to lay blame?"

I moved away from him. "Give me an hour. I'll have them fixed."

Because as God as my witness, I'd never allow anything to happen to her. Naomi wouldn't get hurt because of an oversight on my part. I had underestimated her. We all had. But now that I understood her abilities and what she was capable of, I knew how to protect her.

Especially from herself.

17

RANGER

A FEW DAYS LATER

"Are you fucking serious?" Bury asked.

Lancer stood to his feet. "A cop? That bitch's fiancée is a cop?"

"Watch it," Trooper warned.

"Technically, she's no longer engaged to him," Dutch said coolly, his feet propped up on the wooden conference table upstairs that I made with my bare hands.

"Does he know that?" Lancer spat.

"Enough," I said curtly. "Everyone, take a seat. This is church, not a cock fight."

Coffin, who usually stayed silent during church meetings and took everything in, spoke up for once in his damn life.

"We got a plan as to how we're gonna handle this fucked up situation? Or is this another Alicia moment?"

The fact that he dared to even mention her name forced anger up the back of my throat. "Speak her name again and I will end you. Understood?"

Yet Coffin remained unwavering. "Tell me you're not falling in love with someone caught up in our bullshit that you feel weirdly protective over all of a sudden, and we'll be fine."

I pinned him with a glare that made his eye twitch. "Let's not forget what happened to her on your watch."

Coffin shot to his feet. "I had nothing to do with her jumping in front of you. *She* wanted to save you from that bullet, and you put her in a situation where she felt she had to. That ain't on me. That's on y'all. So, what I'm asking is, are we gonna have to bury another woman because you can't—?"

"You were supposed to hold her back, Coffin!" I said as I stuck my finger in his mousey little face. "You said you had a grip on her! She wasn't even supposed to be in the fucking clubhouse! What the hell happened to that!?"

"Enough!" Trooper exclaimed. "Sit the fuck down and shut the fuck up! All of you!"

Normally, I would have put his ass on the ground for that. We were in church, and that was my motherfucking domain. But, with the guys all bent out of shape, I got it.

We were in shit territory with that woman in our basement.

Still, they sat down. One by one, they turned their attention back to me, their President. The person they trusted to have all the answers.

And I had none when it came to Naomi.

"Now that we're all done pitching our weekly fits," I said as I stared each of them down, "do you guys wanna hear about our new buyer? Or do you want to keep playing chicken shit around some girl?"

Bury grinned. "That was quick."

I shrugged. "The fuck did you expect? We're businessmen, so we do business."

"Who's the buyer?" Lancer asked.

Coffin went back to keeping his mouth shut. And honestly, I preferred it that way. Most people who brought up my ex in any way, shape, or form found themselves attached to concrete and headed toward the bottom of the fucking ocean while screaming for mercy.

He'd be no different if he said her name again.

"Code name: Mercenary. Got a group of guys interested in some of the new stuff. Dutch and I are headed to a meet with them tonight to get a handle on what they're looking for before officially place our order, but it should be a good haul for a typical trade-off."

"How many?" Lancer asked.

"Seven."

Bury whistled. "You sure only two of you should be going?"

"We're not meeting all of them," I said with a roll of my eyes. "We're just meeting with their interface. They have a hierarchy, like we do. We're respecting it with the assumption that they'll respect ours."

"And if they don't?" Trooper asked.

I smirked. "We show them why they should have."

"How much?" Coffin asked.

The only question he ever asked, and it was a damn good one. "Haul should be around three mil."

He nodded as he picked the dirt from beneath his fingernails with a pocketknife. "If you need another person, let me know."

Not a fucking chance. "You know I will. Anyone got any questions?"

The room stayed silent.

"Any other gripes, or complaints, or bullshit I should know about?"

They all looked around the room at one another, but still stayed silent.

"Good," I said as I clapped my hands together three times. "Then, church dismissed."

Normally, the guys stayed to chat for a while. You know,

crack open some beers. Throw some rocks out into the ocean while shooting the shit on the back porch. But, today, their anger got the better of them. They all stormed out of the clubhouse, leaving the three of us to listen to their heated boots clunking against our expensive floors before they busted out the front door. The roar of motorcycles gearing up and revving down the road damn near shattered the fucking windows of our clubhouse. But I simply shook my head.

"Fucking temper tantrums," I murmured.

"They're right, you know," Trooper said.

I shot him a look. "Be careful with your next set of words, Troop."

He stood to his feet and made his way to the door. "We have to figure out what's going on with Naomi. We need to know if she's a risk that needs to be handled."

I scoffed. "Seems like you and Dutch have been handling her just fine."

Dutch finally stood up. "We still know the drill, though."

His gaze locked with mine as I drew in a deep breath. "I'll figure it out. And when I do, I'll let you guys know. But until then, she's been no threat, and there's been no attack on us. Hell, for all we know, her fiancee--."

"Ex-fiancee," Dutch said.

I waved my hand in the air. "What the fuck ever. Whoever the hell that man is to her, for all we know, he's grateful she's out of the picture. So, quit bellyaching and go get ready for the job. We've got a long night of preparations ahead of us if all goes well with the meet-up."

Trooper called out from the hallway. "I'll get on those patrols. We need to make sure our regular routes are good to go."

"Dutch?" I asked as he slipped through the doorway himself.

He paused, his shoulders pulled taut. "I've doubled down

on security and shored up those empty spaces Naomi talked about."

I nodded. "Good. Then, all three of us can go tonight. Let's get to it."

"Hey," Trooper said as he stuck his head back into the room, "anyone feed Naomi before we started church?"

The three of us looked around at one another before I groaned. "Fine, I'll put together something for her. Just go do your jobs. I'm tired of looking at you."

Troop smirked. "That makes two of us."

"Three," Dutch said as he finally turned to face me.

The look of anger behind his eyes gave me pause. "You got something you want to say?"

His jaw moved, almost like he was chewing on his tongue or some shit. "No."

"Good. Then, get the hell out of my hair and go do your damn jobs. I'll get the girl fed."

"You should know that she didn't eat dinner last night, either, then," Trooper said.

I closed my eyes and pinched the bridge of my nose. "Any particular reason why?"

"No clue. Just figured you should know," he said as his voice faded away.

"Anything else?" I asked.

When I was met with silence, I opened my eyes and found myself all alone in the third-story conference room. Dutch had slipped away at some point in time like he always did, and as Trooper practically leapt his way down the staircase, I pointed myself toward the kitchen. My stomach growled to life, finally getting hungry after hours of being up. So, I set my sights on a couple of nice sandwiches with some chips and some fruit.

Only to find the basement empty as I stood there with the fucking tray of food in my hands.

"Naomi?"

Silence answered me as I stepped over the threshold. "Naomi!?"

And yet, nothing.

"Goddamn it," I murmured before I cleared my throat. "Naomi! Where are you!? I've got--!"

What did I have, anyway? What was the last meal she had eaten?

"Brunch!" I called out.

I sure as hell wasn't tearing that basement apart just to find her. I was tired of chasing her down every time it became our responsibility to feed her. If she wanted to starve? That was just fine with me. She was a grown-ass woman with roaming privileges. She could make her own motherfucking food.

"Naomi!" I bellowed.

With two more motorcycle engines fading into the distance, I found myself alone at the clubhouse with a silent woman playing hide-and-seek. I marched up the stairs; the food rattling around on the tray as I walked down the hallway. I knew damn good and well that she wasn't on the third floor, and if she wasn't in the basement, then there was only one other place she could have been. So, I started throwing open all the doors to the guest bedrooms.

Until I found her perched on one of the beds with a book in her hand.

"There you are," I said as I dropped the tray of food on the top of the dresser that sat next to the door. "Got you some lunch."

Her stare darted over the words on the page before she flipped it. She has her legs tucked beneath her as she sat there, hunched over the book that sat against the black sheets. She looked to be in her own little world, light years away from where we were in our own space and time. And as she sat there, moving rhythmically with each page turn, I let my eyes roam along her body.

Drinking in her curves.

Delighting in her delicious scent.

My hands begging to tug on that hair while I emptied my balls into her.

But the woman had an attitude a mile long and—.

"Cat got your tongue?" Naomi asked.

She finally peeked her gaze over at me and I simply nodded toward the food. "Brunch time."

She looked at the food before her stare fell back to her book. "Not hungry."

I snickered. "With those curves? I'm pretty sure you're starving."

She turned another page. "Thanks. You can leave it there."

I clicked my tongue. "Troop said you didn't eat dinner last night, either."

"I'm shocked you even care, honestly."

I stormed toward her and ripped the book off the bed, slamming it closed. "Just because you want to fight doesn't mean I do. Eat the food, or starve to death. I don't care which."

She looked up at me with apathy in her face before snatching the book right back out of my hand. "Interrupt me again, and you're going to be sorry you did."

I swear, I can never resist a taunt. "Really, now?"

She started searching for her page. "That's a promise."

"Good."

I reached down and took the book from her, only that time I turned around and threw it against the wall. It knocked over the drink I had poured for her, sending ice water spewing everywhere. I chuckled as I turned to face her. I waited for my punishment. For whatever wrath she thought she could bring down upon me. But, as I stood there, my arms opened wide, I--.

"Motherfucker," I hissed as her fist landed straight against my gut.

My arms came down slowly at my sides as my head tilted. The ticklish sensation wafted throughout my body, and I couldn't help the grin that crawled across my face. I had to admit, I wasn't sure she would have done anything. She was brave, I'd give her that.

But she was stupid.

And it would get her killed if she wasn't careful.

"Is that all you've got?" I asked.

Her gaze slowly panned up to my face, and the look of determination etched in her features quickly melted into one of fear.

Oh, that's the good stuff.

I took a step toward her, cloaking her in my shadow. "Are you afraid of me, girl?"

Despite her widened eyes, she held firm. "My name is Naomi, thanks."

"I don't give a damn what your name is. What I want to know is why."

"Why... what?"

It was the one question that had lingered in the back of my mind for days. Ever since she had thrown herself at us. Ever since I had seen those luscious tits of hers enter her father's bedroom before she did, gripping onto that damn shovel, she thought she could actually swing around.

There was one question I still couldn't answer for myself.

"Why did you take your father's place?" I asked, as my voice lowered.

She didn't hesitate to answer. "It's my father, Ranger. He's ill. He would've never survived a day without his meds, much less the week that I've been here."

A week? Feels longer than that. "And yet, you've managed to make your rounds with two of my men."

The grin that slid across her face lit up those gem-colored eyes of hers. "Not my problem. You guys are my only entertainment."

I shook my head. "Not any longer. You've gained access to our relaxation room, and now this room. It's your fault if you're still bored."

She stood on the bed, putting her at eye level with me. "Say what you want and get the hell out, Ranger."

"I swear, that's the cutest part about you?"

She blinked. "What is?"

I reached out and tucked a strand of hair behind her ear. "The fact that you think you have control."

She yanked away from my touch the second the words fell from my lips. "I've always got more control than people give me credit for."

"Including your fiancée?"

That seemed to suck the breath out of her lungs. She opened her mouth to speak, but nothing came out. Open, nothing, closed.

Open, nothing, closed.

Like a damn guppy in a goldfish bowl.

"You want to know what I think?" I asked as I pointed my finger at her chest.

She fell back down to the bed, her thick curves dancing for my viewing pleasure.

"No," she said as she scrambled to get to the other side of the bed.

Her answer broadening my grin. "I think you wanted to get captured because you wanted to get away from your life. You're running, and we gave you the ability to run without ever having to make the decision for yourself."

She scrambled to get onto her knees as she puffed her chest out in pride. "I did this for my father. You three idiots would've killed him at the drop of a hat, not knowing about his medication."

I held my arms out. "I think you're just a coward who couldn't make a decision for herself, so you placed the decision with us."

"I did this so my father could live!" she exclaimed. "And it doesn't shock me one fucking bit that you don't understand that kind of love!"

Her words snapped something inside of me, and everything went black. I didn't know how long I was out, or how much I missed. But when my vision cleared, I found her pinned beneath me on the bed with my knee pressed between her legs and her arms pinned above her head.

"You," I glowered, "have no idea about the people I have loved."

She snarled up at me, her teeth gnashed together. "And you know nothing of the life I left behind in order to save my father from whatever fate you three had for him. I had a house with my fiancée, and a father that loves me, and a career I loved. I had no reason to run away."

I lowered my face into hers until I felt her breath pulsing against my lips. "I think I know why you ran away."

She scoffed. "Then why don't you enlighten me?"

My lips moved to the shell of her ear as a growl practically bubbled up the back of my throat. "Boredom, sweet girl. That's why you ran."

It was the first time I had rendered her silent, and I considered that my victory. It was a shame, though. I had hoped she'd be a bit more complex than that. But she was just some scared little girl who had made stupid decisions in her life to go with the flow of the status quo instead of taking what she wanted by the balls.

She was another scared member of society.

It was honestly disappointing.

"So," I said as I hopped off the bed and made my way for the bedroom door, "if you're really that fucking bored, there's a bar not too far up the road. Bury, one of the guards outside, can take you there if you want to get out and have a drink."

I strode out into the hallway as her voice followed me.

"Aren't you worried that I'll make a break for it!?"

I chuckled as I drew in a deep breath. "No. Because I know I'm right. And because I'm right, you'll come back every single time. Anything to cure your boredom, really."

And as silence followed me down the stairs, I tucked my victory into my belt and focused my sights on the evening.

We had a mission to fulfill, after all.

18

———

NAOMI

The pride in his voice made me want to punch him again. "No. Because I know I'm right. And because I'm right, you'll come back every single time. Anything to cure your boredom, really."

I ground my teeth together as I snatched the book up from the bed. What the hell was wrong with that man? How in the fuck could the other two stand him? He didn't know what the fuck he was talking about, and it wasn't worth fighting with someone who always thought they were right. After all, I had never won a fucking fight with Gordon that ever ended with me being heard if he came into the conversation thinking he had already won.

And I sure as hell didn't intend to engage in another one of those arguments.

"Stupid fuck," I murmured as I started flipping through the pages of the book.

I found my place in the book, but I couldn't focus. There was a bar? That I could go to? God, it sounded lovely, the idea of getting out and getting a drink. All the time, I used to take my lunch breaks at the bar and grill across the street just to steal some time to myself. And while the book in my hand wasn't the one still in my purse back at home, the thought of being anywhere but the fucking house pulled me off the bed.

Except, I had no money for a drink.

"Here," Ranger said as he stuck his arm back through the door.

I watched him slap something against the dresser before he poked his head in.

"You know, in case you actually want to eat there as well instead of starving on our watch."

I looked at the wad of cash he had left behind, almost like he had read my mind. "Thanks."

"You're welcome," he grumbled as his boot steps faded down the hallway.

I waited until I couldn't hear him. I waited until I thought he was down the steps for good, then I raced over to the tray. I scooped up the money and unfolded it, trying to organize it into some semblance of understanding. And as I counted it out, my eyes widened.

Jesus fuck, the man had given me three hundred bucks.

"This is such a bad idea," I murmured to myself.

You know, before I stashed the money in my bra.

A smile overtook my face as I raced out of the room. I held the book tightly, making my way into the basement to try to scrounge an outfit together. Over the past few days, Dutch and Trooper had brought me some things. A pair of sweatpants. Some t-shirts. Troop brought a summer dress he thought I'd like, even though it fit me horribly. Still, they tried, and I picked through the few straggling things before I found that a comfortable set of leggings and a fresh t-shirt was perfect for a relaxing day in the corner booth of a bar.

I was going to make it a day of drinks and snacks while I read a book. A day for me. A day for myself that I hadn't taken in so long. A day off where I didn't have someone to entertain, or someone's friends to put on a face for, or a father to take care of that needed a care facility more than he did a loving, doting daughter. I slipped into the soft leggings and pulled the shirt over my head. It was baggy as hell, but I didn't care. It gave my body room to breathe, which was something it hadn't had lately, and it made me step outside with a smile on my face.

It made me hopeful for the first time in... years.

"Now," I said as I threw open the front door, "which one of you is Bury?"

Six men shot to their feet and practically barricaded me inside.

"Ranger told me someone named Bury could take me to some bar up the road for a drink?" I asked.

The man in the middle folded his arms over his chest. "Did he now?"

The dingy looking man with dirt on his face attempted to pin me with a look, but I was much too immune to that. Every single one of these guys had a stare that could have killed, but the problem was that I didn't care.

At the end of the day, they were just boys.

And boys didn't frighten me one bit.

"Yeah, he did," I said as I took a step toward him, "so, are we heading out? Or do I need to ask someone else to take me?"

The guys all turned their stares toward Bury, who raked his gaze up and down my body.

"Well?" I asked.

He sighed as he stepped off to the side. "Get in the car. I'll drive."

I smiled politely. "Thank you, Bury."

"Yeah, yeah," he murmured.

I sauntered toward the car, knowing damn good and well those guys were staring at me. Men were so easy. A little sway of the hips. A little flutter of the eyelashes. A little hair flip before a nice "thank you," and they were putty in your hands. These guys were no different. They enjoyed salivating over a woman, just like the next guy did.

So, I decided to give them a show.

A show that never made them question who really had control.

I busied myself with my book as the car lurched forward. I swear, it sank closer to the road whenever Bury shifted himself, and I wondered if we'd even get there before the engine started scraping against the black asphalt. It was humorous, honestly. Like a clown car stuffed to the brim with giants from the top of the beanstalk.

Still, when we pulled up to the bar, a giddy sort of excitement flushed its way through my veins.

"I'll be outside when you're ready to head back," Bury said as he parked the car.

My finger held its position on my current page as I looked up. "And if I decide to make a break for it?"

He pulled a gun off his hip and cocked it. "Then I get to have a bit of target practice."

"Seriously? You're going to kill me?"

He placed the gun back in his holster. "If you run, yes."

"Did Ranger give you that order, or something?"

He craned his gaze over his shoulder to look at me. "You haven't pussy-whipped everyone, you know."

I slammed the back door open. "Whatever."

"One more thing," Bury said.

I stood to my feet and stuck my head back into the car. "What?"

He turned his gaze forward. "The bartender's one of ours. He knows you're coming. So, my advice to you is to not do anything rash."

"Jesus, you're like fucking fruit flies," I whispered as I closed the door.

Bury chuckled. "We're everywhere, and you'd do well to remember that."

I wasted no time in getting myself inside and picking out my favorite place in any bar: the corner booth. Kudos to any bar whose lights over their corner booths weren't working. I didn't want people staring at me. I didn't want them knowing who I was.

All I wanted was a bit of peace and some fucking junk food.

"Hi there," a cheery waitress said as she came up to me, "what can I getcha?"

I didn't even need to look at the menu. "You guys got wings and fries here?"

"We sure do."

I nodded. "I'll have some wings in buffalo sauce, a double order of fries, and a bottle of chianti."

She scribbled things down onto her little notepad. "Anything else?"

I cracked my book open. "Not for now."

"Perfect. I'll go get that bottle. You want it chilled?"

I flipped the page. "That sounds amazing, thank you."

"My pleasure."

I lost myself in the words of the book. In the adventure unfolding in front of me. I was a sucker for a good fantasy novel, and the way the author described her ice-wielding powers sucked me in. Icicles poured from her fingertips, slicing and dicing through enemies as they attempted to cross the threshold into her kingdom. And as all of her loyal subjects awaited their fate, I--.

"Here ya go," the waitress said as she placed my food in front of me.

I looked up and found that there was also a glass of wine on the table, completely untouched.

With that bottle of chianti sitting in an ice bucket.

"I didn't even realize, sorry," I said.

"Ain't no big thing," the waitress said as she put my food down. "Been a while since a read a good book. You keep on doing your thing, and I'll come back around in a bit."

I smiled up at her. "Thanks. I really appreciate it."

She winked. "Us girls always gotta stick together. You enjoy."

The second those buffalo wings tickled my nostrils, my stomach let out the most insane growl. I had to look around the room to see if anyone else had heard it, because surely the damned thing had a bullhorn up to its mouth. I placed my book down, marking my spot with a bit of a paper napkin that I quickly tore off from my silverware. And as I reached for a wing, I slathered it in the ranch before bringing it to my lips.

And that was all it took.

"God, I'm starving," I murmured to myself.

I was almost embarrassed as to how quickly I tore through those wings. My stomach cried out for more. Cried out to be filled after barely eating a meal a day as it was. I sucked the meat off those bones and dipped my fries in the remaining sauce, refusing to come up for air until everything had been sopped up, mopped up, and devoured.

And as I used the little wet wipe that had come with my meal to wipe my hands, the waitress magically appeared again.

"Good?" she asked with a soft giggle.

I leaned back. "It was fantastic."

"Ya want anything else?" she asked as she gathered up the empty plates.

I finally reached for my glass of wine. "Got anything for dessert?"

The waitress winked at me. "I'll bring you my favorite."

I held my wine up to her. "Cheers to that."

But I didn't even get the wine to my lips before a voice sounded in front of me.

"A girl who's got an appetite. That's rare in this world."

I flickered my gaze toward the booth in front of me and found a man sitting on the edge of the booth, his head crooked around the corner.

"Thanks, I think," I said as I took a long pull from my drink.

He stood to his feet, and I got a good look at him. He seemed ordinary enough. Not at all like one of the guys who supposedly were keeping an eye on me at all times. He had some gray at his temples and a basic collared shirt tucked into a set of khakis that looked to be two sizes too big for him. His smile was kind, though. Unassuming.

It reminded me of the first time I'd ever met Gordon.

"Mind if I take a seat?" he asked, his hand pointing to the empty seat in front of me.

"Mind if I take a seat?" the boy in the leather jacket asked.

I looked up at him, my lunch still hanging halfway out of my mouth. Was he talking to me?

"Yes," he said as he sat down, "I'm talking to you, Library Girl."

I chewed quickly and swallowed. "Yeah, yeah. Sure. You're good."

He smiled, and it disarmed me. "I'm Gordon."

"Naomi."

"I know," he said.

My cheeks flushed. "Y—you do?"

He nodded. "I do."

It should've been my first red flag. My first glimpse into the fact that something had always been wrong with Gordon. After all, who in the hell knows someone's name before they're ever introduced?

I don't know, maybe it was a common thing. Maybe some women even swooned over that kind of thing. But, after everything I had found out about Gordon—about the man that had swindled me all my life—the interaction with the kind man at the booth had me on high alert.

"All right," the man said as he sat down, "let's start with an easier question. What's your name?"

I followed my gut for once. "Debra."

He smiled. "Beautiful name for a beautiful girl. Whatcha reading?"

I held up the book so he could see the cover before I turned my attention back to reading. Maybe if I ignored him long enough, he'd get fed up and go away. I dragged my glass of wine behind the book and sipped it, all the while wondering where in the hell that waitress had gotten off to with my dessert.

I needed an exit strategy, and quickly.

"There we are," the man grunted as I felt my book being pushed down and out of my view. "Don't wanna cover up those eyes of yours. They're your best feature."

"Look," I said with a sigh, "I'm sure you're very kind. But all I want right now is to enjoy a nice afternoon out."

He leaned back. "Then, it's a good thing that's all I'm trying to do as well."

Jesus Christ, why the fuck did men always have to ruin shit?

Just answer his questions until the waitress comes, and then he'll leave.

"The book I'm reading," I said before I cleared my throat, "is about a young woman meant to be queen, but she has to battle a great evil in order to secure her seat on the throne."

The man nodded. "Sounds interesting. Is it a series?"

"The whole book is the trilogy."

"So, it is."

I shrugged. "Depends on how you want to define the word 'series.'"

He chuckled. "I like you. You're quick-witted."

Well, I don't like you. "Thanks."

"So, what does a girl like you enjoy doing around here? Taking a dip in the ocean or something?"

"No," I said plainly.

"Seeing a movie, then?"

I sighed as I peered over my book. "Look, I'm sure you're really nice, but I just want to enjoy my wine and read my book."

"Doesn't mean you can't hold a conversation."

"Yes, it does. I have to focus on my reading, or I'll lose my place."

The man's smile grew almost comically large. "Then we can keep each other company."

I didn't know if he couldn't take the hint or didn't want to take the hint. But, either way, I started looking for that waitress. It felt like she had been gone an entire fucking hour. Where the hell was she with that dessert?

I needed help, and I had no one to ask.

Which sent a shivering chill up my spine.

"All right," the waitress said as she finally came out of the kitchen, "one large slice of piping up chocolate cake with all three of our drizzles. I love dunkin' them. It's so good, especially with the raspberry stuff we've got here."

Relief washed over me. "Thank you so much. Can I also get my check?"

She eyed me carefully. "Is... everything all right?"

The man answered for me. "Everything is fine. Can I get a-."

I interrupted him. "Just the check, please. And a to-go box for my dessert. I'm ready to head out."

She peeked back over at the guy before patting my shoulder. "I'll get right on it. You hold tight."

Thank fuck. "Thank you. It's much appreciated."

"You can just put her stuff on my tab, Ramsey," the man said.

Jesus Christ, I wanted to punch him in the throat. "That isn't necessary. I've got my own money, so I'll pay my own bill."

"Look, I insist," the man said as he cocked to one side and pulled out his wallet, "it's the least I can do for--."

"No," I said plainly.

The man tossed his wallet onto the tabletop. "You seem nice, so I'll be honest: all I'm saying is that I wanna treat you to something. You look like you haven't been treated to anything in a while, and that's all I wanna do. Promise."

I locked eyes with him as I reached into my bra. I pulled out my cash and fiddled with a few twenties before handing it to the waitress. I didn't have the energy to put up with that man a second longer. If I wasn't going to find a shred of peace in the bar, then I'd go back to the clubhouse and get it there.

"Keep the change," I said as I finally turned to face the waitress, "and the slice of cake. I'll be back around soon, and I can try it then."

"You want me to cork your bottle of wine so you can take it with you?" she asked.

The man heaved a heavy sigh as I shook my head. "You take it. You look like you could use a drink just about as much as me."

She held up the money before placing it in her apron. "Thanks for the tip."

I nodded before I turned toward the man. "When a woman says 'no,' that's exactly what she means. No matter your intentions, the fact that you ignored mine negates every good thing you wanted to try and do here. Learn the lesson and remember that for next time."

I'd had enough food and wine for one day, anyway. The last thing I needed was to be stumbling drunk in a bar with a man who didn't want to stop breathing down the back of my neck. I heard him mumble something beneath his breath, but I didn't catch what it was. And I didn't care, either.

All I cared about was getting back home.

Even if I didn't know where home was any longer.

I picked up my book and caught a side exit out of the corner of my eye. Perfect. A quick getaway back to Bury and the car. I wasted no time in walking over to the door and shoving my arm into it. I spilled out into the alleyway, turning left to head back toward the parking lot. With every step I took, my relief became greater. Any distance put between me and that asshole who didn't understand the English language was a win in my book. It was the kind of distance I should have placed between me and Gordon, instead of succumbing to whatever book fetish had told me it was possible for someone like him to ever want someone like me.

Gordon always looked out for number one.

For himself.

And damned be the consequences if anyone else got caught up in his shit.

"Good ridd—AH!"

My head fell back before my body stumbled on its feet. A hand clapped over my mouth before my face went soaring toward the brick wall, and had it not been for a last-minute turn of my cheek, I would have absolutely broken my nose. Panic gripped my throat. Something shoved the back of my head, sending my forehead banging into the brick. And as bile crept up the back of my throat, I felt my book tumble from my hand.

Before a set of shoes attached to a khaki-laced leg crushed it into the muddy waters at my feet.

"So, this is what I get for being nice to the bookworm, huh? Embarrassed in front of everyone for being nice?"

I raked my fingernails up and down the brick, trying my best to find leverage.

"Well," the man hissed as he spun me around, "maybe you'll think twice before being such a grade-A bitch."

I spat in the man's face. Hell, I didn't even have to look at his face to know who the hell it was. The gray at his temples flashed in the sunlight as his collared shirt sat cockeyed on his shoulders. I fought against him, batting his hands away and doing my best to cry out for help. But every time I parted my lips, his hand clamped around them.

Keeping me silent as his hand gripped my shirt.

"Let's see where all of that food goes, shall we?" he asked.

His smile was crooked and his eyes were filled with malice. I'd never seen a look of pure evil before, but as I stood there—pinned between his disgusting erection and the brick wall—I found myself face to face with it.

"Get—off me!" I cried out into the palm of his hand.

His free hand worked its way up my shirt and tugged at my bra. "Ah, there we go. Just what I was looking fo—SHIT!"

I opened my mouth as wide as I could and bit down against his hand. I dug my teeth into his skin until I tasted something warm and metallic against my tongue, and he ripped his hand away. I started screaming. I screamed at the top of my lungs as I started running toward the parking lot. But yet another yank of my hair sent me tumbling to the ground.

Soaking my stomach in the stale, muddy waters of the alleyway.

"Stupid bitch," he growled.

He slammed his fist into my lower back, and I cried out in pain. He threw me around like a damn rag doll, picking me up from the ground and tossing me back against the wall. My legs gave way, sending me plummeting back to the concrete. But not before the back of his hand smacked me against my cheek.

Sending tears to blind my vision.

"I'm going to have fun with you," he said as I heard the clattering of a belt buckle in front of me. "And when I'm done with you, maybe you'll learn some goddamn manners along the way."

"Maybe it's you who needs some manners."

Bury's voice came out of nowhere and I crumpled to the ground. I curled up into a ball, sobbing into the waters that drenched my skin. My clothes. My book. The tears fell like raindrops from the sky. Big, heavy teardrops that held the sins of my past, my present, and probably my future. I blocked out the sounds. I focused on the way the wind kicked up, sending microscopic ripples of that muddy water against my cheek.

Almost as if it were caressing my tears away as I cried them.

Suddenly, I felt a set of hands on me. I flailed around, screaming and crying and beating my fists against anything I could touch. I kicked my legs. I spat a mouthful of blood down onto the ground before shoving my shoulder into someone's gut. At least, I thought it was their gut.

It wasn't until Bury tossed me over his shoulder that I heard his voice.

"We have to get out of here. I'm taking you home."

And as that word echoed off the corners of my mind, relief took hold as more sobs poured forth.

Home.

Bury was taking me home.

Home, to the only place that had felt safe since I had moved out of my childhood home.

Maybe I really am better off inside with the guys.

19

RANGER

"Ranger!"

The sound of Bury's bellowing voice brought me to my feet.

"Ranger! We have a problem!"

I took off running down the stairs, and when I saw Naomi tossed over his shoulder, I froze.

"What happened?" I asked as I rushed over to him. "Tell me everything."

"Ra—ra—Ranger?"

I furrowed my brow. "What's wrong? Why is she crying?"

Bury placed her down on her feet and grabbed her shoulders. But I wasn't nearly ready for the sight to be had when he turned her around. Blood dribbled from her mouth as a bruise continued to darken against her cheek, right in front of my eyes.

"Look at her hands," Bury said.

My furious gaze dropped to her fingernails, and I saw that she had ripped some of them clear off her fucking nail beds.

My vision dripped with red. "Tell me everything. Now."

"There was a guy at the bar that wouldn't leave her alone. Ramsey said he kept dodging her efforts to tell him to piss off, but politely. You know the shit girls do sometimes."

I kept my gaze trained on Naomi as she stared at my chest. She had blood dripping down her neck, she was missing actual fingernails, and yet she simply stood there. Blank-faced. Not making a sound. No moaning in pain fell from her lips. No tears streaked her cheeks. None of her breathing was choppy, like she'd been crying on the way back.

She just stood there, seemingly lifeless. No yelling. No fighting. No arguing. No explanation.

As if she had given up on everything around her.

"What does he look like?" I asked as my gaze lifted to Bury.

"I snapped a picture of him before I got her back to the car. I sent it to your phone."

I dug it out of my pocket and forced my gaze down to the picture. "Oh. That rat bastard."

"Yes. That rat bastard."

I turned off my phone and placed it back in my pocket. "Naomi, can you hear me?"

If she did, she didn't make a move. No blinking. No nodding. No... nothing.

The anger I felt welling up within my body threatened to consume me. It was so great. I'd kill that motherfucker for what he'd done to her. Bury didn't even have to finish the story for me to understand why she looked the way she did.

So, I scooped her into my arms and tried my best not to focus on how limp her body felt in my grasp.

"Bury?" I asked.

"Yeah, boss?"

"Round up the guys from the field," I said as I made my way to the basement door. "We've got work to do."

When I got downstairs, I perched Naomi on the closed toilet seat. I opened the mirror above the sink and pulled out some peroxide, some bandages, and a few cotton balls. I had to do something. I had to keep myself busy while Dutch and Troop got back to the house.

Because when they got here, we had hunting to get done.

After gathering everything I needed, I knelt in front of her. Her gaze stared squarely into mine, but she didn't look to be home. It was as if her body were on autopilot, simply going through the motions without registering a damn thing around her.

I poured some peroxide onto the cotton balls before gripping her chin.

"He'll pay for this," I growled as I dabbed at the blood dripping from her lip.

She finally made a sound, and it was a scoff. "I didn't think you cared."

Her words lingered in my mind for a while, trapped between the two of us. I got the blood cleaned up enough to realize the blood was inside of her mouth, so I folded down her lip to make sure she had all of her teeth. Her gums were split, so I discarded the blood-soaked cotton ball in favor of some plain gauze.

And after tucking a small piece against her injured lower gumline, I folded her lip back into place.

"No one touches what is ours," I glowered.

That snapped her back into her body. "I'm not your property."

I gripped her chin. "I never said you were."

Her gaze danced between my own. "Why are men always like this? Always—ruining good things?"

She reminded me so much of my Alicia that it damn near made me sick. "I don't know."

She pulled her chin away from my grip before her gaze fell to her lap. "I'm fine. I just need a moment."

"Hey," I said pointedly as I crooked my finger beneath her

chin.

I raised her gaze back to mine before stroking my thumb along her cheek, catching a rogue tear as it slipped from her beautiful green gaze.

"You're better than that," I said as I held her attention. "Act like it."

That was all it took. A simple directive to dig down deep into her gut for that well of strength she had no problems show-casing. And when she did, she sat there for me while I cleaned her up. I finally got her mouth to stop bleeding, though she'd be sore and bruised for a few days. Despite her hissing and jerking, I managed to clean the rocks and dirty water from her exposed fingernail beds before wrapping them up in gauze. It took every-thing inside of me not to tremble with fury as I thought about all of the ways I'd skin that motherfucker at the bar alive for what he had done to her.

And after retrieving an ice pack for the bruise on her cheek, I scooped her back into my arms.

"I think it's time to lie down," I said as I walked her over to the bed.

She relinquished herself to me, her head placed softly against my shoulder as I settled her down on the mattress. She turned her back to me, resting her cheek on the ice while prop-ping it up with the pillow. I eased myself down and pulled her legs into my lap. I took off her shoes, tossing them to the floor before peeling the soaking wet socks off her feet.

"Do you want anything else off?" I asked.

She shook her head. "No."

I placed her legs back down onto the bed. "Do you want me to stay?"

"Where the fuck is he!?" Trooper exclaimed.

He slammed through the basement door with Dutch hot on his heels.

"Where is she?" Dutch asked. "Is she all right?"

I stood to my feet, shielding Naomi from their prying gazes. "Calm down."

"Calm down? Calm down!?" Trooper asked as he threw his hands into the air. "Bury just said Naomi was almost raped at the bar, and you want me to--."

"Oh, my God," Naomi choked out.

Her soft crying filled the room around us as Trooper pushed me off to the side. He crawled onto the bed, getting into Naomi's face as he stroked her hair off to the side. Dutch wrapped around to the other side, standing there with his hands balled up into fists. And when I saw the droplets of his own blood soaking his fingernails, I snapped my fingers.

"We've had enough bleeding for one day," I said.

He unfurled his fists. "And one more will bleed before the day is done."

"Naomi, it's me," Trooper said softly as he settled into bed next to her. "I'm right here. So is Dutch. Would you like to see Dutch?"

"Where is the son of a bitch?" Dutch asked.

His voice was much too calm for that question, and if I had been a fearful man, it would have shaken me to my core.

"I have his picture. He won't get far," I said.

"What are you guys going to do to him?" Naomi asked through her sniffling.

Trooper kissed her forehead. "You let us worry about that, pretty girl. Okay? You let us take care of him."

"Ranger?" Naomi asked.

Even Dutch seemed shocked that she had asked for me.

"Yes?" I asked.

I saw her stick her hand up into the air. "Can you come here?"

I nodded, motioning for Troop to get up so I could sit down.

He leapt off the bed, standing next to Dutch who was practically vibrating with the same anger that bubbled my blood in its veins. I sat on the edge of the bed. I placed my hand on the other side of her body, hovering over her in the hopes that my presence made her feel safer.

And as she turned onto her back, I knew what she was going to say before she even said it.

"I'm sorry," she said softly.

I picked up the ice pack and held it to her delicate cheek. "We'll bring back some dinner and we can eat out on the back porch. Watch the sunset. How does that sound?"

"Do we have to talk?"

I shook my head. "Not if you don't want to."

She turned back onto her side, her back toward me. "That sounds nice."

I nodded as I stood. "Guys? Upstairs. Now."

"We're just going to leave her here? Alone?" Troop asked.

"I want to be alone for a little while. It's why I went to the bar. So, if I could get it now, that would be nice," Naomi said plainly.

"You heard the woman," I said as I thumbed over my shoulder. "Let's go."

It took us no time at all to scale those stairs. I had to do something. I had to move around. Get out of the house. Track down that slimy motherfucker and chop his head right off his fucking shoulders after I relieved him of his pathetic little dick. I needed to do something with this energy. With this anger, I couldn't abate.

"Bury!" I exclaimed.

He came soaring through the front door. "How is she?"

"About as good as you can expect," I said as Dutch and Troop gathered around us.

"Your orders?" Bury asked.

My face hardened into stone. "Find him and bring him to the warehouse."

"Well, he's already in the trunk," Bury said with a straight face. "Want me to get him set up for you?"

I peered around his body and watched as the car buoyed around on its chassis.

"Good work," I said as I brushed past him. "We'll take it from here."

"Help! Somebody, help me! Anyone! Heeeeelp!"

Troop dragged the man out of the trunk, kicking and screaming like the pussy he really was. If he thought for one second he was ever going to be good enough for a woman like Naomi, he had another thing coming. He was nothing but a spineless rat bastard that didn't know his asshole from his dickhole.

Dutch propped open the door to the warehouse as Troop dragged the walking dead man inside.

"Where to?" Troop asked.

"The hook," I said plainly.

That made Dutch smile. "My favorite.

"No! Please! I'll do anything. Anything! Just let me gooooooo!"

I walked inside behind the belly-aching bitch before Dutch closed the door behind all of us. Darkness encompassed us, and I swear to God I'd never heard a man sob the way that man did.

"Take the long way around," I said as I split off from them. "I want him good and ready for when it's my turn."

"Please. No, no, no—nooooo! Stop it, please!"

Hearing that man's screams echoing off the metal walls of the warehouse brought a smile to my face. I walked exactly twenty-two paces before shoving my shoulder into the wall to my right, and as the door slammed open, a singular light got triggered.

Shining a harsh spotlight down onto the meat hook hanging from the ceiling.

The sound of punches intoxicated me as the man stopped screaming and started gurgling on his own blood. Trooper, no doubt. That man loved a good boxing ring. The sound of crunching bones and cracking knuckles backdropped my stretching as I reached my hands toward the sky. My back popped into place. My fingertips tickled the meat hook before I jumped up, grabbing it with both of my hands.

I swung my hips around, releasing the tension I'd been carrying around since snatching up Naomi in the first place.

And as the door on the other side of the room slammed open, I watched Dutch drag the mumbling man toward me.

"Broken jaw," I said as Troop stood in the open doorway. "Nice."

He shook out his hands. "Think I broke a rib or two as well."

I backed away from the meat hook. "You want to do the honors, Dutch? Or should I?"

That statuesque man, with his long arms and his tight grip, hoisted our bleeding wannabe rapist up there without even breaking a sweat.

"I'll take the honor this time," he said as he gazed up at his latest prey.

I held my hands up in mock surrender. "Hey, suit yourself. I'm just glad I get to strangle the guy."

"Please," the man choked out, "you've got the wro—aaaa-AAAH! HOLY FUCK!"

Dutch threaded that meat hook through the space between each of his collarbones, linking him permanently to the swinging structure. The man couldn't even get his arms over his head to grab onto the rope above him, and when he tried, the sound of snapping twigs for bones made me come alive. Dutch moved like lightning, scooting a chair just beneath the man's foot so he could tiptoe around for his life.

And as Troop finally made his way into the room, he got one more sucker punch to his lower back.

"That's for Naomi," he glowered. "You know, the girl you tried to rape at the bar today."

"What?" the man sputtered. "I-I-I—I didn't do—I'm not--."

"So, you don't know who this is?" Dutch asked.

I watched him shove his phone into the man's face, no doubt with a picture of Naomi on it. And when recognition sprouted behind his eyes, it only confirmed what we already knew.

"That's what I thought," Dutch said as he tossed his phone to the ground.

While Trooper enjoyed a brutish touch, Dutch enjoyed his finesse. Maximum pain for minimal work, like watching the man dance ballet on his tiptoes so that his collarbones wouldn't rip clear from his body.

"You know," Dutch said as he circled his prey, "they say that the artery running along the inside of one's thigh, when nicked, can force someone to bleed out in a matter of seconds.

He brandished a knife that seemed to sing as he held it to the inside of the man's leg.

"But that almost seems too merciful for someone like you," Dutch said.

I folded my arms over my chest and watched the show as Dutch filleted the man out of his khakis. His boxers. His shirt. He took his time undressing our appetizer, and the bruises Troop had left behind shimmered in the spotlight. Sweat dripped down the man's brow, carrying with it every last drop of life he clung to.

Then I watched as Dutch grabbed the man's balls and

pulled them out as far as they could go.

"No, no, no, no. Please. Oh, Jesus Christ. I did it, okay? Do you want me to admit it? I did it, and I'm so sorry. I'll never do it again. I swear to fuck on high, I never will."

Dutch paused, the blade of his knife right against the man's wrinkly sack of skin. "Promise?"

The man whose name we didn't bother to know nodded vehemently. "Yes, yes, yes. I promise with everything I am."

Dutch tilted his head. "I don't believe you."

His knife sliced through that man's nut sack like butter and the scream that poured from the back of his throat filled me with a need deep within the pit of my gut. Blood dripped from between the man's leg as Dutch stepped off to the side, beckoning to Troop with his knife.

"Want some target practice?" Dutch asked.

And he sure as hell didn't need to tell Troop twice.

The man soared away from my side, almost as if wings carried him across the ground. He sank his balled-up fist against the man's dangling dick, and the pain muted the man. He gasped for air, his face turning blue as his body grew limper. His collarbones cracked. His skin broke. The white of the bone started protruding as Troop slammed his fist against the man's gut, forcing him to breathe.

Forcing him to take in life when he no longer wanted it.

"No one touches what is ours," Dutch said as he wiped the man's nut blood off on his pant leg.

"And Naomi is absolutely, unequivocally, ours," Troop glowered.

Then they both turned to face me.

"Well, then," I said as I walked up to the man, staring at him, eye level to eye level. "I guess you've found yourself in quite the predicament."

He coughed up blood before he choked out the words. "Are

you going to kill me?"

I reached one hand out and wrapped it around his throat. "Yes."

He whimpered. "Will it at least be quick?"

I smiled as I wrapped my other hand around his neck as well. "No."

I pivoted, wringing my hands around the man's neck while Dutch stepped back up to the forefront. I squeezed my hands, feeling him struggling for life as I drew in a deep breath. Dutch grabbed the man's dick before yet another slice of his knife dropped the useless piece of meat to the ground. And as Dutch laid another punch toward the man's nonexistent groin, his pain made him seize.

He shook in my grasp, his body flailing around like a fish out of water. And as I tightened my grasp, I placed my lips to his ear.

Making sure my voice was the last he heard.

"No one. Touches. What is ours," I growled.

Before his entire body went limp.

With a twist of my hands, I snapped his neck. The sound reverberated throughout my entire body before I stumbled back, my head tilted toward the sky. Life flowed through my veins, coursing through my system as it stood my cock on end.

He'd never lay hands on my Naomi again.

On *our* Naomi again.

"Make sure no one finds him," I said as my head came down out of the clouds.

Troop chuckled. "Same place as always?"

Dutch shook his head. "I say we cook the man."

I pointed at Dutch. "Bingo. Leave no trace."

"Never to be seen again," Troop said.

Just like the rest of our victims that believed they held ownership over what was rightfully ours.

20

————

NAOMI

With the fluorescent light buzzing overhead, I finally found the strength to sit up. My head pounded in pain and my mouth felt like it was on fire. But it still didn't stop me from looking down at my left hand. It didn't stop me from studying my left ring finger, clocking the stark tan like across my skin. I didn't even tan easily. I always burned more than anything else. I was freckled from head to toe from sun damage as a child, and yet the tan line was clear as day.

For years, I'd been wearing a promise to Gordon that he had never once anted up on. We should've been married years ago, but he always kept finding reasons to put it off. His career, or Dad's health, or the move into the house, or something with his friends.

There had always been something more important than our wedding day.

That is, until he had sprung that "surprise" on me.

"Selfish bastard," I murmured.

It wasn't the tan line that struck me as odd, though. Well, it was odd, but it didn't explain how light I felt on my feet. Removing that ring from my body had released me from a burden I never once realized I had been carrying around. I felt so flipped upside down, and I couldn't make sense of it. I was free, but not at the same time. And yet, every time I thought about returning to my life, it scared me. Being held as an actual prisoner had shown me just how jailed I had been in my relationship with Gordon. At my job. In the fight to keep my father from death. Everything in my life had trapped me, and I never understood how bad it had gotten until those guys had removed me from it.

Until I had a reason to step away from it.

Since when did I hate my life so much?

Footsteps above my head ripped me from my trance. I turned around, forcing my pain into the back of my mind as I made myself face the door. I slid to the edge of the bed, still holding the melted ice pack to my face. And when Ranger appeared in the doorway, my heart skipped a beat.

"Hey," I said softly.

He stood in the doorway, his body filling it up as his head fell off to the side. "You'll never be bothered again at the bar."

I swallowed hard. "Does that mean what I think it means?"

He started walking toward me. "Do you really want to know?"

I tilted my head back to keep him in view. "I don't get any of this."

He knelt in front of me, crooking his finger beneath my chin as he gazed into my eyes. "Neither do I."

"I don't—I don't understand anything, anymore."

He stayed there, unwavering and unmoving, as his finger held me hostage.

"I just--," I said breathlessly.

"Take your time," he said.

I had no more energy to fight. "It's like... just... everything...

it was all a lie, you know? With Gordon, a-a-a—and... and everything."

His finger moved before he cupped his hand on top of mine, holding the ice pack to my cheek. "I think you need another one."

I snickered. "Yeah, I think so."

A shadow of a grin ticked his cheeks. "Sometimes, sweet girl, no one knows what they want until they're staring it in the face."

My gaze searched his. "Yeah?"

He nodded. "Yeah. That's how it was with me and my crew when I first pledged."

I shrugged. "Maybe you can tell me the story sometime."

"Maybe over breakfast."

I scooted closer to the edge of the bed as my voice fell to a whisper. "Maybe."

"Fucking hell," I growled.

The first thing I felt was his arms. The strength of them. The mountainous form of their existence. They wrapped me up and pulled me close, and yet not once did their grasp hurt me. I curled my aching fists into his leather jacket. I pulled him close, arching my face up to his as my lips searched for somewhere to land.

And as his mouth fell to mine, our teeth clattered together in an unwavering kiss.

"Mmmm," I moaned.

"Mine," he growled.

My back hit the bed, and I didn't care that it hurt. I didn't care that my body felt like it was on fire. All I wanted was to block it out. All I wanted was to focus on something else. Anything else. Anything other than the constant pain, I couldn't sort out. He sucked on my lower lip. His nibbles worked their way down my neck as he sucked on patches of skin that damn near sent me hurtling through the ceiling. And as my hands tangled into his pitch black hair, I found those steel-gray eyes of his hovering over me.

"If I hurt you, say something," he said.

I shook my head. "I'm not sure that you ever could."

His lips dropped to mine once more and my legs spread as wide as they could go. Jesus Christ, the man was a mountain, and part of me wondered if I had to dislocate my hips just to make room for him. I felt his thickness pressing into my thigh. His tongue, teasing the roof of my mouth as his bricked girth stroked my clothed pussy.

"Ranger," I gasped.

"My sweet girl," he grunted.

He peeled me out of my clothes, one by one, and cast them to the floor. I'd never felt so exposed, yet so cloaked, in all my life. As each of his articles of clothing fell to the floor, his chiseled muscles came into view. And for the first time, I understood what a personified mountain looked like. His chest swelled with the strength of ten thousand men. His arms bulged with angry veins that looked as if they were fleeing his body in desperation. His thighs twitched, girding a rock-hard dick with veins that matched his pulsing forearms.

I found myself entranced by him.

"Ranger," I whispered.

He laid down beside me and reached for my hand. "Up."

I scrambled to get onto my knees. "Now what?"

He grinned as he pointed to his mouth. "Sit."

I blinked. "What?"

He yanked me toward his body, causing me to fall against him. "Don't make me repeat myself, sweet girl. You won't like the punishment that comes if you do."

I was overwhelmed by him, but my body obeyed. I climbed up his body like a goddamn mountain trail before placing my knees on either side of his face. The smile that streaked across his cheeks seared itself into my memory. He looked like a kid ready to open his Christmas presents. And as he gripped my hips, he pulled my pussy down to his lips.

Before piercing my folds with his tongue.

"Oh, my God," I gasped with shock.

My hands slammed down on the top edge of the headboard as I hung on for dear life.

"Fuck yes," he growled.

I rocked my hips. "Shit, to the left. A little bit—there. Right there. Oooooh, Range."

His fingertips curled against my skin. The sound of him lapping up my juices held me hostage as my hips swirled around on his face. His growls encompassed me. The heat of his touch seared his fingerprints onto my skin. My toes curled and my head fell back as an animal rose up within me. An animal that wanted nothing more than to mark what was mine.

"Mine," I whispered.

"Mine," he grunted.

"Mine," I whimpered.

"All mine," he growled.

I bucked against his face so hard that it shifted the bed. I braced myself against the headboard as it started banging against the wall. I succumbed to my desires. To the sizzling pleasure rushing through my veins that blocked out all the pain I couldn't seem to stomach. His tongue eased me. His stubble tickled me. And as his hands massaged my ass cheeks, I couldn't take it any longer.

"I'm coming!" I cried out to the heavens.

Before my body unleashed.

"That's it," he grunted as he came up for air. "Give it all to me."

"Oh, fuck," I whimpered as I collapsed against him.

Every muscle in my body gave way, sending me plummeting toward the bed. And yet, somehow, Ranger managed to catch me. He contorted my body, being careful to mind my bruises, as he lowered my shaking body to the mattress. The world tilted around me. It was as if the bedroom had its own axis, and it was spinning at a thousand miles an hour.

I tossed my arm over my half-hooded gaze in an attempt to quell the surreal sensation.

Before I felt my legs being spread.

"Ranger?" I asked breathlessly.

He slid my legs on top of his before his fingers parted my pussy lips. "Mm, mm, mm. Look at that."

"Range?" I whispered.

He slowly eased a finger into my soaking wet entrance. "Ugh. I can't wait to fill you up."

I gasped softly. "Oh."

"You like that?"

My walls clamped around him. "So much."

I felt another digit pierce my opening. "I can tell. You're soaking my fingers in your wetness."

"Fuuuuuuck," I groaned.

I staked myself on his fingers as his chuckle wrapped around me. It cloaked me in the heat of the moment, and before I knew what I was doing, I found myself fucking my body on his fingers. His thumb pressed into my clit, his hand staying stationary as my body wiggled around. Trying its best to find that perfect pattern.

And yet, it wasn't until he wrapped his free hand around my neck and took control that I finally found it.

"Sometimes, Daddy knows what's best," he said.

His steely stare stilled my movements, but it didn't still his fingers.

"Shit," I hissed as my eyes rolled back.

He tightened his grasp against my pulse point. "Eyes open."

I forced them back open. "Range, I-I-I--."

He bent down into my face. "Keep those eyes open, sweet girl. Don't think I haven't forgotten about your punishment."

With every stroke of his fingers, my gaze wanted to shut. With every circle of his thumb around my clit, my eyes wanted to flutter closed. It took every ounce of strength I had to keep my gaze open, but goddamn it, I wanted to make him proud. I wanted to make him smile. I wanted to seek an end against his fingers before he licked me off his skin and praised me for being his good little girl.

I wanted nothing more than to lose myself in him—in all of them—so that I never had to come up for air ever again.

"Range," I choked out.

"Oooooh, there it is," he glowered.

"Fuuuuuck," I groaned.

"Come for me," he commanded.

I bucked ravenously against his hand. "So close. So close. So close."

"Come for me, sweet girl."

I raised my hips into the air. "Yes. Yes. Just like that. Just like —Ranger! Yes! Holy hell!"

His mouth dropped to mine as he swallowed my sounds. His fingers played me like a fiddle, pulling rolling orgasms from my body as my toes curled so deeply that it cramped my calves. One after the other soared through my system, drenching the sheets beneath me in my own sweet mark. I clung to him, throwing my arms around his neck and pulling him down to me, forcing his hand away from my pussy.

And as he scooped me close to him, pulling me into his lap, my head fell against his beating heart.

"Wow," I whispered.

I heard him sucking at his fingers. "Mm, mm, mm. Delicious."

Goosebumps sprinted across my body as I listened to his sounds. I nuzzled beneath his chin, wanting nothing more than his attention as he cradled me in his grasp. It felt like God Himself was holding me, blanketing me away from the cold, harsh world I had always known.

And as a yawn dropped my jaw, I felt myself moving. Gliding. Suspended in the air.

Until Ranger placed me down on the bed and tucked me in.

"What about dinner?" I asked through yet another yawn.

"Sleep, sweet girl. That's what you need."

I felt him move away, and I reached out for him. I grabbed the first thing I found, which just so happened to be nothing except his thumb.

"Please, don't leave," I whispered.

"Naomi, look at me."

I peeked an eye open and found worry in his gaze. "You're safe here with us."

"Please, don't leave," I begged him.

He nodded. "All right, but only for a bit."

He crawled over me, his body creaking the bedframe as he settled against my back. I wiggled back toward him, my ass seated against his pelvis as his arm snaked around my waist. I pulled the sheet up to my face. I felt him bury his nose into the tendrils of my hair as his heated breath pulsed along the nape of my neck.

Had I not been so tired, it would have prepared me for another round.

"I've got so much on my mind," I said softly.

He nuzzled his nose against the crown of my head. "You're safe with me. Sleep."

"What about dinner plans, though?"

He chuckled. "Like I said, there's always breakfast."

And for the first time since I had been taken, I felt free. Protected. Safe and cared for. It closed my eyes and relaxed my body long enough for darkness to overcome me.

While Ranger's presence chased away the nightmares that had plagued me for days.

21

NAOMI

The first thing I felt was an ache. A deep-seated ache with no particular source or destination. My foggy head lifted up as the room spun around me. My body felt as if it were floating high into the sky before being slammed down into the bottom of the ocean. I eased my feet over the edge of the bed, trying to plant myself so my stomach would stop turning over onto itself.

Then, everything hit me like a ton of bricks.

"No," I murmured, "there's no way."

Thoughts of Ranger spun through my head. His pulsing muscles, blanketing me as he slurped me down. His fingertips curled into my excess as he held me to his face. My hand gravitated to my thigh, stroking the place where the phantom lingering of his body heat raged against my skin.

I pressed the heels of my hands into my eyes to try to pull myself together.

But all I felt was a searing pain that rocketed through my skull.

"Careful," Ranger said, his voice heavy with sleep, "it's gonna be there for a while."

I peeked an eye open and found him carrying a massive

tray of food toward me. I watched with my hand cradling the side of my head as he sat the tray to my left before pivoting to sit down.

"Did we...?"

I wiggled my finger between the two of us, and his smirk told me everything I needed to know.

"Don't tell me you already forgot. That'd be a first for me."

I snickered, but I couldn't help the smile that crossed my face. "Never, apparently."

"Good," he said as he picked up a mug of coffee. "Now, drink. It'll help with the bruise on your eye."

I took it from him. "How does coffee help with a bruise?"

He shrugged. "Don't know. Always helps me, though. Make sure to eat something, too. I know you're starving."

I looked down and found myself at a specific loss for clothing. Holy shit, I hadn't dreamt it. Ranger and I had slept together. My cheeks blushed furiously as I reached for a pillow, slamming it down into my lap. I held it against my stomach, teetering the fresh, creamy coffee in my off-hand as I tried to cover myself as best as possible.

And the entire time, I felt him watching me. "Self-conscious?"

I peeked over at him before grasping the mug with both of my hands. "Something like that."

He picked up a breakfast sandwich. "No need to be. You're beautiful."

He said it so plainly. So simply. Like it was some universal truth.

"Thanks," I said before I took a long pull of the caffeinated drink.

"Have you always lived in the area?" he asked.

The hairs on the nape of my neck stood on end. "You mean we're still in town?"

He shrugged. "Yeah, pretty much. Just on the other side of it."

Why the hell was he telling me any of this? "Yeah, born and raised. You?"

He took a gargantuan bite of his sandwich. I mean, he devoured half of the damn thing!

"No. I grew up in a pretty rough neighborhood in California."

"I'm sorry," I said softly.

"Got any siblings?"

I found myself intrigued by his line of questioning. "No. Only child. You?"

He nodded. "Got a younger sister. Well, *had* a younger sister."

They seemed to all have that in common, their rough pasts. "What happened to her? I mean, if you don't mind me asking."

He polished off the other half of his sandwich before reaching for his coffee. "She got herself into a bad situation with a guy she liked. He was in a gang, slinging drugs, and she thought he was--."

"Her world."

He stared down into his coffee. "Yeah, something like that."

I reached out and placed my hand on his bare thigh. "If you don't want to talk about it, you don't have to. But I'm here if you do. Okay?"

He stared at our connection for a long time before he placed his hand on top of mine. "He came over one evening to hang out, and I knew what that meant. It made me sick that Mom was totally okay with them snorting shit off one another in the basement, but I think she liked it because they always gave her what was left over."

"Jesus," I whispered.

He started squeezing my hand. "I woke up to Mom

screaming one morning. Just... just this blood-curdling, shrieking sort of sound that... God, when I first woke up, I thought..."

I knew where it was going, but I gave him the silence he needed in order to get it out.

"Turns out, her and him both OD'd one night in the basement. And I never forgave myself for that."

I shook my head. "You know it's not your fault, right? You couldn't have possibly–."

He turned his heated gaze toward me. "They were getting high in the basement, and I allowed it. I allowed my drug-addled mother to usher my sister down that exact same path, and it killed her. *He* killed her."

I swallowed hard. "I'm so sorry, Ranger. Honestly, I am. I can't even imagine."

His hand started trembling, but he kept his stare locked with mine. "I killed them, you know."

I froze. "Killed who?"

His hand grew even tighter around mine. "The gang responsible for her death. I slaughtered them all for what they did to her, and I was only nineteen at the time. I had nothing to lose, and I acted like it. Does that scare you?"

"Does what scare me?"

"The fact that I'm a murderer?"

Even though it was hard to move my hand, I turned it upward and allowed his palm to fall against mine. "No, it doesn't scare me."

He turned his gaze forward quickly. "Well, it should."

And yet, his fingers threaded through my fingers instead of letting them go.

"We all have our dark sides, Range."

He scoffed. "You don't."

"Seriously? You think I don't entertain the idea of killing people from time to time?"

"Ever done it?"

"I almost did."

He snickered, almost as if to challenge me. "When?"

I didn't hesitate, either. "When you guys had my father hostage."

That whipped his gaze back to me, and the shock was evidence enough.

"Before you say anything," I said as I pushed the food tray up the bed a bit before scooting closer, "I know I would have never succeeded. But it didn't stop me from allowing that to be a viable option if it meant trying to save my father. That's why I don't think you're a terrible person. You went after the guys who hooked your sister on the drugs that ultimately killed her. You did it for family. That's the difference for me, because I'd kill for family, too. In the blink of an eye."

His gaze traveled down my body before he turned to face the basement door again. "That's how Skurge found me, you know."

I blinked. "Who's Skurge?"

He grinned. "Our former President. The longest-running president of our crew. After I stormed into that drug house and put a knife into everyone's stomach, I was on the run from the police. Stumbling around, covered in their blood, trying my best to stay hidden. He came across me in a ditch about five miles outside of my hometown."

"What happened when he found you?"

He shrugged. "The man pulled me up onto my feet, dusted me off, and said I had a choice. I could choose to keep running until I was caught, or I could stop running and never have to run again."

"Seems like an easy enough choice."

His thumb started stroking my skin. "He gave me the ability to be in control and protect those I loved. He trained me. Put me through the ringer. Convinced me to leave everything behind, even my clothes, and come with him for a fresh start."

I couldn't help but to ask. "What happened to your mother?"

He sighed heavily. "I still send her money regularly. She's... well, she's as good as she can be for snorting up every other night. But I make sure she's got enough for food and things that she needs. Though, I'm sure she just blows it on more coke."

I saw a side of him I never thought would have existed. A tender side. A loving side. A side that cared beyond anything I had ever experienced or seen in my entire life. He loved just as big as his mountainous form, and I felt honored that he was comfortable enough to open up to me.

"Your turn to spill your guts now," he said with a cheeky grin.

I blinked. "Wait, what?"

He turned to face me, propping his thick thigh up onto the mattress. "You've got my story. Now it's your turn to give me yours. How does a girl like you end up in a position like this?"

"You mean, how do I end up kidnapped and down in this basement?"

His head tilted to the side. "You know what I mean."

I slid my hand away from his and stared off over his shoulder. I didn't even know where to begin. Thoughts of Gordon raced through my mind, and it made me regret ever meeting him in the first place.

"I don't even know where to start," I said breathlessly.

Ranger placed his hand on my knee. "Start at the beginning, if you don't know where else to start."

So, I did. I cleared my throat and closed my eyes, hoping that my past didn't change the way he looked at me.

Because I found myself becoming fond of the way Ranger looked at me.

"I met Gordon when we were in high school," I said.

"Ah, high school sweethearts."

I snickered before I heaved a heavy sigh. "Yeah, something like that. It was such an odd pairing, too. I mean, he was the resident bad boy who thought being hard was throwing a drink at a teacher's feet, and I always had my nose stuck in a book."

"How long did you two date?"

I shook my head. "Forever, it seems. It was sort of this whirlwind thing that turned into us... it just..."

He squeezed my knee softly. "Got away from you?"

I opened my eyes and was shocked when I didn't feel tears streaking my cheeks. "Yeah, kind of. I mean, I didn't see any reason not to be with him, and I loved him. I really did. It just..."

"Yeah, I get it," he murmured.

I groaned. "Anyway, we kept doing our thing, and eventually I started applying to medical schools."

"Doctor. Nice."

I shrugged. "You'd think. But all of the medical schools I applied to were so far away, and Gordon didn't like that."

"Oh, boy."

I rolled my eyes. "It should've been my first red flag, but Gordon and I never really fought, you know? Not up until that point, anyway. We fought about it. He talked about how he had always wanted to be a police officer in his own hometown. Maybe make detective someday. And how he wanted me by his side the entire time. Medical school didn't fit into that plan, and at the time I loved that he wanted me in his future, so I shelved the idea of being a doctor and went to a nursing school about forty-five minutes from here."

"You gave him way too much."

"Don't I know it. I just... I loved him. He had always been

there for me at the drop of a hat, and so in my immature little brain, it made sense. He had been there through every tragedy, dried every tear, so the least I could do was show him that I was willing to stand by his side as well. Right?"

"Wrong."

I giggled softly. "Yeah, I know. At least, I know now."

"What happened after that?"

I clicked my tongue. "The usual. Once I gave in that first time, he wanted me to give in every time. The fights grew. The tension mounted. We worked through some things, compromised on others, and the rest of the time, it was me just... giving. Giving and hoping for something in return."

"I'm sorry. You deserve better than that."

I pinched the bridge of my nose. "This last fight of ours actually happened the day I met you guys."

He paused. "What did you fight about?"

My hand flopped into my lap. "My work schedule, of all things. He didn't tell me about some stupid cookout with his friends, and when I told him I had to work, he went off on me. Talked about how work always came first and how he always had to come up with excuses for why I couldn't attend shit with his friends, but I always expected him to come to Dad's house whenever we were invited."

"That's bullshit, and he knows it."

"Right!? And that's not even the worst of it, Range. The worst of it is that once I finally gave in and told him I'd use a sick day to call in sick, he hits me with the fact that he booked our wedding venue without my knowledge, without consulting me, without asking me how I felt about it. Just took the money, made the deposit, and thought that surprising me with it would be a good idea. And then got pissed that I got upset with him!"

I finally looked over at Ranger and found his face red with

anger. "He's a narcissist and a manipulator. He knows what he's doing."

That sucked the air out of my lungs. "You—you think?"

He scooted so close that our thighs touched. "I've met many men like him in my line of work. Men that think they rule the world they live in. Men that think they can get their way by fucking over others and convincing them it's their fault. It's not on you, Naomi. This is him. This is what men like him do."

I shook my head softly. "Honestly, being removed from him these past few... how long have I been here?"

He chuckled. "A little over a week."

"Right. Yeah. I just... having this time away from him, it's given me time to think."

"About?"

My gaze danced between his. "About how a life with him isn't really what I want."

He reached up and gripped my chin. "I tell my men this all the time: sometimes, people don't know what they really want until it's staring them in the face."

His touch ignited something within me. "Yeah?"

"And here, I thought you only used that line on me," Dutch said with a chuckle.

I smiled as I nudged Ranger softly. "Didn't know you swung both ways, handsome."

Ranger wiggled his eyebrows. "Don't knock it 'til you try it."

My head fell back with a cackle as he barked with laughter, and the sound overwhelmed me with goosebumps. It was the most glorious sound I had ever heard, and it lit up his features in a way I never thought I'd see. His face became almost boyish. Those hardened edges softened with every bout of laughter that fell from his lips. It was a warm sound, like hot cocoa on a cold winter's day. And as I leaned my head against his shoulder, he threaded that big, strong arm of his around my waist.

"Do you ever make noise when you walk, Dutch?" I asked.

Dutch winked at me. "It's part of my appeal."

"Hey, now," Troop said as he came bumbling down the stairs, "sounds like there's a party happening down here without me. That's rude."

I smiled so hard my eyes closed. "Have you guys eaten breakfast yet?"

Dutch and Troop both shook their heads.

"Well, don't just stand there," Ranger said as he stood to his feet, "get some food. We can take breakfast out to the back porch."

"Hell, yeah!" Troop exclaimed as he slapped Dutch's shoulder. "Come on, I think Range left us some eggs on the stove."

Dutch rolled his eyes. "You know damn good and well Range didn't leave us shit."

"You coming?" Range asked as he held his hand out to me.

And when I slid my hand into it, a burst of happiness filtered throughout my body that I'm not sure I had ever experienced in my life.

"Yeah," I said as he helped me to my feet, "I'd love to come."

"Don't we know it," Dutch said.

The guys fell apart in laughter as I balked. "Hey, now! It's not my fault you guys keep coming onto me like that."

Troop stuck his head back down into the doorway. "Not our fault you're too sexy to pass up."

Range tucked a strand of hair behind my ear. "If you want to get out a bit later on today, we could all head up to the bar for a drink. There's supposed to be a thunderstorm rolling in later, and if you sit at one of the booths, you can see the ocean while the storm's coming in."

"It's a great perch spot," Dutch said.

I paused. "Shouldn't we stay clear of that place for a while because of what happened?"

Troop smiled. "Not when we own the place. We'll be fine."

For the second time that morning, I found myself scraping my jaw up off the floor in shock.

"Well, you guys are just full of surprises, huh?"

And as Range dipped down into my ear, my entire body shivered with the heat of his breath.

"You haven't seen anything yet."

22

TROOPER

"Seriously, this makeup you guys got me is *not* doing the job," Naomi said.

Dutch ushered her into the bar. "Don't worry, we're going to be sitting in a back corner, anyway."

Range held the door open for us. "People won't stare, anyway. You're with us. They know better."

I brought up the rear as lightning flashed off in the distance. "Besides, it's your fault you trusted a couple of guys to go get makeup for you."

Naomi whipped around as she balked. "I told you I'd go with you if you wanted me to."

"Face it," Range said as he started back toward the booth, "Troop's shoulder massage had you attached to that chair."

I grinned as I let the bar door close. "Among other things."

Naomi shot me a look, but the glimmer of mischievousness in her gaze stopped my heart. She was one of the most beautiful women I had ever set my eyes on, and I swear to any God that may have existed that she almost looked to be in her natural state. With every day that passed, she relaxed a little more. With every night that went by, I found myself longing to be at her side. Did it freak me out that I knew she'd also been with Dutch and Ranger as well? Not one damn bit. It wasn't the first time we had shared someone.

It was just the first time I hoped she'd be the last.

"Here," Dutch said, "no one will see your bruises under this kind of light."

Naomi scooted in and I quickly took up the seat beside her. "Hope you don't mind."

The smile she afforded me was unequivocally brighter than the sun. "Not a damn bit, Troop."

"All right," Grady, the head bartender, said as he came up to the booth. "What would you guys like to drink?"

Range leveled his gaze at the man. "That all you want to do?"

Grady shrugged as he pulled out his pen and pad. "I'd talk about how things will go differently next time, but there won't be a next time. Not while I'm at the bar."

He turned his attention to Naomi.

"Got it?"

Relief crossed her face as she nodded. "Thank you. I really mean that, too."

Grady nodded. "Now, what can I get for the VIPs of the afternoon?"

Naomi lifted her finger into the air. "A margarita on the rocks, sugar on the rim instead of salt."

I slid my arm around her waist. "I like a woman who knows what she wants."

"Oh, oh! And can I get another order of those buffalo wings? Those were amazing," she said.

Ranger pointed at her. "I'll have one of those, too."

"Double the order, got it," Grady said.

"I'll have a Guinness and some fries," Dutch said.

Grady continued scribbling on his pad. "And for you,

Trooper?"

I drew in a deep breath. "Just bring enough wings and fries for the whole table and get a pitcher of margarita made up the way she likes. I think I'll have one with her."

Naomi giggled. "A man after my own heart."

Grady stuffed his pen and notepad away. "Coming right up, guys!"

As thunder boomed and lightning lit up the darkened world around us, I found myself entranced with Naomi. She laughed with Dutch and snickered with Ranger, and the entire time I couldn't stop thinking about how well she seemed to fit in. The bar kept an eye out for her. Grady seemed to take a liking to her. Hell, even the guys that kept up our security around the clubhouse had started chatting with her whenever she roamed around.

I wonder if she'd consider...

Nah. She had a life to get back to, anyway.

You know once it was safe for us to release her.

"You really did that!?" Naomi exclaimed.

I'd never heard Ranger laugh so much in all my life. "I know it's hard to believe, but when Dutch poured that ice cold water all over me to get me out of bed, I slammed that fucker into the wall and damn near choked him out before I realized what had happened."

"Serves him right, too," Dutch said with a nod of his head. "He got me last time by pouring—get this—fucking spaghetti sauce on my feet."

Naomi's nose wrinkled. "Water seems a lot tamer than fucking spaghetti sauce."

I held my hand out. "See!? That's what I said. I think Dutch should have another go at it."

Ranger shrugged. "If he wants to gamble with his life like that, fine by me."

Naomi nudged me. "What about you, Troop?"

I loved it when she used my nickname. "What about me?"

"Are you a prankster like them? Or do you just enjoy watching things go haywire?"

Dutch scoffed. "You better tell her now before I do."

Naomi furrowed her brow. "Tell me what?"

I leaned back into the booth seat. "There was this one time."

"One time!?" Ranger asked.

I barked with laughter. "Okay, there's *more* than one time, but there's only one time worth talking about."

"What happened?" she asked as she took a sip from her third margarita.

"Hey, Grady!" Range exclaimed. "I could use another one over here!"

"I'm trying to tell a story here, if you don't mind," I said playfully.

"Yeah, guys," Naomi said with a smirk on her face, "he's trying to tell me about the time he saran-wrapped the toilet and made you guys pee all over yourselves."

Dutch chuckled. "You say that like he hasn't already done that before."

Range growled. "I could've killed you for that one. Those were my nice jeans, too."

I threw my head back with laughter. "It's an oldie, but a goodie."

"You know what's a good one?" Naomi asked.

"Oh, please tell me you've pulled a prank or two. That would just make you sexier, in my opinion," I said.

"So long as you don't do them to us," Dutch murmured as he reached for his beer.

Naomi smiled brightly, and I couldn't get over how beautiful it made her. "So, Dad loves orange juice, right?"

"Naturally," Range said as Grady exchanged his empty

drink for another one.

"Well, did you know the power shit that comes with Kraft Macaroni and Cheese? When it's mixed with water, it looks just like orange juice."

My mouth dropped open. "You did not."

Range grimaced. "Now that's just nasty."

Naomi cackled with laughter. "He grounded me for an entire weekend for it. But, it was so worth it. I'd never heard my father cuss in my life, but he did when he took a swig of that nasty shit."

In any other world, you'd be ours forever. "Not gonna lie. I don't see your father as the cursing type."

Range shook his head. "Me, either. Your father's a stand-up man."

Naomi's face sunk a bit. "I miss him. I hope he's taking his meds."

I shot a look at Ranger, but it was Dutch who stood to his feet.

"We need to go. Now."

Thunder cracked overhead as Naomi paused. "Wait, why?"

But I knew that tone of voice. I knew that look on his face.

"All right," Ranger said as he lifted his hip, "I'm going to calmly pay for our tab, then we'll walk out the same way we came in. Got it?"

Naomi peered over the top of the booth. "Seriously, what's going on?"

I turned to face her and took her hands in mine. "Do you trust us?"

She nodded. "Yes, I do."

"Then, don't ask questions. Just come on."

I slid out of the booth and offered my hand to her, but Dutch intervened. He took her hand from mine and helped her to her feet, pulling her close as he slinked his arm around her waist. In any other situation, I would have decked him for a move like that. But when I followed his gaze, I clocked him.

The man sitting at the table by the front window.

"Oh, my God," Naomi murmured.

"Range?" I asked.

"I see him," he said as he brushed past us to move to the bar. "Just stay calm and let me get our stuff paid for."

"Don't look too hard," Dutch said as he turned Naomi away from the man.

She reached her lips up and kissed his cheek. "Make it look like I'm fine, yeah?"

Dutch grinned. "You're good at this, you know."

"Isn't she, though?" I asked as I shoved my head in between the two of them.

Dutch paused, looking down his nose at me. "Do you mind?"

I smiled brightly as I turned my head toward Naomi. "You okay?"

She kissed the tip of my nose. "Never better. Let's go."

"Wait," Ranger said.

He stepped in front of the three of us, tucking his wallet back into his pocket.

"What is it, Range?" Naomi asked.

I furrowed my brow. "Yeah, what gives?"

But Ranger's gaze didn't waver from her face. "This is your one chance."

"I'm sorry, what?" Dutch asked.

"What chance?" Naomi asked.

"Range, think about what you're doing," I hissed.

He didn't budge, though. "We all know who that man sitting in the corner is. And we know why he's here."

Naomi nodded. "That's Gordon's partner, I know."

Range sighed. "So, this is your one shot. This is your one

chance to leave."

"Hell, no," Dutch said curtly.

Ranger shot him a look of death before taking Naomi by the shoulders. "This is your one chance to leave and get back to your life. We can leave you here, in this booth, and you'll never see us again. You can go back home, back to your life, and get back on track."

"Are you insane?" I whispered.

"What if she talks?" Dutch asked lowly.

Naomi scoffed. "I'd never do that to you guys. Not in a million years."

I shoved Ranger out of the way and cupped her cheeks, unable to contain my musings a second longer. "Does that mean you'll stay, then?"

"It's her choice, Troop," Range murmured.

"Does that mean you'll stay with us instead?" I asked breathlessly.

Time seemed to suspend itself in space. Everything stopped. No one breathed. At least, I sure as fuck wasn't breathing. I couldn't stand the thought of letting her go. Of allowing her to go back to the beast she had finally escaped from. She'd never be happy. Not like she was when she was with us. And for the smallest of seconds, her gaze darted over my shoulder.

I thought that was it.

Until...

"Let's go," she said as she took mine and Dutch's hands, "for all we know, Gordon has already been alerted that we've been spotted. Range?"

"Out the back is best. He can intercept us now that we've been standing here for too long," he said.

Naomi nodded as she pivoted. "Out the back, around to the bikes. I'll get on with Dutch this time in case we were spotted coming in. Let's go."

23

NAOMI

"Hang on," Dutch said as he struck up his bike. "Peel outs can be a bitch."

I wrapped my arms clear around his waist and gripped tightly to his leather jacket. The squealing of tires had nothing on the revving of their engines that rattled my ribcage. Riding with Troop to the bar had been a fantastical moment. Feeling his body heat so close to mine while the wind whipped through my hair was unlike anything I had ever experienced. The dark clouds above hung low, threatening to open up the heavens on us as we raced toward the clubhouse.

"I'll take the long way with Naomi. You two split up and take our other two routes," Dutch said.

"Who are you talking to!?" I called out.

He simply tapped his earpiece before leaning forward. It dragged my body with him, and I felt myself sort of suspended. How I was able to float while catapulting myself through the air at seventy miles an hour, I'd never know. But being on the back of that bike with Dutch was an unmistakable high. Riding with Troop had been relaxing. He leaned back, filling the spread of my legs as we leisurely gazed out over the ocean. Watching the storm roll in with clouds as high as the Eiffel Tower. With Dutch, though, it was different. There was a concentration that sucked me in. The way his back because almost a board for my support made me feel cared for, even when I was behind him.

I'd never felt that way with anyone before. being safe with them, even when their arms weren't wrapped around me.

It made me wonder what riding with Ranger would feel like.

I closed my eyes and listened to the cracking thunder as the sky pierced with lightning. The storm raged the ocean beneath us, battering waves against the cliff side. With every crash, the smell of the ocean grew fierce. With every gust of wind, Dutch counteracted its force by weaving with it instead of fighting against it. There was a finesse to the way he drove, just as there was a finesse to the way he moved.

I swear, the engine of his bike made noise simply because Dutch wasn't capable of it.

Still, once I felt the smooth concrete give way to gravel, I knew we were back at the house. I opened my eyes and found a war waging in the sky above my head. Rain dumped into the ocean, miles away from where we were. And yet, it felt like, at any moment, we'd be drenched by the same water that filled the ocean to its core.

"Come on, we have to get you inside where you're safe," Dutch said as he took my hand.

"Everyone, listen up!" Ranger bellowed as we made our way inside. "We've got an impending attack! Hostiles in the area, and they spotted us at the bar!"

Trooper held up his hands. "We took emergency routes back to the clubhouse, but we need to be prepared. These are police officers coming after us, so we have to step cautiously."

"Come with me," Dutch murmured.

"Dutch!" Ranger barked.

"Recon after I get her settled, got it!" he called out.

I glanced over my shoulder and the crack in my voice gave me away. "Range?"

His face softened ever so slightly. "You'll be okay. You have my word."

"Come on, let's get you behind a closed door," Dutch said softly.

He pulled me up the stairs before taking a hard left. The hallway dead-ended with two doors to my right, but I should have known better with these guys. Dutch held his hand out and pushed the wall in, and I heard it catch against the rollers. It raised up, revealing yet another hallway that Dutch quickly snaked me down.

Before taking a hard right into a bedroom with floor-to-ceiling bookshelves.

"Wow," I whispered.

"This is essentially a panic room," Dutch said. "The door won't lock on you or anything, but the rolling door will. We'll come get you when it's safe, okay?"

I whipped around to face him. "Wait. What if you guys need help?"

He scooped me into his arms and blanketed his mouth with mine. His tongue pierced through my lips, holding me hostage as mine battled his for dominance. I draped my arms around his neck. His hands roamed my body, clinging to my clothes. He trembled with a need. His cock thickened against my pelvis. And in that moment, I wanted nothing more than for his naked body to comfort mine.

"Sorry to interrupt," Trooper said as he came racing into the room, "but we really need that recon."

Dutch released my lips, but not my body. "You listen to us and stay here. You're not going to get caught up in this."

"But what about protocols?" I asked.

"That's what we're doing," Ranger said as he stalked into the room. "Troop's on traps while Dutch is gonna be out doing recon. I'll be here with the guys setting up a perimeter to--."

I shook my head as I pulled away from Dutch's grasp. "No, no. I mean, Gordon's protocol. The police precinct. They won't head here straight away."

Ranger locked his gaze with me. "You know their protocol?"

I scoffed. "I've been with Gordon ever since the beginning of his career. He talks about all of this shit because he thinks it impresses me."

Troop grinned. "Sounds like it just gets on your nerves."

I shot him a playful look. "Because it does."

Dutch chuckled, but it was Ranger who commanded my attention.

"All right, so what's their next move?"

"Well, Gordon's partner, Dogma? He was in his uniform. And assuming he knows everything about what Gordon has gotten himself into with whatever the fuck he's doing, he's going to have to keep his nose clean with this. So, even if he's radioed into Gordon that he's found me, he'll still have to give proof and get permission to run an op from his boss before he can head out."

"So, we've got some time, is what you're saying," Ranger said.

I nodded. "Some time, but not a lot. When Gordon is intent on something, he can rally people quickly. With the time we spent at the bar, there's no telling how long Dogma watched us before radioing it in. So, it could be hours before they find us, or it could be less than that."

"Anything else you can tell us, lucky girl?"

I smiled at him. "Protocol states that at least five men have to run an op. Two to partner up, and one to call the shots from a safe zone. That safe zone is usually a cruiser parked a quarter of a mile from the supposed crime scene. But Gordon has mentioned a few times that he just parked his fucking cruiser right in their damn driveway."

"Shocker," Dutch murmured.

"One last thing," I said quickly. "Unless they get official sign-off with the Chief of police, they're just coming with their issued guns. They need someone higher up to sign off on tactical gear, and that usually takes a while. So, if they roll up today, chances are they won't have tactical gear."

"Unless they're coming with Griggs," Ranger said.

That gave me pause. "Do we have any reason to believe that?"

He shrugged. "It's not off the table, that's for sure."

I sighed heavily. "But that's protocol for a situation like this. I wouldn't be surprised if my face made it to the local media as well, now that I've been spotted."

"Jesus, you're amazing," Dutch said.

He scooped me back into his arms and I couldn't help but kiss him. The command in his lips clattered our teeth together, and the way his hands roamed down my back made me want to throw him onto the bed and stake myself on his dick. We had to focus, though. Gordon was coming for us, and I knew it wouldn't end well.

It never did when Gordon was pissed.

"Stay safe, okay?" I whispered against his lips.

Dutch smiled as his nose nuzzled against my own. "Always. After all, I got my lucky girl as my charm."

I took a step back from him. "Troop?"

"Yeah?" he asked.

"Maybe do a bit more than pranks for the traps."

He threaded his fingers into my hair and pulled me close. "Anything you say, pretty girl."

Our lips crashed together in a searing kiss that damn near buckled my knees. But, it was Ranger's arms that caught me. Those strong, bulging arms that damn near filled my torso as he held me up onto my feet. Troop's tongue caressed the roof of my mouth, sending a moan straight from mine and down his throat.

I wanted nothing more than to keep them at my side, so I knew they'd be safe.

"All right, all right," Ranger said as he broke our delectable kiss, "leave some for the rest of us."

And when I turned to face my Mountain Man, he gripped my chin.

"You stay here until we come for you. Be a good girl for me, okay?"

I melted into his body. "Just come back to me. It's all I ask."

He placed the softest kiss on my lips. His thumb stroked my lower lip as my mouth parted for him. I sucked on his tongue, eager to taste him one last time in case--.

No, they'd come back to me. There wasn't another option.

Because any other option just might kill me in the process.

"Now, go," I whispered.

"You heard the woman," Ranger said as he pulled away from me, "let's head on out. Dutch, I want to know everything we don't already know about Gordon and his whereabouts."

"On it," Dutch said as he marched out of the room.

I heard them talking down the hallway as Ranger kept barking orders. "Troop, you get started on this house. I want every crevice, entry point, exit point, window, and room stacked to the nines with traps. Motion sensors. The works."

"Got it," Troop said.

The last thing I heard was that door at the end of the hallway rolling closed. The hissing of the hydraulics sealed me inside, and silence blanketed me. It was as if they had stuffed me into another universe. A little pocket to stow away their most precious goods in case something ever happened. A chill shivered its way down my spine. With everything they had figured out about Gordon, I didn't know what he was capable of any longer. Nothing and everything, all at the same time.

The fear brought tears to my eyes as I turned inward toward the room.

"At least I've got a lot of books to keep me company," I whispered.

I wiped the tears away and cleared my throat. They needed me to be strong. They needed me to be okay. So, I set my sights on a colorful book spine that caught my eye. It glittered with gold and shimmered with an illustrious blue that forced my fingertips to its presence. And as I plucked it off the shelf, I smiled at the title.

"*My Three Men.*"

The smile that soared across my face came with a daunting thought. My three men? Since when had those guys become *my* men? I walked over to the bed and perched on its edge in somewhat of a daze. The silence was deafening, as if my part of the house had been cordoned off in a completely different country. And yet, as I sat there, staring down at the beautiful cover of the book, my fingers kept gracing the edging of the title.

My Three Men.

My Three Men, fighting for their lives while trying to protect mine.

"Please, stay safe, you guys," I whispered.

I placed the book down beside me and walked over to the bay seating that separated the two bookcases on the wall opposite of the bed. There was an outline of what once looked like a window, but it had been sealed off and painted over. I reached out, fingering the colorful windowpanes that had been painted to look like stained glass. And yet, not a shred of light bolted through.

I sat down, easing onto the cushion so I could close my eyes and breathe for just a moment.

But I sat on something hard, and it made me gasp.

"What the fuck?"

I quickly stood and found a dirty, muddy book sitting there. With a furrow of my brow, I reached for its existence, and even though dirt continued to fall from it, I recognized the cover.

It was the book I had dropped at the bar.

"Where did you come from?" I asked mindlessly.

I flipped through the pages, trying to see how much damage had been done to the book. But instead of focusing on the book, I focused on the little note etched into the back corner of the book's last page. The penned ink looked fresh, standing out from among the dried, curling pages that still had yet to be freed of the dirt that muddied its words.

And as I read the note to myself, tears of joy crested my eyes for the first time in years.

_L.G.,_

This is a good one. Enjoy the ending.

• Dutch

"L.G.," I whispered.

After all, I got my lucky girl as my charm.

Panic gripped my throat. "Dear God, please come back to me."

Because after everything I had been through—every tear shed, every degree earned, every job taken, and every time I moved—I finally knew where I belonged. I finally knew where I was meant to be. Who I was meant to be with. Where I wanted to spend my days. For years, I had lost time wandering about, trying to fulfill a life everyone else expected of me while ignoring my wants and needs. I had been away from my old life long enough to figure out what I wanted for my new one. A fresh start, with a home I could be proud of.

And it all hinged on my three men coming back to me.

24

———

DUTCH

I hated taking cars to do surveillance. They were bulky and easy to spot. But, with the kind of noise our motorcycles made, I couldn't risk it. Not now that we had been spotted. I went back to the bar and cased it, making sure no one had been harassed or otherwise questioned unnecessarily.

But when Grady told me that the man had just closed out his tab only moments before I walked in, I rushed back out to the car.

"I got you, you stupid fuck," I growled.

Finding people was usually half of the battle, but that fucker made it easy on me. With his police cruiser soaring down the road with his lights going, I simply made sure the sound stayed in my ears. I sat back, with the radio on and my surveillance equipment littering the back seat, and followed the searing sound of that idiot's blazing siren.

But I didn't track him where I assumed he'd go.

I figured he'd head back to the station. You know, loop in his boss. Maybe even Gordon himself. However, that isn't where he went. He missed the turn for the police precinct, and that piqued my interest.

"Where are you going, you squirrelly motherfucker?"

I reached down and turned off the music. I needed to focus. Dogma had already deviated from protocol, which meant that the information my lucky girl had provided for us wouldn't work for shit.

Which also meant that Ranger's theory might be right.

"Fuck," I hissed.

I saw Gordon before I saw where his partner turned into. They weren't at anyone's house, or in anyone's neighborhood, or anywhere near their place of work. Instead, they were at a café across town, sitting at a wrought-iron table sipping fucking drinks.

I scrambled to get my surveillance equipment out so I could listen in on what they were saying.

"All right," I murmured as I set up the recording equipment to capture everything, "let's sink these bastards."

"So, I was right," Gordon said.

I settled in for the conversation, keeping my head low as I pointed my listening dish toward the windshield.

"You were right, yet again," the older man said.

Right about what?

"God, this is going to make our careers, Barker. You know that, right? Fucking taking down the Twisted Metal? They've practically tortured our captain his entire career."

A bit overboard, I thought. But it wasn't good that they knew our crew. That meant we were all targets.

Every single one of us.

"Should we tell the Captain? You know, get our resources together?" Barker—or Dogma—asked.

"Nah," Gordon said before he damn near slurped his entire drink down, "we need more information first. You said you saw her? With your own eyes?"

"Yep."

"And you're sure it was Naomi."

"It was her, all right. You're not gonna like the other tidbit I have, though."

Oh, boy.

"What?" Gordon asked, his voice a bit curt.

Barker sighed. "It looked like she was being pretty sweet on them."

"The hell does that mean?"

My eyes widened at his tone of voice. I mean, I say tone, but what I mean is a damn demon started inhabiting his body. It was almost as if someone else had started talking. Someone maniacal. Someone with a vendetta.

His anger was more than prevalent as well.

"I mean, she didn't look to be in any sort of duress. They had their arms around her, but not controlling her, right? Not tugging her around. Not throwing her about. She didn't look like she was captured, Gordon. She looked like she was..."

"Don't say it," I whispered.

"Like what?" Gordon glowered.

"Like she was happy, man," Barker said weakly.

The pause was so long that I almost peeked over the dashboard to see what in the fuck was going on. But, when I heard the crashing sound of glass in my headphones, I knew exactly what had happened.

"That fucking bitch!" Gordon exclaimed.

I forced myself to swallow my fury down. I couldn't get out of the car. I couldn't go defend her honor. But goddamn it, I wanted to put a bullet in that man's skull for calling her that.

No one called her that.

Not unless they were about to make her cry out in ecstasy.

"You got pictures, Barker?" Gordon snapped.

"Duh," he said.

"Let me see them. Now."

Shit.

They had surveillance photos of us. I had to get back to Ranger. I had to let them know that not only had our faces been seen, but they had been captured.

"See? That's Naomi. Look at how that guy's holding her," Barker said.

"That skinny motherfuck. Who the hell does he think he is, touching my girl like that?" Gordon asked.

"He's really not that skinny," Barker murmured.

I smirked at the comment. I couldn't wait to fuck that man's girl in front of him.

If Naomi approved, of course.

Still, none of this was good. If there was picture evidence of us with a missing woman, we were sunk. They'd come after us until there was nothing left. Until they had chased us out of town, out of the state, and out of our damn bodies.

I quickly pulled out my burner phone and shot a mass group text to the guys.

Me: They have surveillance photos. Naomi's in them. They've got proof.

"All right," Gordon said as I stashed the phone back into my pocket, "here's what we'll do."

"All ears," Barker said.

"I want to personally pay these fuckers a visit before we go see the Captain."

Barker paused. "Uuuh, are you sure that's smart?"

"Of course, it's not smart!" Gordon said as he banged his fist against something. At least, I thought it was his fist. "But I want to see for my own eyes. I have to. I don't have any other choice."

"What do you think you're going to find?"

"I don't know, but I need to see it. Where they've kept her. What they've done to her. I want to see why the fuck she looks so comfortable with Pipe Cleaner over here."

Barker sighed. "You want to see what they have that you don't."

"Trust me," Gordon growled, "there's nothing they've given her that I already haven't. She's as selfish as they come."

"Then, let's go to the Captain first. Let's do this right."

"You're either in, or you're out."

Barker scoffed. "You know who you sound like right now?"

Gordon's voice was damn near feral. "Don't you ever reference that man out loud in public. You hear me?"

Holy fucking Christ, his partner knew, too.

I've got to get back.

I had to get back to Naomi. I had to get back to the house. This was so much bigger than any of us could have predicted, and we were all in a hell of a lot of trouble. The fury that vibrated through the marrow of my bones had nothing on the fear I had for Naomi's safety.

So, I pulled my cell out and shot off one last text.

Me: Gordon's coming. Be ready. He wants to see us before he goes to his captain with the evidence.

As I started disassembling my phone to be tossed into the ocean as I blazed by in the car, a commotion started outside. Women started screaming as glasses fell to the ground, and I peered over the steering wheel to figure out what the fuck had happened. I didn't see much with everyone racing by, fleeing their half-eaten meals. But, what I did see what Gordon hovering over his partner as Barker laid there on the concrete.

Still as stone.

"Loyal, my ass," Gordon murmured.

Before he spat on his partner and walked away.

I forced myself to wait as long as I could. I waited for what seemed like hours until I knew without a shadow of a doubt that

Gordon was gone. Cars peeled out of the parking lot as waiters and waitresses surrounded Barker, who laid there on his back, completely unconscious.

I didn't even know if the man was alive.

That is, until I heard someone yell.

"He's got a pulse! Someone call 9-1-1!"

"Come on," I murmured as I tossed my equipment into the back seat. I needed an opening. I needed everyone to leave, just for a second, so that I could grab those pictures. If that reel made it back to the precinct, we were fucked. We'd have to pack up shop, lest we risk an all-out war with the department itself.

And thank God, people were idiots during emergencies.

"Everyone inside! Now! Give the man some room to breathe!"

Someone started calling out orders, and it provided me with the perfect opening. I shimmied out of the car and snaked through the throng of people that came running at me, keeping my head down as much as possible. I leapt over the railing to the outside deck and knelt down next to Barker's head. I placed my fingers against his pulse point, making sure he was actually alive before relief washed over me.

"Are you a paramedic?" a man barked at me.

I peeked up at him before removing my hood. "I was jogging by and heard the commotion. Figured I'd come check him out before my colleagues got here."

The man's voice immediately softened. "Is he going to be okay?"

I fiddled with the man's temple and checked his pulse on his wrist. I busied myself with untucking his shirt and opening the buttons at the top to give him some room to breathe. Thank fuck, I'd been obsessed with magic as a kid. Being intrigued with sleight-of-hand shit got you beat up on the playground.

But it made retrieving the digital camera of pictures—along

with the man's cell phone—effortless.

"Yeah," I said as I quickly tucked his things into my hoodie pocket, "he should be good. He's concussed, though, so don't move him until the ambulance gets here. Time will be of the essence."

The man grew frantic. "What can I do in the meantime?"

I pointed back inside as I stood. "Go get some cold water. Get a washcloth on his head, and a warm washcloth on his chest. It'll help with the swelling and keep the blood circulating through his heart."

The man nodded. "I can do that. Be right back."

And the second the man disappeared, I tore back to the car and got the fuck out of there.

The first thing I did was destroy Barker's phone. I sped toward an alcove just off the highway and cracked the screen over my knee. I wiggled it back and forth, finally getting that damned back panel off so that I could remove the SIM card. I fractured everything into pieces, crumbling it in my hands as specks of blood pierced through my skin. I tossed it over the cliff side, down into the angry ocean as the storm raged louder than ever above my head.

Then, I did the same thing with the digital camera.

Making sure that no one could ever retrieve those damning pictures again.

"Now, let's hope that old fuck doesn't know how to use a cloud," I murmured.

Everything inside of me wanted to speed back to the club-house. But I knew that my recon wasn't done. If Ranger found out that all I did was sit at the restaurant for a little while, he'd be pissed. So, I forced myself to turn my sights to another destination.

I needed to get inside Gordon and Naomi's house.

"Let's do this," I murmured to myself.

I pulled the battery and the SIM card out of my burner phone, but I didn't discard it. I was concerned that I'd need it before I started back to ground zero. I set it on the front seat and weaved in and out of traffic, trying to get to that house just a tad quicker. With Gordon on the road, most likely headed for the clubhouse, that meant I'd have ample time to case the joint.

That also meant I'd be able to grab a few things for Naomi in the process.

Getting to the house wasn't an issue. Getting in through the back door wasn't an issue, either. Why most people kept their back door unlocked, I'd never know. But holding back my anger as I walked through their house was one of the hardest things I'd ever done in my life.

"You didn't love her one bit, you son of a bitch," I hissed.

Every step I took throughout the house, there was evidence of him. A coffee mug sitting out with his damn face on it. Pictures of him in his uniform with dates beneath for every promotion he had ever received. There was a trophy case in the living room that had his name etched and scrawled over everything from 'Best Boyfriend Ever' to 'Graduate of the Academy.'

Yet, there was nothing there to symbolize Naomi.

She was nothing but another trophy to you.

By the time I finally made my way up the steps to the second floor, I had turned my sights toward packing up some of Naomi's things. There was no way in hell Gordon was stupid enough to hide anything incriminating in his home. Everything was pristine, like something out of a magazine, despite the fact that two people who supposedly loved one another lived inside. Hell, even the fucking hallway was lined with either scenic pictures or baby pictures or grown-ass adult pictures.

And none of them had Naomi in it.

"What a fucking prison," I whispered.

It made it sick, is what it did. She deserved so much better than that. So much better than all of this. I made my way to the end of the hallway and threw open the door, finding myself face to face with the master bedroom. And yet again, it was devoid of anything even remotely resembling Naomi. She had such a colorful personality, and yet the colors of the room were dark. Gray. Dead. I peeked into the bathroom off to the side and found a plethora of men's products, and alongside that was a little caddy with a few colorful bottles inside of it.

Jesus Christ, the woman didn't even have her own place at the sink.

"I should fucking kill him just for that," I growled.

I walked into the bathroom and snatched the caddy off the counter. I ripped the curtain to the shower back, making sure there wasn't anything in there that she needed. I reached for a pink loofah sponge that looked to have a measly bar of soap in it, and I did my best to stomach my anger as I searched the cabinets for anything else that could have been hers.

Then I threw open the closet, pulled out a leopard-printed suitcase, and started stuffing it with her things.

I threw open the dresser drawers and pulled out her clothes. I stuffed lingerie that still had the tags on it down into the bottom. And fucking hell, the man needed to be arrested just for that. I held up a royal blue pair of boy shorts with no crotch and damn near came in my pants right then and there. With Naomi's juicy body smashed into these?

God, it was almost too much to bear.

"Focus," I murmured as I dropped them into the suitcase. "She still needs you, Dutch."

I made quick work of gathering some of her things, minus her electronics. Those could be tracked, and it wouldn't have shocked me one bit if Gordon already had a tracker on them to watch her every movement. After packing the suitcase so tightly that I had to sit on it to get it zipped, I did my best to put the room back in working order.

But something underneath the bed glinted and caught my eye.

"Now, what do we have here?" I whispered.

I dropped to my knees and peered underneath the bed, only to find a lockbox staring me in the face. I grinned as I reached for it, sliding it out and holding it on its end by the handle. Surely, there was something important in there that she'd need for herself. And even if it wasn't hers, she was entitled to it anyway, in my opinion.

Then I gathered her things, snuck out of the house, and threw her stuff into the trunk.

Before speeding back toward home.

25

TROOPER

"Shiiiiiit," I groaned as I read Dutch's latest text. "Ranger!"

"What!?"

"We got a problem! Check your phone!"

Silence filled the house before--. "God fucking damn it, that motherfucking asshole!"

I nodded. "Yeah! That!"

Ranger barreled down the stairs. "Bury! Lancer! I want you in trees! Dutch will be your point man once he gets back and gets up there with you!"

"On it," the two men murmured.

"Troop, how are the traps?" he asked as he came strolling up to me.

I pointed to the basement. "Got that place littered with them. I don't know what kind of surveillance we've been under, so I'm working under the assumption that they know everything there is to know about this place."

"Should we move Naomi?" he asked as he dropped his voice.

I shook my head. "That was the first door I trapped. You know the code?"

He nodded. "Do you and Dutch?"

I nodded back. "Anyone presses that door from the outside, and they go up in smoke."

"And Naomi will be unharmed?"

I scoffed. "The hell do I look like? Gordon?"

He grinned as he patted my shoulder. "Keep at it. We know he's headed this way. And make sure our men know they can fire at will if things get hairy. No one makes it out alive if he comes in hot."

"Got it," I said as I turned around on my heels.

I grabbed the road spikes from the porch and dragged them behind me. I jogged half a mile in either direction and laid out equal patterns of them, three on each side, just in case multiple people attempted to assault us from different directions. I shot out call signs for the guys in the trees, relaying messages from Ranger. And when they shined the laser scopes on their guns, I watched them blink three times at the ground.

Telling me they understood.

"Good," I murmured as I turned around and went back inside.

I made my rounds, checking the trip wires and land mines we had stacked all around the outside of the house. We needed to know their entry points and what directions they were coming from, and that was the only way to do it. Booming sounds caught everyone's attention, including the other police. And if Gordon was coming alone, he'd be pissed if someone from another precinct rolled up and saw him raking us over the coals without permission from his boss. Then I made my way upstairs and punched in the code that disarmed Naomi's door.

I had to see her one last time.

You know, just in case.

I drew in a deep breath and practiced silencing my footsteps. Dutch constantly trained us in stealth techniques, though some of us caught on better than others. Ranger damn near gave up about halfway through our yearly training, but I did my best to cling on. And as I stood in the doorway, watching Naomi sitting in that bay window curled up with that muddy little book of hers, I couldn't help but smile.

She looked so peaceful, and it made me wonder what kind of chaos she had come to terms with when she lived with Gordon.

"I'm pretty sure you're the calmest one of all of us."

She peered over her shoulder. "You don't move as quiet as Dutch does."

I chuckled as I made my way toward her. "Guilty as charged."

She dangled her legs off the edge of the window as I sat at the foot of the bed.

"Seriously though," I said as I clasped my hands between my legs, "how are you so calm right now?"

She shrugged. "I just... I'm not sure how it gets much worse than this. So, I'm trying to take solace in that."

I chuckled. "Never say never. The world always has a way of making you eat your words whole."

Worry crossed her features. "You really think so?"

I stood to my feet and bent forward, placing a soft kiss on her forehead. "We've got you, I promise."

But her heavy sigh told me she still felt burdened.

"Whatcha reading?" I asked as I sat down next to her.

I pulled those luscious legs of hers into my lap and traced faceless patterns on them. I committed every single feeling to memory. The way her excess molded to me. The way her smile brightened her worried gaze. The way she snuggled the crest of her ass against my thigh, teasing me even at the height of our fears.

God, what a woman she was.

She was a woman worth dying for.

"Honestly?" she asked as she closed her book. "I've been reading the same damn page for a while now and I've got no clue what's on it."

I took the book from her and set it off to the side. "Naomi, look at me. I want you to hear me when I say this."

Her glorious green gaze met mine. "Yeah?"

I reached out and rested my hand on her shoulder. "So long as we're alive, you're safe from Gordon and whatever he's got up his sleeve."

She started blinking back tears. "I don't think I ever knew who he was. How terrible is that? That I was so blind as to--."

"No."

"No?"

I shook my head. "Don't you dare do that to yourself. Men like him are good at what they do. They prey on people. Unsuspecting people. He took advantage of you and your kindness, and he knows it. He's losing a grip on what he can control, and it's spinning him out because that's all he cares about. It says nothing about you, but it says *everything* about him. And anyone who could ever want to hurt someone as precious and as breathtaking as you as deep issues that have absolutely nothing to do with you in the first place."

She reached her lips down and kissed my hand. "Thank you, Troop."

I stood up, feeling her legs slide off my lap before I placed one last kiss on her pillow lips. "Now, stay here until one of us comes to get you. And if anyone walks through that door, that isn't us? Use this."

I reached behind me and pulled out the piece I had stowed away behind my back. I brandished it for her, holding it in the palm of my outstretched hand. Her eyes widened as a gasp fell from her lips. She shot to her feet so quickly that it damn near knocked me off mine. But, as I gathered myself, I kept the gun held out in front of her for her to take in.

"I've never even shot a gun, Troop. How the hell am I--?"

I took her hand and placed the gun in her grasp. "You point and pull the trigger. It's got a full magazine, and the safety is off, so be careful with it. Don't point it at anything you don't want to harm."

"I-I-I—I don't know if I can do this. I don't know if—if I could—I'm not like you guys. I just can't."

I smiled as I cupped her cheek. "You've always been like us, pretty girl. It just scares you. So, make the decision to no longer be afraid. That's all you have to do. Okay?"

Her gaze fluttered up to mine. "Just like that?"

"Believe it or not, it's just like that."

I bent down and stole one last kiss from her lips. One last warming touch to carry me through the hellscape that was about to drop down onto our heads. I had no idea if we'd make it out. I had no idea if Gordon was coming with an army, with the mafia, or was stupid enough to come all by himself. But one thing I knew for certain was that we couldn't underestimate him.

Doing so would cost us our lives.

"Remember," I said as I started backtracking toward the door, "point and shoot if it's anyone other than us."

She nodded quickly. "Yeah, yeah, yeah. I—I got it."

I winked. "Good. I'll see you soon."

"You fucking better, Troop."

The seriousness of her tone pulled the words out of my mouth. "I love you, too, pretty girl."

Then, I closed the door and didn't stop until I had that hidden doorway rolled down and armed.

"You ready?" Bury asked, as he came up behind me.

I turned toward him. "No one gets in this house while we're gone, understood?"

Bury nodded. "You sure you don't want someone posted up here?"

I brushed past him. "Just take up your spot on the porch and stay there. I've got everything else handled. Range!"

"You coming or what!?" he called out.

I perched on the banister of the steps and slid down, planting my feet in the middle of the foyer. "One last round before the show starts?"

Range whipped the front door open. "It's about damn time. Thought you were wanking one out real quick."

I grinned as I slid past him. "Nah, that's more Dutch's thing."

Ranger chuckled. "Bury! Make sure this door gets closed!"

"On it!" the man called out.

But, as we headed toward our bikes to do one last round through our escape routes, I couldn't help but look back over my shoulder. Up to the second story. Up to where our princess had been stashed.

Where she waited patiently for our safe return.

26

NAOMI

As I sat back down at the bay window, I planted my feet firmly on the floor. I curled my toes into the plush carpet, trying to ground myself as fear threatened to choke me out. The gun felt heavy in my hand. Even though it was only the size of my palm, it felt as if the weight of the world had been placed against my skin. I hated it. I hated looking at it. I hated clinging to it. And yet, I found myself slipping my trigger finger into the loop against the gun's boom switch.

"Let's see how it feels," I whispered.

I quickly stood to my feet and pointed the gun at the door. It fit the size of my hand perfectly, and it didn't feel as if I were holding onto any sort of excessive weight. What happened when I pulled the trigger of a gun? What happened whenever it went off?

I whipped around and pointed it at the bathroom door before I debated on whether to pull the trigger.

"Maybe a pillow will make it quieter?" I asked.

I leapt onto the bed, forcing my trigger finger to stay put. The more I moved around with it, the more comfortable I became with it, and as I knelt down onto the edge of the pillow,

I used both of my hands to aim at its bulging center. I closed one eye and opened it. I closed the other eye and opened it. I watched the gun seemingly switch positions right in front of my stare, and I wondered which one was more accurate.

The left eye being open, or the right.

"Just shoot the pillow," I whispered.

And yet, I couldn't. Even though I knew the pillow wasn't a living thing, nor would it ever hurt me, I found myself unable to trip the trigger. I groaned as I slid off the bed, making sure to keep the gun an ample distance away from my body. I twirled around, dancing on my feet, trying to do anything to familiarize myself with the newfound weight I felt sitting against my palm.

It felt like hours of silence had gone by. Hours of waiting, and tiptoeing around, and holding my breath. Waiting for something to happen.

Then, I heard it.

Those glorious footsteps coming down the hallway.

I scrambled to get onto my feet. Somehow, I had found myself laying on the floor, pointing the gun right up to the ceiling. The second I heard that amazing sound, though, I scrambled to get to my feet. I took my finger off the trigger. I held the gun at my side, ready to give it over to someone—anyone—who was much more versed in firearms than I.

And when the doorknob turned, a smile peeled across my face.

"God, I didn't think you guys would ever get back up here," I said as I walked toward the door.

However, when the door fell open, I was greeted by none other than the Devil himself.

Who had a gun pointed straight at me.

"Hey there, sweetheart," he said as he steadied his gun. "I missed you."

My arm quickly raised up, pointing the barrel of that gun

straight at his chest. I moved so quickly that it almost shocked me.

Almost, being the key word there.

"Brainwashing," he said with a chuckle, "that'll be a fun charge to oversee."

I shook my head. "I'm not brainwashed. You know that as much as I do."

He took a step through the door's threshold. "Well, you're currently holding a gun to your fiancée's chest. So, I'd say something has happened."

I took a step away from him. "What happened was the truth. The truth about you finally came out, and I'm disgusted with what I see."

He holstered his gun and held up his hands in mock surrender. "Whatever it is you think you know, I promise you don't know the half of it. So, can you put the gun down so we can talk?"

He wanted to talk? Fine. But I was cutting straight to the chase.

"The mafia, Gordon? Seriously?" I asked.

He stopped dead in his tracks as his face turned a shade of red I'd never seen in my life. "What? You're just going to shoot your fiancée? The man you love? Over some dumb bullshit a bunch of criminals have shoved down your throat?"

"I saw the proof," I said flatly. "I saw you with that Griggs guy."

His eye twitched. "Clearly, they've done something to you. And I don't know what they've done, but if you'll just come with me--."

I took another step away from him. "I'm not going anywhere with the likes of you."

He scoffed. "Do you even hear yourself right now? I'm here to save you! I'm here to take you home, Naomi!"

I held my head high with pride. "I don't need saving. I'm right where I'm supposed to be."

Where the hell was everyone? Where were the guys? And the guns? And the traps? And the guards?

Something was wrong, and I had a hell of a time fighting back tears of fear as Gordon stood there, unimpeded by any tactics the guys may have set up.

"You're out of your mind right now, sweetheart," Gordon said as he tilted his head, "and I don't know what they did to you, but--."

I didn't want to kill him. I didn't want to gun him down. But dear God, he needed to hear me. He needed to realize that I was serious. So, I lowered the gun to where I thought his crotch was and I pulled the trigger.

Before the kickback of the gun stunned my shoulder, as a bullet pierced the ground just in front of his toes.

"What the fuck!?" he exclaimed as he jumped back.

"How long?" I asked as I raised the gun to his head.

He threw his arms into the air. "How long what, you crazy bitch!?"

My hands tightened around the gun as I shook with fury. "How long have you been in bed with the mafia?"

"I don't know what you're talking about," he glowered.

"I've seen the pictures, Gordon. I heard the conversation you had with Tommy Gun or whatever his name is. In the back alley? When you were talking about mountains and rivers and shit? Oh, what was it that you said?"

"Don't," he warned.

"Ah, I remember. 'The mountains weren't as beautiful as I figured they would be, but at least there was a nice lake to jump into every once in a while.' Jog your memory at all?"

And when his face sank, I knew I had him pinned.

"How long, Gordon?" I asked, as my voice cracked.

I watched as any love or feelings Gordon had for me vanished completely. His features contorted into anger as he pushed off his feet and came barreling toward me.

"Gordon, no!" I exclaimed.

"You stupid bitch. Why the fuck do you always ruin everything?" he growled as he reached out for me.

I pointed the gun at him as he bent forward, trying to knock me off my feet. Then, without thinking, I pulled the trigger.

BOOOOOOM!

"You think you can kill me?" he grunted as he slammed into me.

I started screaming at the top of my lungs. "Let me go! Let me go, you fucking idiot! Help me! Somebody stop him!"

His elbow came down against my forearm, knocking the gun out of my hand. Everything happened so quickly that I didn't have much time to process anything, but as I watched a hole develop in the ceiling, the crack of the gun echoed off the caverns of my mind.

BOOOOOOM!

"You're mine, Naomi," he grunted as he wrapped his arms around me. "Even Tommy knows that you chase after what's yours."

I snarled in his face. "You sent that mafia bastard after my scent, didn't you?"

He chuckled wryly. "And he sent me straight to you. All that code. All that smooth talking. It was for you, Naomi. For you! And you're just... going to throw it all away? This is how I make my money! This is how I keep you comfortable! And all you are is a selfish fucking bitch."

He picked me clear up off my feet and I flailed around, trying to throw him off balance. "Ranger! Dutch! Trooper! Help me!"

He groaned as he dragged me toward the door. "In time,

you'll come to forget all about this once I can give you the life you deserve. Once Tommy pays me the money I'm owed for all the shit I do for that bastard."

I threw my elbow back into his gut, but it didn't do much. "I'd rather eat lead than ever live a life with you, you traitorous dirty rat!"

He slammed me into the wall next to the opened bedroom door and pressed his lips to the shell of my ear. "Now, I can give you what you've finally been screaming at me for, Naomi. I can give you a life of rest. Of shopping. Of relaxation and vacations that make you smile and all the shit you complain about to that useless father of yours that you refuse to put in a home. Endless books along every single wall of our home with the money I'm about to rake in with those asshats. They're idiots, Naomi. Just a bunch of underground criminals--."

"He's the bogeyman of the West Coast, Gordon! You can't beat him!"

"Well, once I'm done? We'll have the entire world at our fingertips. I'll get the promotion I've always wanted. They'll cut my hours at work, and we'll have more time to spend together. We can travel the world. See all of those places you've always wanted to see."

"What happened to you, Gordon?"

"How's that sound?"

The desperation in his voice broke my heart. I had no clue when Gordon had turned into that person. A person willing to trade in his moral code for a stack of cash. At least Trooper, Dutch, and Ranger lived by their moral code. Morally gray, at best, but never something they considered compromising.

I trusted them because of that.

I'd never trust Gordon again because of what he'd done.

"I would rather die," I hissed as I bucked back against him.

He ground his pelvis against my ass cheeks. "Don't tease a

man if you're not willing to put out. You're always so bad at that."

"I swear to hell on high—AH!"

He yanked me away from the wall and shoved me out into the hallway. I slammed into the wall, my head bashing into the pristine white plaster before something wet and warm started dripping onto my lips. My head felt dizzy. I teetered on my feet as I brought my hand to my face. And when I pulled it away, I saw red.

Red blood all over my palm.

"Of course," Gordon said as he stepped out of the bedroom. "You'll need some time in the psych ward to make it all seem plausible. But, it'll be easy to sell the brainwashing aspect to the Chief of police after that."

I started backing down the hallway. "I'll never let you get away with it. I'll never let you win."

He smiled, as if he were victorious. "And when I've destroyed every last shred of evidence, I'm going to destroy them."

"No."

"I'm going to throw them behind bars in a maximum-security prison--."

"No," I practically growled.

"Oh, yes," he said as the Devil himself took over Gordon's features, "and I'm going to let them rot in hell for the rest of their days."

"No, you son of a bitch! I'll never let that happen!" I shrieked.

"Then," Gordon said with a sigh, "I guess you'll simply have to die in the crossfire. But either way, this doesn't end with you living a happy life with those assholes. You either live it with me, or you don't live it at all, because I didn't compromise everything ingrained within me just for some selfish know-it-all to ruin it because she's not getting dicked enough."

I finally backed into a wall and turned to find that the hidden doorway I thought he had entered from was still closed.

So, how in the fuck did Gordon get inside in the first place?

"Someone help me!" I cried out as I started slamming my fists against the wall.

That gave Gordon the opportunity to rush up behind me, though. And when he fisted my hair, he slammed my face into the wall again. Breaking my nose as pain unlike anything I had ever experienced ricocheted through my face.

"Oh, my God," I whimpered as tears streaked my face.

"Now," Gordon said as he cracked his knuckles, "it's time for you to come with me."

I stumbled around, trying my best to get back onto my feet. Where in the actual fuck was everyone? How the hell could I have ever committed myself to that monster? How had I not seen it before in him?

Where were my men?

Had I been played?

Again?

"I'll never let that happen," I said as I covered my blood-spewing nose, "because I will never be yours."

"Your engagement ring says differently, sweetheart."

I finally stumbled back onto my feet and turned to face him. "You mean the engagement ring that I threw into the ocean?"

He leveled his gaze with mine. "Tell me you weren't that stupid."

"I'll die before I ever go back to living a life at your side. I'll never give into you, Gordon. You're a sack of shit I should have never trusted, and when my father first told me that you were going to be trouble, I should've listened to him."

His fists clenched at his sides. "You really should watch your language with me."

"Why? Because you're going to kill me? Good. Because I'd rather be dead in this house than spend another second in the prison we bought for ourselves. You should've never been trusted, and when I'm done with you? You'll be the one rotting in prison. So, you better go ahead and kill me, because none of this ends the way you want it to. I'm going to make sure of it, whether I'm alive, or whether I'm dead in the process."

And as the wall behind me came alive, sliding up to reveal the rest of the house, I heard the most amazing voice behind me.

The most wondrous, reassuring voice I could have ever heard.

"Well," Ranger said as he stepped up behind me, "would ya lookee what the cat dragged in."

27

RANGER

With Dutch and Trooper on the task to figure out exactly how that man got into our house without coming in through any of the armed sides, I made my way up the stairs. From the first gunshot that popped off, I knew exactly what had happened. And I prayed with everything inside of me that Naomi could hold her own long enough for me to reformat the guys. I had to get them into position. With Gordon already slipping underneath our noses, we needed to make sure there wasn't a way in hell he'd be able to get out of the house without going through one of us.

Then, I pressed that wall in and rolled it up to find the pot-bellied asshole standing there with a gun flashing on his hip.

"Now, we can talk," I said as I stepped in front of Naomi, "man to man."

Gordon quickly pulled his gun off his hip and aimed it at me.

"No!" Naomi exclaimed.

"I don't think that's a very good idea you've got going for you," I said plainly.

Gordon narrowed his eyes. "Get out of my way. I'm taking my fiancée home."

Dutch stepped out of the bedroom behind Gordon. "I found how he got in. He scaled the backside of the house and came in through the bathroom window."

I clicked my tongue. "Told you we should've boarded that thing up."

Dutch pulled out his knives and shrugged. "We figured she could use the sunlight. Innocent mistake."

Gordon peered over his shoulder. "You gonna filet me for dinner or something?"

Dutch chuckled. "You know what's interesting?"

Gordon pivoted and aimed his gun right at Dutch's head.

"No, please," Naomi said as she came out from behind me, tears marring her voice. "Gordon, just stop."

"What's so fucking interesting, dickweed?" Gordon spat.

I heard footsteps rushing up behind me before Trooper slid onto the scene with two guns in his hand.

Both of them aimed at Gordon.

"What's interesting," Troop said as he cocked both of his guns, "is that you're not the only one in bed with someone you shouldn't be."

When Gordon whipped back around, I figured he was about to aim his gun at Trooper. Because why not? He had aimed it at me. He had aimed it at Dutch. All that was left was to aim his sights at Trooper before he realized he was hopelessly outnumbered. However, when the gun stopped shy of him and aimed itself directly at Naomi's forehead, I paused.

"I wouldn't do that if I were you," I warned.

"Why?" Gordon asked as he took a step toward Naomi. "Because you'll kill me if I do?"

"Something like that," Dutch said.

Gordon scoffed. "Well, if I am to die today, then let there be fire."

"No!" Naomi shrieked.

"Get down!" I roared.

The second Gordon's forearm twitched, all hell broke loose. I dove for Naomi, trying to knock her out of the way. The problem with that was Trooper had the exact same idea in mind, and we collided just shy of Naomi's arm. She lunged toward the madman as Trooper and I slammed into one another, tangling ourselves up and trying to figure out our left from our right. Not our finest motherfucking moment, I can assure you. But, when I saw Naomi knock that gun clear out of Gordon's hand, I'd never been so impressed in all my fucking life.

"Dutch!" I bellowed.

"I see it!" he exclaimed.

"Stop this! Now!" Naomi shrieked.

As Gordon's gun hit the floor, it went off, splintering the wall and causing Naomi to yelp. Dutch kicked off, running toward Gordon and slicing the backs of his thighs open as the man tried leaping to get to his gun. Naomi was quick, though, and she darted her foot out in order to scoot it further away from him.

And when Gordon hit the floor on his stomach, Trooper leapt through the air and brought his knee down straight into the fuckwad's back.

Before pointing both of his guns at the back of the man's head.

"Goddamn it," Gordon groaned as he wiggled around. "Get off me, you son of a bitch!"

FWEET!

I pressed my tongue to the back of my teeth, letting out a high-pitched whistle. I peeked over at Naomi, clocking her wide eyes and her frozen stance. She seemed suspended in space, unable to look around, or move, or damn near breath. Had it not been for the rising and falling of her shoulders, my want to shake her back into reality would have taken over.

But maybe it was better that she was frozen in time rather than panicking up a storm.

"You summoned me?"

Gordon peered up before his face paled. "Sheriff Barnes?"

I smiled as the suited man approached my side. "Sheriff Barnes. Not a moment too soon. How are you this afternoon?"

The man harrumphed. "Wondering why the hell you interrupted a private luncheon for my daughter's engagement."

Despite Trooper holding two guns to the back of his head, Gordon scrambled to get to his feet. "Sheriff Barnes, I'm so glad you're here. These men, th-th-they—they captured my fiancée. They took her, right from her father's home."

"Did they, now?" the man asked.

"That's the story," I said.

Gordon circled his pointed finger around in the air. "These men, all of these men, they've had their hands on her. Raping her. Brainwashing her. She doesn't even recognize me as her fiancée right now. I'm shocked she even knows my name!"

The sheriff turned to face Naomi. "Is that true?"

The question pulled her out of her trance. "I took off my engagement ring when these guys were kind enough to reveal the true nature of this man. Did you know he's in bed with the mafia, Sheriff?"

"What!?" Gordon exclaimed.

"See, that's my concern here," the sheriff said as he walked toward Gordon. "I've seen some very interesting video footage. Great audio, too. And I'm wondering why you're talking with Tommy Gun in the first place while using the exact language you magically decoded for me in order to receive the promotion that I just gave you."

"Wow," Troop said with a snicker, "hell of a coincidence if you ask me."

"Sir," Gordon said as he lowered his voice, "these men are trafficking weapons. You know as well as I do--."

"You got any proof of that?" the sheriff asked as he got into Gordon's face.

The man's jaw pulsed. "No, sir."

"Interesting," the sheriff said as he stalked around the man, "because I've got plenty of proof of you working with the assholes that fill our streets with drugs, and death, and blood."

And that's when Gordon switched tactics. "That's rich, coming from you. You're in bed with the same assholes that fill our streets with illegal weapons. I've been chasing those fucking weapons down my entire career, and you're working for them!"

"No," the sheriff said as he stopped in front of Gordon, "I'm not in bed with them. Not like you are with Tommy Gun Griggs. I do, however, use this crew and its members as C.I.'s to keep me updated on who's moving into the city."

Gordon balked. "That's not true. I've gotten you all of those leads. I've gotten you all of those wins."

Sheriff Barnes shrugged as he backed toward me. "How do you think I verified all of your information?"

I smirked. "Surprise."

Gordon pointed his finger at Troop. "I can prove that these motherfuckers deserve to be arrested. That they're good-for-nothing assholes that—."

The sheriff held up his hand. "Sometimes, Gordon, C.I.'s are a dirty means to a clean end. I keep them out of trouble, and they point me in the direction of their buyers."

"That is—you—that's not—fuck!"

"You, on the other hand, have been lining your pockets with money from the mafia and keeping the same weapons you claim to hate out on the street."

Gordon threw his hands into the air. "That's the same fucking thing!"

Sheriff Barnes walked up to him and, to my shock, ripped that man's badge right off his fucking hip. He held it up to Gordon's face, with the damn thing shaking in his hand as rage filled his body. I slowly reached out for Naomi. I pulled her toward me, tucking her behind me once more so she didn't have to watch. So she didn't have to see the shitshow that I knew would happen.

Because Gordon struck me as the kind of guy that wouldn't go down without a fight.

"If you can't see the difference," the sheriff hissed as he shook the badge in that motherfucker's face, "then you don't deserve to wear this badge."

And Gordon erupted. "You stupid, empty-headed bitch!"

His heated gaze flickered around to find Naomi, but I blocked her from view.

"Sorry," I said with a shrug, "can't look at the goods without paying the 'good boy' toll first."

Dutch and Troop came over, brushing past the angry man to come stand at my side. With Dutch's knives shimmering in the hallway light and Troop's guns still at the ready, they stood on either side of me.

Blocking the whole of the woman we had come to love, and respect, and admit.

"Gordon," the sheriff said as he plucked Gordon's own fucking handcuffs of his tactical belt, "you're under arrest for conspiracy, coercion, attempted murder, harassment, and a host of other things I'm sure we'll figure out soon enough."

"Bye - bye," Dutch said as he wiggled his fingers at the man.

"You have the right to remain silent," Sheriff Barnes said as he yanked Gordon's arms behind him. "Anything you say can, and most certainly will, be held against you in a court of law."

Sheriff Barnes was much stronger than he looked, too, because when he yanked Gordon toward the hidden doorway to walk back out into the house, he damn near pulled Gordon straight off his feet.

We pivoted with the scene, cloaking Naomi from all of it as she stood behind us.

"You have the right to an attorney. If you can't afford one, one will be appointed for you. If you decide to answer questions now without a lawyer present, you have the right to stop answering at any time."

And as the two men made their way toward the main house staircase, I couldn't turn around fast enough.

"Naomi, are you all right?"

Dutch whipped around as well. "Did he shoot you at all?"

Troop scoffed as he holstered his weapons. "Jesus, your nose. It looks broken. Here, let me take a look at it."

But she held up a hand, stopping our movements in their tracks. She drew in a deep, unimpeded breath through her mouth, and the way her entire body started vibrating worried me.

"I'm okay. I mean, my face hurts, but I just—I just need—."

"Here, wait just a second. Hold on," Dutch said.

As the sheriff's voice faded into the background, Dutch blew past all three of us. With his knives holstered, he tore down the hallway and took a hard left, and for the life of me I had no idea where the fuck he was going.

"You got any clue?" I asked as I eyed Troop.

He simply shrugged. "Not a fucking clue."

But it didn't take Dutch long to come back. And when he did, he was carrying a leopard-printed suitcase.

"My suitcase? Where did you--?"

Dutch dropped it at her feet. "You need any of your creature comforts right now?"

Naomi's brow furrowed deeply as she crouched down. Her trembling fingers unzipped the bag, and its contents were revealed to all of us.

"Oh, my God," she whispered.

I chuckled as I reached over and patted Dutch's shoulder. "Good job, man."

Naomi gasped as she pulled out a fuzzy robe. "Oh, my God. Where did you get this?"

Dutch crouched down and smoothed a bit of blood off her lips with his thumb. "I did a bit of recon on the house. Just to make sure there wasn't anything else there that we could've used against Gordon. And I figured, since I was there, why not grab a few of your things?"

But, as she started pulling out clothes, she tossed them to the floor. She ripped them out, some of them so fucking quickly that tags ripped off of some pretty scandalous articles of clothing. I grinned as I thought about the many ways I'd tear those pieces of fabric from her body. I imagined her tied up for me, wiggling around in a pair of those--.

"Dutch, go get Gordon," Naomi glowered.

I blinked. "Wait, what?"

Naomi shot to her feet, and her face was so red that the blood on her skin blended in. "Now, before the sheriff leaves."

"Why?" Troop asked as he raced around to get in front of her. "What's wrong?"

Dutch pointed to the suitcase. "Is it something I picked up?"

And when she grabbed a handful of that lingerie, she shook it in his face. "These aren't mine, Dutch. I've never seen those fucking things in my life. Now, go get Gordon, or I will. I want him to look me in my fucking face when I make him tell me who he bought these for."

His gaze simply dropped to the flimsy fabric in my hand. "The tags. That's why they weren't taken off. Because he hadn't given them t—."

"Now," I commanded as I shot Dutch a look.

28

———

NAOMI

Everything started swirling. Like a vortex, threatening to swallow me whole. As I crouched there, staring at the handfuls of tagged lingerie I'd never once seen in my life, something overcame me. Not anger. Not fear. Not bloodlust. No. Peace came over me. A peace unlike anything I had ever experienced. A peace that settled my gut, focused my gaze, and breathed like back into my mind.

I was going to kill Gordon, and I had peace about it.

"What's that?" Ranger asked.

I looked up and found the tip of his finger pointing toward the corner of the suitcase, and when I looked, I found something shiny. Something sharp. Something I'd never seen before. My hand navigated toward the item, smoothing along its rough exterior. The cold metal matched the chill of my heart as it pounded relentlessly against my chest, and as I gripped it with my stable hand, I pulled it out to study it.

And found that it was a lockbox with a six-digit combination.

"This should be easy enough," I said breathlessly.

My gut reaction was to try my birthday, but that simply

made me snicker. The old me would have tried that. The old me who had hope. Who thought Gordon was a stand-up citizen. Who thought that fighting alongside her man, despite the fact that he always fought her, was what I was supposed to do. The naïve little girl inside of me would have tried my birthday, but Gordon was clearly more selfish than that.

He didn't care enough to keep his dick tucked into his pants.

So, why the hell would he care enough to make my birthday one of his passwords?

"Gordon's birthday should work just fine," I murmured as I pushed against the small, metal Rolodex of numbers. They clicked into place, one after another, and when that lid popped open as the last number fell into place, I didn't even feel shocked.

I simply felt more ready for what was coming.

"What's in there?" Ranger asked.

The first thing I did was I picked up the gun. It looked like just any old handgun. Black. Official. Heavy in its weight. The bottom looked longer, though. As if someone had attempted to shove more bullets up its ass than ever before.

"An extended mag," Ranger murmured as he crouched beside me. "Interesting."

I moved it to the other side of the rectangular box, and it revealed wads of cash. And not just any cash, either. Different currencies. There was pink money, and green money like ours, but it sure didn't look like ours. I picked up a passport and flipped it open to find Gordon's picture, but none of his information.

"Mikey Leeway?" Ranger asked with a scoff. "Jesus, you could Google a fake name better than that."

The more I uncovered, the more certain I became about my decision. A man like Gordon didn't need to be walking around this planet, infecting it with his disease. He had destroyed enough lives. He had destroyed enough of mine, that much was for certain. And as I picked up a journal from the very bottom of the lockbox, I flipped it open to find that same coded shorthand I remembered listening to from around the corner.

Rivers and lakes. Mentions of mountains. There were dates with timestamps followed by things like 'two lakes' or 'pristine rivers.' There was even a sale for 'four and a half mountains,' whatever the fuck that meant.

"I'll just... keep this," Ranger said as he plucked the wad of U.S. currency from the lockbox.

I merely shrugged, though. I didn't care what they took. I just didn't want to look at it any longer.

"Hey!" Sheriff Barnes barked.

I whipped my gaze up and stood to my feet as he charged back through the hidden doorway.

"Everything all right?" Ranger asked.

The sheriff pointed his finger in the man's face. "Where's Gordon? I know you've got him, and if you want this to play out the way we discussed, you'll turn him over right this second."

"I have no idea what you're talking about," Ranger said.

I saw the shadow of that grin on his face, though, and that's when I knew what Dutch and Troop had done.

They had taken Gordon right from beneath that man's nose. *God, my guys are good.*

"Ranger, this isn't how this is going to go," the sheriff warned. "Either you give me back that man, or I bring you up on charges."

"Of what, exactly?" Ranger asked kindly.

I'd never once heard him ask anything kindly in the time that I had known him. But when it dripped from his lips, it almost sounded sarcastic.

Which made me snicker.

"I believe you're going to want this," I said as I kicked the lockbox and its contents toward Sheriff Barnes.

The man looked down at it before he hiked up his suit pants in order to crouch down. A groan fell from his lips before he picked up the gun, and he turned it over before heaving a heavy sigh.

"Numbers have been filed off," he murmured.

I pointed. "The passport is fake as well."

The sheriff picked up the pink currency. "Well, this is just fucking great."

"There was a journal in there, too," I said as I tossed him the book.

He barely caught it in his hands as he stood back to his feet. "What's this?"

"Open it up. I'm sure you'll recognize it."

And when he did, his eyes damn near bulged out of his fucking face. "Holy shit, these are transactions. This was in that box, too?"

I nodded mindlessly. "Yep."

"Where was this lockbox originally? I'm assuming you haven't always had it."

"I honestly don't know, and I honestly don't care. But I think your business is done here, Sheriff."

"Naomi?" Ranger asked.

I walked past everyone and stood in the doorway that was supposed to be hidden, but had been advertised to the entire world.

"You know how to get out, I'm sure," I said with as kind of tone as I could.

Sheriff Barnes looked at me with apprehension in his features. "I still have to find Gordon. I know he's still here."

"I don't care where he is, but you've got all the proof you need to bury the man for good in the palm of your hands. Get your guys on it. Start your own search. Tear this place apart, for all I care."

"Naomi," Ranger warned.

I shot him a look that told him to shut his fucking face before I turned my attention back to the sheriff. "Whenever you're ready."

"I have to come after them if anything happens to Gordon. You know that, right?"

I simply shrugged. "Good luck with everything. I hope you find him. He deserves everything that's about to come his way, as far as I'm concerned."

The man snickered. "Don't I know it."

"Quick question, though."

Sheriff Barnes eyed me carefully. "You mean, outside of where Gordon currently is?"

I bypassed his question. "Lakes. Mountains. Scenery. They spoke in so much code. Do you have any idea what it means?"

The sheriff snaked his gaze down my crooked figure. "How do you know that?"

"Does that matter?"

His stare snapped back up to mine before he relented. "Tommy Gun is known for turning cops against their own in order to get to their evidence lockers. It's how he establishes his dominance in an area. His M.O., so to speak. Then, he convinces those same cops to steal and pillage for things that can be sold on the street: guns, cars that have been readied for sale after cases are closed, drugs, cold hard cash confiscated at crime scenes. Things like that."

"So, that's probably what Griggs was having Gordon do?"

"Most likely. Though, it'll take time to break down what their arrangement actually was. But I'd be shocked if it was anything other than the standard stuff. Griggs is nothing, if not predictable."

I looked up at Ranger and did my best to stomach the bile rising up the back of my throat. "I'll be in the room if you need me."

With a nod of his head, he turned toward the sheriff. And his damned body was so massive that it completely blocked my movements. I passed by the gun that had been knocked from Gordon's hand, and I peered over my shoulder to look at the men behind me. They were whispering to themselves, no doubt striking up some sort of a deal. And while I almost couldn't stomach it, the moment gave me enough time to snatch that gun up and take it back into the bedroom with me. Where I quickly tucked it away behind my back. In the belt loops of my pants.

Just like I'd seen my men do so many times before when they thought I wasn't looking.

"Ah, there we go," I groaned as I sat back down in the bay window.

I stared at the wall and pictured the ocean waves undulating out toward the horizon. I closed my eyes, imagining the white caps that softly crested against the waters before battering against the edge of the cliff side. Maybe one of these days, I'd make my way down to one of the many private beaches that scoured the cliff's edge along the entire state. Maybe one of these days, I'd start enjoying myself instead of simply surviving.

But I had one last thing to do before I could move forward.

"I thought I'd find you in here, pretty girl," Troop said.

I opened my eyes and found him making his way toward me. Seeing him pulled a smile across my face, but it was a weak one. My mind was much too preoccupied with other things. That didn't stop Troop from sitting beside me, though. It didn't stop him from pulling my legs into his lap before his hands gracefully massaged my feet.

"Ugh, that feels amazing," I groaned as my head leaned against the painted window.

"Figured you could use one. It's been a long day."

"For all of us," I murmured.

"Dutch wanted me to let you know that you're not going to be the one to kill him, by the way."

My gaze snapped toward his. "What?"

Troop held his hand out. "So, give me the gun you picked up in the hallway."

"How could you possibly—?"

He wiggled his fingers. "Come on, don't make me come over there and take it from you."

I grinned. "And if I make you?"

His gaze grew dark as he moved my legs off his lap. He stalked toward me, his hands and knees pressing into the cushion of the bay window as I leaned myself back. He quickly wrapped his arm around me, shaking his head from side to side as he held me hostage with his gaze. And as he slid the gun out from the back belt loop of my pants, he captured my lips in the softest kiss.

"Wouldn't want that going off unexpectedly on you," he whispered.

"I want to kill him so badly," I said breathlessly.

He hovered over me, quickly ejecting the bullets from the gun before popping one out of the barrel. "I know you do, and you have every right to. But we can't let you do that."

"You guys took him, didn't you?"

I watched as he continued to take the gun apart, piece by piece. Then, he threw the contents onto the ground at our feet before he pulled me quickly into his lap.

"Come here, I gotcha."

I tucked my tired head beneath his chin. "You guys took him, didn't you?"

He rocked me softly in his embrace. "Just breathe for me."

"I can breathe just fine. Just tell me what you guys did."

"What you don't know won't kill you."

And that was all I needed to hear.

"Knock, knock," Ranger said as he rapped his knuckles against the door.

I snickered. "Since when do you knock?"

Dutch chuckled. "That's a damn good question, if I ever heard one."

I reached up with my lips and kissed Troop's jawline. "Let me up for a second."

"Anything for you."

He released me from his embrace, and I planted my feet squarely on the floor. I pushed myself up, leaning toward Dutch as I damn near threw myself into his arms. He caught me, his entire body cradling my fall. And as I got my feet underneath me, I pressed myself up to my tiptoes.

Before smashing my lips against his.

"God, I'm so glad you're all right," I whispered down the back of his throat.

He gripped my ass cheeks, pulling me closer into his growing thickness. "I'd do anything to keep you safe."

I peered over my shoulder and reached out for Ranger. "Come here."

Dutch stepped off to the side, passing me into Ranger's longing embrace. He picked me up and swung me around, causing me to wrap my legs around his waist just to hold on for the ride. I climbed him like a fucking tree. I scooted up his body until my face hovered over his. And when I cupped his cheeks, the words fell effortlessly from my mouth.

"I love you," I said.

His gaze widened before he sat on the edge of the bed. "I love you too, Naomi."

I reached out for Dutch and felt him take my hand. "I love you, Dutch."

He closed the distance between us and kissed the top of my head. "I love you too, lucky girl."

"Troop?"

He came up behind me and threaded his hands through my hair. He pulled my head back, crashing a kiss to my lips from upside down. I groaned down the back of his throat. I felt Ranger's dick rising to the occasion between my legs as Dutch feathered his light fingertips over my exposed skin. And as Troop's lips parted from mine, I wasn't the first one to speak.

"I love you, pretty girl."

I reached up to cup his face any way that I could. "I love you too, Troop. I love you all so much, and I don't even know how it happened."

Ranger chuckled. "That makes two of us."

"Three," Dutch said.

Troop shrugged. "It's not so hard to figure out."

I returned to my upright position before sliding off Ranger's lap. "Really, now? Fill me in, then."

Troop shrugged. "Simple. I'm awesome. They're awesome. You're sexy as hell, and very awesome yourself."

"Agreed," Dutch said.

"Hell, yeah," Ranger said as he stood.

Troop closed the distance between our bodies. "And now you can do whatever you want. Love whoever you want. Be whoever you want to be without that asshole breathing down the back of your neck."

Ranger took my hand and slowly turned me around. "You're free, Naomi. Free to stay, or go. Free to find another home, or make yours here."

"But the important thing," Dutch said as he crooked his finger beneath my chin and turned my attention in his direction, "is that you're free of him. Forever. So, whatever you choose, we'll support."

"Because that's what people do when they're *actually* in love," Troop said.

I turned back around, not knowing who to focus on as the whole of reality settled onto my shoulders. These men. These dark, dangerous men who led their life in the gray area of society had somehow swept me off my feet after stealing me away from a home I thought I loved. A home I thought I enjoyed. A home that I thought held my future. I couldn't believe it. It was almost too good to be true. And yet, as I reached my hand up to cup Troop's cheek, I knew I couldn't leave them.

I knew where my future lied, and it didn't lie where I thought it did.

"What's this?" I asked.

I smoothed my finger over a freckle I'd never seen on Troop's face before. But when it came off on my finger, I held it up to my face. It was more red than brown, and when I brought my other hand to my face to the dried blood beneath my nose, a chunk broke off. My hands sat in front of me as I compared the two. Comparing the dried blood on my face versus the dried blood on Troop's face.

"Are you bleeding anywhere?" I asked.

"He's not the one bleeding," Ranger glowered.

At that point, I knew. I knew what they had done. I knew what they had accomplished. As I wiped the dried blood off on my pants, realization dawned upon me.

I couldn't kill Gordon because they already had.

They eliminated my fear. They took care of the man that had hurt me. The man who had betrayed me. The man who had sucked away so many formative years from my life because I had allowed him to prey on me for so fucking long.

They took care of the real threat for me, and as I gazed around at the guys, I had the answer for my future.

"I like the idea of staying here, if I'm being honest."

"Well, if that's the case," Ranger said as he bent down and picked me up, tossing me over his shoulder, "then it sounds like we've got some celebrating to do."

Dutch walked by and smacked my ass. "I'll go get my newest set of knives."

Troop damn near giggled like a schoolgirl. "I get to use those tie downs again. What a day to be alive."

Ranger slid his hand between my thighs as he pinned me to his shoulder. "You're coming with us, and you're going to be a good girl, right?"

And as heat ricocheted through my gut, I rolled my hips as much as I could against that callused hand of his.

"I'll always be a good girl for you, Daddy."

Ranger growled. "Then you're coming with us, and you're going to like it."

No, not like it.

I'm going to love it.

29

NAOMI

"There we go," Troop said as he stepped back and surveyed his work.

I tugged at my restraints as I craned my neck up to look around at them. Ranger palmed his cock, and I swear I wanted nothing more than to taste it again. I licked my lips, feeling my pussy heat as his face darkened with nefarious desires.

"Dutch?" Range asked.

I heard the glimmer of his knife as he unsheathed it from his hip. "Already ahead of you."

I furrowed my brow. "Huh?"

When I felt the cool tip of Dutch's blade, I froze. I didn't move. I didn't speak. I barely breathed. It left a cool trail up the inside of my leg, peeling my jeans from my body as if Dutch were unwrapping an orange to be eaten. I slowly pivoted my leg, taking in the way his gaze dazzled upon my body as his fingertips curled back the fabric from my skin.

I watched him slide that knife all the way up to my inner thigh before popping it up.

I jumped. "Jesus, Dutch."

He flickered his hungry gaze up at me. "What a lovely present you make."

I gasped as he cupped my clothed pussy. I groaned as my head fell back toward the pillow, and effortlessly he slid that knife underneath the other leg of my pants. I focused on the sound of the fabric giving way. Like Moses and the Red Sea, the fabric seemed to give way to Dutch's intrusion. To his command of my body as he unraveled the clothes from my form.

And when I felt him pluck at the other side of my pants, the tip of his blade sat against my pussy.

"Dutch," I said breathlessly.

"It would be in your best interest, lucky girl, to stay still."

I swallowed hard. "Yes, sir."

He growled as he pierced my jeans. I squeezed my eyes shut, feeling Ranger's thick fingers stroking through my hair as Troop stood there, admiring Dutch's handiwork. My jeans loosened around my hips. They fell away from my skin as I balled my hands into fists.

Then, with one singular motion, Dutch gripped my jeans and ripped them clear from my body.

"Ta-daaaaa," he said mockingly.

"Perfect," Troop said.

"Now, the rest of her clothes," Range commanded.

I groaned as Dutch took his time with me. Kissing random parts of my skin, like my stomach, or my forearm. I gasped at the warmth of his lips. At the way the cold blade of his knife made my skin pucker before his lips made my body purr. My back arched softly as he freed my tits, tossing the shreds of my clothing to the floor until I was completely bared for them.

And when I opened my eyes, I found all three of them staring hungrily down at me.

"Jesus Christ, pretty girl," Troop said as he started disrobing immediately. "I can't stand it any longer."

Range chuckled. "You make us feral, little girl."

Dutch sheathed his knife and started crawling between my legs. "I call dibs on downstairs."

Troop walked over to the dresser and opened the top shelf. "I want to see her sweat with my teasing."

"What?" I asked breathlessly.

But, that's when Ranger gripped my hair and tilted my head toward him. "And I want that throat of yours."

I licked my lips. "Yes, Daddy."

He bent down and kissed my forehead. "Good girl."

I whimpered. "Fuck."

Dutch lapped his tongue up the slit of my pussy and my hips shot into the air. I tugged at the restraints, wanting nothing more than to cling to his silken blond hair. His icy blue eyes twinkled from above the pooch of my stomach, dazzling as he drank in the way my curves moved as I squirmed for his viewing pleasure. I heard clothes being tossed to the floor, one by one, until Dutch took a break long enough to quickly peel himself out of them as well.

I didn't know who to focus on first. They were all so beautiful, and so goddamn sexy, that I couldn't stand it. Ranger, with his bulging muscles and thick dick that stood rock hard at attention for me. Troop, with his honey-colored eyes and his chiseled features, standing there with his abs glaring back at me. And Dutch, with his lean form and his dexterous fingers already filling me one by one.

I felt someone guide my head toward the side before Range tapped his dripping dick against my lips.

"Open wide, sweet girl," he growled.

The second I unhinged my jaw, he plunged into the back of my throat. I fought against the intrusion, my throat closing around him as he clasped the back of my head with his palm.

"Relax," he coached, "don't fight it. It only makes it worse."

I gagged and sputtered, sending spittle dripping down my chin. But, the second Dutch lapped his tongue against my clit, my entire body settled.

"Do that again, Dutch," Range commanded.

"With pleasure," Dutch grumbled.

"Let's see about that asshole, shall we?" Troop asked.

Something started buzzing, and my eyes widened. Dutch tickled my clit with his tongue, swirling it around the base as he crooked two of his long, dexterous fingers against that pebbled spot within my body. Suddenly, I relaxed. Range's dick filled my throat as I started breathing through my nose, and my entire body rose to the occasion. Something tickled my puckered tits, and I jumped. Range threaded his fingers through my hair and slid his dick out before plunging it back in, stroking my throat with his girth. I tried to see what was vibrating around my tits, but I couldn't move to see anything.

Range had his command over me, and Dutch damn near sent me into the heavens with those long fingers of his.

"Oh, fuck," I moaned around his cock.

"Jesus Christ, sweet girl," Range groaned, "such a good girl for me."

I felt the vibrations rushing down my stomach as Troop spoke. "For us."

"Goddamn it," Dutch growled against my pussy.

"Why don't you raise those hips for me a bit, pretty girl?" Troop asked.

"I can't," I tried to say.

"What was that?" Range asked cheekily.

I shot him a look before I hollowed out my cheeks. He grunted as his eyes widened, and I nuzzled my nose against his tightly wound curls. He pulled his dick back out before sliding back down, and as he started moving my head, I opened my throat as much as possible.

I wanted him to use me.

Fuck me.

Make me cry out his name.

Before he poured every single ounce of his mark down my throat.

"Here," Dutch murmured as he removed his fingers from my depths, "try this."

He slid his hands beneath my ass and raised my hips. As if I weighed nothing, he parted my ass cheeks as I pressed my heels into the mattress of the bed, and I felt those vibrations closing in on my pussy. My juices dripped down my ass crack. Dutch kissed and licked the dollops of excess on my inner thighs, teasing me in ways that sent electricity soaring throughout my system.

Never in my life had I felt so amazing.

But, when something wet pressed against my asshole, my entire body clenched.

"Fuck!" Range damn near snarled.

"Sh-sh-sh-sh," Dutch said softly as his tongue massaged my clit softly, "relax for us, beautiful."

"I wanna come," I choked out around Range's dick. "I wanna come. Please."

"What do you think, Dutch?" Troop asked. "You think she wants to come?"

I nodded quickly. "Uh, huh. Uh, huh."

Dutch lapped at my clit again. "I think she does, Troop."

Range started fucking my face. "Then, let's let her have what she wants, gentlemen."

The vibrations stayed seated at my asshole as Dutch plunged back down into my pussy. His fingers filled me, pumping with the strokes of his tongue as Range claimed my mouth as his own. I lost control. I bucked against Dutch's face, feeling my asshole slowly claiming something that Troop had held in his hand. The more I bucked, the further my puckered hole swallowed its intrusion. And as Range's dick pulsed against my throat, I felt his hips stuttering.

"So close, sweet girl," he growled. "Fucking Christ."

"Come for me," I murmured.

"Do that again," he commanded.

"Come for me," I said as I moaned around his dick. "Come for me, please. I need it. I want it."

"Fuck!" Range exclaimed.

His dick burst down the back of my throat, and I opened my body to accept every thread of arousal that shot from the tip of his dick. Dutch sucked my clit between his lips, tickling my tip at lightening speed as I bucked ravenously against his face. I tugged at the restraints, feeling the entire bed rattling as Range's taste encompassed my entire being.

And finally, as Dutch filled my pussy with yet another glorious finger, I finally snapped.

"Yes!" I cried out.

My throat clenched around Range's dick. I milked his balls for all he had to offer as my pussy clenched over and over around Dutch's fingers. I heard him lapping me up, swallowing every droplet I had for him as he devoured me with his tongue. Troop chuckled as the vibrations inched their way further into my asshole. Dutch slid his fingers out, freeing my pussy as my entire body trembled in ecstasy.

And the second I relaxed, collapsing down against the mattress, that toy slid into my asshole.

Claiming the last of my holes.

"Oh, shit!" I cried out.

Range slid his dick out from my throat. "Good girl."

I whimpered at his words. "Yes. Yes. That's me."

He chuckled as he bent down, kissing my cum-stained lips. "Yes, sweet girl. That's you."

"Dutch?" Troop asked. "If you don't mind."

Dutch stood, and I swear to hell on high I heard him wipe his mouth off. "All yours, Troop."

And when I felt his knees settle between my thighs, I couldn't help but raise my head.

Only to see his long, veiny dick dropping toward my pussy.

"Oh, thank fuck," I whispered as my head dropped back down to the pillow.

"Range, why don't you hold this toy steady? I love feeling the vibrations against my dick."

He stumbled around the edge of the bed as he and Dutch switched places. "Can do."

I found Dutch standing at my head, his thick dick drenched in my juices. "Think you got room for me in that throat of yours?"

I nodded mindlessly. "Always."

He threaded his hand into my hair. "My lucky girl."

I smiled. "My Dutch."

"On the count of three," Troop said.

Dutch settled his dick against my lips. "Ready."

His endless legs pulsed with veins that bulged from his thighs. They throbbed with his beating heart, with the raging, wanton lust that had filled our veins. He slid the tip of his swollen cock around on my lips, painting my skin with his pre-cum. Teasing my tongue as it darted out and tried gathering his taste against my tongue. I wanted to wrap my lips around him. I wanted to feel him fill me up from the inside out before his languid presence descended upon me, molding to my excess. I wanted to feel the imprints of his chiseled muscles against my skin, morphing me into none other than a glorified fucking pillow. I wanted the weight of his lean, chiseled form to drown me.

Then, as I opened my mouth and offered him my tongue, he settled the heavy weight of his dick against it.

"One," Troop said.

Range twisted the toy around in my asshole, causing me to whimper.

"Two," Troop said.

Dutch eased his dick inside of my mouth. "Mmph, how warm you are for me."

"One," Troop growled.

Troop plunged into my pussy as Dutch eased his way down the back of my throat, but it was Range who turned up the vibrations on whatever toy had been stuffed into my asshole. Troop's dick spread my walls as if I were being fucked for the first time in my life, and I didn't hesitate to grind my hips against his.

"Told you, pretty girl," he grunted as he gripped my hips tightly, "I knew the second you felt this dick, you'd never want to know anything else."

"Fuck, fuck, fuck," I groaned around Dutch's cock.

"Fucking hell," he choked out as he fucked my throat, "I'll be having this throat more often."

Range chuckled. "It's fantastic, isn't it?"

The toy moved around in my asshole, causing Troop's dick to quiver against my walls. Dutch crooked his finger beneath my chin, raising my gaze to his and elongating my neck. I felt the last inch of him slide down the back of my throat. For fuck's sake, it damn near felt like he was in my fucking stomach.

"I want you to look at me, and don't you dare close those eyes," Dutch demanded.

I nodded quickly as I swallowed. And he had to catch himself against the headboard to keep from falling over.

"Jesus, Naomi," he croaked, "you feel so fucking amazing."

I tugged at my restraints as my body begged to hold my

guys. My family. My men. The people that had saved me from a life of solitude and depression. I owed them everything, and yet all I wanted was to cling to them while they took every hole in my body until they were satisfied themselves. Electricity blinded me, even as I kept my gaze on Dutch. His blond hair fell into his face as beads of sweat dripped down his brow, and I swear to fuck on high I'd never seen a more beautiful picture in all my life.

But the sound of wet skin slapping wet skin overtook me as Troop's dick slicked my pussy in ways I'd never experienced before.

"So fucking wet for me," he growled. "Fuck!"

My walls clenched around him. "Come for me."

Dutch groaned at my murmurs. "Keep that up and I just might."

Troop pounded against me, slamming the headboard against the wall as Range fucked my asshole with that damned toy. They synced their movements, with Troop pumping first before Dutch moved his dick, followed by Range easing the toy in and out.

In and out.

In and out.

"I'm gonna come," I choked out. "I'm gonna come. I'm gonna come."

"Stop saying it and just do it," Troop hissed.

And when he spanked the slope of my ass, I was a goner.

"Fuck!" I cried out around Dutch's dick.

He cupped the back of my head and sank my throat around his length. His dick bulged with the threads of hot arousal that shot down the back of my throat. He collapsed against the wall, physically holding himself up as his entire body shook. His legs locked out and his abs shivered for me, his form giving way to my mouth.

And as Troop filled my pussy to the brim, Range reached up and tugged at my puckered tits.

"You our little cum dumpster?" Range asked.

I nodded as Dutch slid his dick from the back of my throat. "Uh, huh."

"You a little whore for our juices?" Range growled as he smacked my breast.

I whimpered. "Fucking hell, yes. I'll do anything. I just want to feel you. All of you. Please."

Troop pulled his dick out from between my legs, and I felt the rush of our intermingled juices as they flooded my ass crack. The vibrations turned off, leaving my body buzzing all on its own as I tilted my head toward the ceiling. The world undulated around me. It spun on its axis as someone's fingers dipped into my juices. They slid their fingers up and down my ass crack, taking great care to lube up my asshole.

Before Dutch took Troop's place.

"Oh, God," I said breathlessly.

"There's no God here for you tonight," Dutch warned as he frogged his legs out in between mine.

It slid my thighs over his as he stroked his dick up and down my pussy. I watched as Ranger held up that toy for me to study, and I found a small vibrating plug staring back at me. He grinned as he inched it toward my pussy. He teased my stomach, causing me to jump as he cycled through the different vibrational settings on the toy itself.

Then, I watched him walk over to the dresser and abandon the plug for...

Shit, is that what I think it is?

"Why don't you put that right... there?" Dutch asked as he parted my pussy lips and pointed at my clit.

Range chuckled as he turned the wand to its highest setting. "Don't mind if I do."

Troop stood at my head, stroking his veiny cock as he grinned down at me. "I think I'll watch this time."

Ranger shrugged. "Suit yourself."

"Now," Dutch said curtly.

"Oh, God. Oh, God. Oh—oh, fuck!"

The second he breached me, Ranger placed that toy against my clit. It sent my eyes rolling into the back of my head as my hips came clear up off the bed. My pussy swallowed Dutch's dick in one swift motion, like the hungry little bitch it had become. And as Dutch held my hips tightly, curling his fingers into my thickness, he fucked me so hard that his ball sack bounced off my juicy ass.

"Jesus Christ, what a show," Troop said breathlessly.

"Goddamn it," Range growled, "such a good girl for us. Our little cum whore. Our dick slut."

"Yes!" I cried out. "Holy fuck. Just like that. Dutch, oh fuck."

"I love it when you say my name," Dutch growled.

I'd never heard him so feral in all my life. Range held that toy against my clit, pulsing my walls around Dutch's cock as Troop taunted me with nicknames I never thought I'd be called in all my life. His muscles raked against my body. His veins pulsated, pressing into my excess with every swirl of his pelvis against my own. His muscles expanded and contracted, swelling with his efforts as his body brought plea-sure to mine. Gone were the languid movements as he crashed his body against mine. Gone was the unassuming strength as his etched strength consumed me. Gone was the silence of his movements as the sounds of soaking wet skin slapping soaking wet skin sounded between our bodies. Our souls, lost to one another as his athletic structure, gave way to the brute force behind the muscles that pulled taut over his bones.

It was too much in all of the best ways, and I found myself spiraling into an endless, darkened abyss.

One I never wanted to be pulled from.

"That's it. Clench that pussy around my dick," Dutch hissed.

"So wet for us," Range said as he traced the toy around the base of my clit.

"Open wide for me, pretty girl," Troop singsonged.

I turned my head toward him and found his dick ready to explode. He stroked it quickly, squeezing his base as the tip of his dick bulged for me. I opened my mouth. I stuck out my tongue. I readied myself for the load he had for me. And as he settled his dick against my tongue, I felt his threads of come shooting toward the back of my throat.

Before I sucked him down and hollowed out my cheeks.

"Fuck!" Troop cried out.

"Mmmmmm," I hummed around his dick.

"Someone's hungry tonight," Range growled.

But, it was Dutch that started to shutter next. "Yes. Yes. Naomi. Jesus, fuck. I'm gonna—I'm gonna—."

And as Range's lips sank to the shell of my ear, my body exploded.

"Come," he simply said.

I unraveled for them. All of them. One by one, as they stuffed me full and played with my body in ways I had never experienced. The world rocked around me as I collapsed against the bed. Dutch's dick filled my pussy as the last of Troop's mark leaked down the back of my throat. I felt our intermingled juices spilling onto the sheets beneath my ass while Range turned off the vibrating toy and tossed it off to the side. Someone stroked my hair, but I didn't know who. With my gaze closed and my ears buzzing with the blood rushing throughout my body, it grew hard to differentiate who was who.

I felt the restraints falling from my appendages, and I found myself sorely disappointed that everything was done. I mean, I hadn't even had a chance to feel Range yet!

That is, until someone rolled me onto my side.

"Can you look at me, sweet girl?" Range asked.

I peeled my half-hooded gaze open and found him laying in front of me.

"Give me your leg," he said.

I held my leg up for him and he guided it over his pelvis. "Dutch?"

I felt someone shifting behind me before Dutch's long arm snaked around my waist. "I'm good."

"Troop?" Range asked.

I felt someone guiding my head upright before I found myself gazing into Troop's amber stare. "Ready and eagerly awaiting orders."

Range kissed the slope of my neck. "Just relax, sweet girl. Can you do that for us?"

I nodded mindlessly. "Always."

"Good," Dutch said as he parted my ass cheeks.

"Just—just go slow? Please?" I asked, my voice quivering with exhaustion.

Dutch kissed my shoulder. "Whatever you need, lucky girl."

The second he breached my asshole, my entire body clenched. That is, until Range's fingers started massaging my oversensitive nub.

"Relax," he whispered as he kissed my forehead.

My muscles gave way to his strokes before Dutch eased himself in a bit further. Range tickled, and Dutch eased, until his dick plunged itself all the way into my asshole. It was such a different sensation. One I hadn't experienced before. And even though I was overwhelmed with new things to take in, there wasn't anyone else I wanted to be with.

I was with the men that I loved.

And I'd do anything so long as I was with them.

"Jesus," I whispered.

Dutch nibbled along the nape of my neck. "Dutch is just fine."

I snickered. "Cheeky bastard."

He spanked my ass, and it made me moan, but when Range plunged his dick into my pussy, it made me cry out.

"Range! Fuck!"

Troop fisted my hair and turned my gaze up to his. "Open wide, pretty girl."

I drew in a deep breath before I dropped my jaw and stuck my tongue out, accepting Troop's gift as he slid into my mouth. I hollowed out my cheeks, sucking him down as my throat fought against him, gagging and sputtering as spit decorated my lips. Dutch rolled his hips against my ass cheeks. Range pumped his cock deep into my pussy as his finger teased my clit.

And when my body finally stopped fighting, euphoria overcame me.

"Oh, my God," I groaned around Troop's dick.

They all moved in tandem, fucking my holes at once as I laid there like a damn sex doll, ready and willing to accept them. The bed creaked and groaned with our movements as they stuffed me full, and I swear I'd never felt so complete in all my life. Sweat dripped down my body. Their sweat dripped onto me, challenging my own sweat to races down the crooks and crannies of my curves. Range growled and Dutch panted along the shell of my ear. Troop groaned and hissed in pleasure, and I had no clue where to place my hands. I gripped Range's muscles and reached up for Troop's balls. I reached back and threaded my fingers through Dutch's pin straight, beautiful hair, and I pulled his face into the crook of my neck. He sucked at patches of skin, leaving marks behind for me to admire as I drank them all in.

I never wanted it to end, them and I.

I wanted to stay like that forever.

No matter the cost to my own life.

Curses and moans were slung around as my body started to clench. My asshole clamped around Dutch's dick and my pussy fluttered around Range's thick cock. Even my throat closed around Troop, causing his hips to stutter as his fingernails slid against my scalp. I didn't care, though.

All I wanted was to come with all of them.

Feel all of them at once as we unraveled together.

"So close. So close. So close," I groaned.

Troop hissed. "Fucking hell, I'm gonna blow."

Range growled. "Come with us. Be a good girl for us."

But it was Dutch that whispered in my ear. "I love you, Naomi."

I whimpered as my heart came alive. "I love you too, Dutch."

"Jesus Christ, I love you, girl," Troop choked out.

"I love you too, Troop," I gasped.

Range reached around and spanked my ass, causing me to yelp around Troop's dick.

"Goddamn it, I love you so much," Range growled.

Tears crested my eyes. "I love you, too, Range."

"Fuck, I can't take it any—longer," Troop choked out.

"Come," I hummed around his dick. "Mmmmm, come for me."

"Fuuuuuuuuck," he droned as his head fell back.

Troop was the first to burst, his threads of come sliding down my eager throat. I fucked my throat against his dick as he held himself up against the wall, his legs shaking and his arm vibrating with a need to collapse. I milked him dry, lapping up every last drop he had for me as Range's hips began to stutter.

"Shit," he hissed before he thrusted into me one last time.

"Goddamn it, yes," Dutch groaned before he bit down into my shoulder.

"Yes!" I cried out as my body locked out.

I spiraled. I'd say that I orgasmed, but it was so much more than that. Troop collapsed around my head, stroking his fingers through my hair as Range and Dutch poured themselves into me. My muscles contracted and quivered, shivering me to my core as my orgasm rocketed all around my body. Silver stars burst behind my tightly closed eyes, a private show just for me as my heart soared into the heavens. I couldn't speak. I barely caught my breath. And as I felt Range and Dutch collapse around me, my jaw quivered as my pulsing body pushed them both out.

Before I collapsed, sinking into the mattress with my limp body spent.

"Blanket," Range said as he snapped his fingers.

I felt Dutch move before something cool, and soft, and majestic fell over my body.

"There we go," Range murmured as he covered me up, "that's better."

"Oh," I sighed.

It was the only thing I could say. The only ounce of energy I had, and I hoped they heard it. I hoped they heard how much I loved them. How much I appreciated them. How much I adored them. Dutch peppered my bare shoulder with kisses where he had bitten down on me. Range captured my lips softly, sucking on my lower lip as his fingers traced my puckered peaks.

"I'll have to give those more attention next time," he murmured down the back of my throat.

But it was Troop who found the strength to push himself up and kiss my forehead.

"Get some sleep, pretty girl," he whispered.

"Mmmmmm, okay," I murmured lazily.

Dutch nuzzled his nose along the shell of my ear. "We'll stay until you're asleep."

"Well," Range grunted as he shifted away from me, "I think this is as good of a time as any to get her up to her room so she can sleep soundly."

I peeked a tired eye open. "My room?"

Range tilted his head as he slid his arms beneath my naked form. "How do you feel about the room we put you in earlier?"

"Behind the wall?" I asked, as a yawn peeled from my lips.

Range lifted me into the air. "Yeah, that room."

I nuzzled underneath his chin as he cradled me close. "Can we take the paint off that window?"

Troop chuckled. "We can do whatever you want to the room."

"Let me get the door," Dutch said as he scrambled to get up from the bed.

"Of course, we can," Range whispered as he held me in his grasp.

I floated through the air, my body bouncing with the stairs as Range somehow found the strength to carry me all the way up there. I closed my eyes and tried my best to stay awake, but when the comforting sheets of that bed graced my skin, I succumbed to the darkness. It pulled me under, dragging me into a comforting sleep as someone pulled a sheet over my body.

And the last thing I heard was Range's command before it was light's out.

"Troop, go get a paint scraper. Let's get this window ready for her before we leave."

EPILOGUE
NAOMI

The warm sun pulled me from sleep, and the seagulls chirping outside brought a lopsided smile to my face. My aching body rolled over, and I crooked myself enough to see that the bay window was free to shine light inside of the room whenever possible. It made me smile as I pressed myself up. I dragged my feet over the edge of the plush bed and hung my head, waiting for the dizziness to pass.

But, when I lifted my head, I found something green hanging on the closed closet door.

"Huh?"

I planted my tired feet into the soft carpet and dragged my tired ass over to the closet. I had to get closer before it came into focus since my body apparently wanted to protest being up. But, when it came into view, I found the piece of clothing absolutely sparkling.

"What the--?"

I reached out and fingered the silken fabric. The hunter green color shimmered in the morning sunlight as it poured through the freed bay window, and I realized that it was a silken nightgown with a matching robe to wrap around my shoulders. I smiled as I plucked it off the hanger. I wasted no time getting into it, feeling the cool fabric slosh against my skin.

But when I grasped the robe, a piece of paper fell to the ground.

"Always full of surprises," I said with a smile on my face.

I should've known the note was from Dutch. That seemed to be a way that he enjoyed communicating. But the words in the note brought tears to my eyes.

Tears of happiness and joy that reminded me I had chosen correctly for once in my fucking life.

L.G.,

Here's to starting a wardrobe that belongs to you.

• *Dutch*

"Oh, Dutch," I whispered.

I set the note right by my bedside before making my way into the bathroom. I needed to clean myself up and get some water splashed into my face before I attempted to take on the day. But the second I crossed the threshold, the sight of the bathroom woke me up immediately.

Because the thing was fucking huge.

"Jesus Christ, how the hell did they shove all this back here?"

The vanity had not one, not two, but four fucking sinks, each with their own shelving that framed an oval mirror that was placed above each of them on the wall. I slid my fingertips along the marbled countertop, which matched the floors, by the way. In the reflection of the mirror, I caught the hickies Dutch had left all along my neck, and the memory of last night sent shivers down my spine.

My nipples puckered against the silken fabric, and I turned away from the mirror in order to calm my body down.

Only to be faced with the biggest walk-in shower I'd ever seen in my life.

"Fucking hell," I whispered.

Not only was the walk-in shower laden with smooth stone, but it encompassed the whole back wall of the bathroom. With the toilet crooked in a private corner at the end of the sinks, the shower seemed to be at least a third of the bathroom. I walked through the miniature hallway that had been lined with all sorts of expensive body washes and shower toiletry needs, but the thing that tripped me up was the step down.

Two steps down, actually.

Into a massive pit that had a drain toward the bottom.

Holy fuck, it's a shower and a damn swimming pool.

As I gazed around the stone encasement, I found myself smiling harder than ever. Not only was the place absolutely humongous, but it certainly held enough room for all four of us. Whether we wanted to shower, take a bath, or do... other things... we all had the space to completely spread out.

And coupled with the four-sink vanity, something told me they had this room primed and waiting for someone special.

Like me.

"Time to wash up," I whispered as I started my climb out of the stonewalled depths.

After cleaning myself up a bit, I ventured out of my private alcove only to find the smell of breakfast enticing me into the kitchen. I followed the smell of sizzling bacon and freshly scrambled eggs, only to find that the guys were all standing in the kitchen in nothing but their boxers.

And there was a serious lack of security guards walking around.

"Where's everyone else?" I asked as I emerged from the hallway.

Dutch smiled as he turned to face me. "We dismissed the guards for the day."

Troop walked a mug of coffee over to me. "Figured we could all use some alone time after everything that's happened."

I took it from him and stood on my tiptoes to kiss his cheeks. "Thanks."

He chuckled. "No problem."

"Looks good on you, by the way," Dutch said as he raked his gaze down my body.

I tossed him a playful wink. "Now, I just need the rest of the colors of the rainbow."

"That, we can do," Range said as he turned off the stove. "Breakfast is ready, by the way."

"Porch?" Troop asked.

I smiled from ear to ear. "Sounds delightful."

Troop and Dutch guided me out onto the porch, where the sun rose behind our heads, casting beautiful colors all along the waves of the ocean beneath us. The soft crashing of its waters against the cliff side we practically hung off of mesmerized me, and as I sank into a cushioned chair, Range plopped a plate of food down into my lap.

Before hitting a button that scooped my legs out from beneath me.

"Whoo!" I exclaimed in shock.

Range kissed the top of my head. "Bet you didn't know they made outdoor recliners, huh?"

I leaned back and captured his lips in a soft morning kiss. "You guys always seem to find ways to surprise me."

"Like the bathroom upstairs?" Dutch asked.

I kissed Range one last time before he moved back into the kitchen. "You heard me lumbering around up there?"

"Pretty much," Troop said with a grin as he handed me some apple juice. "Here, in case you want something other than coffee."

I took it from him, but not before I reached my lips down and kissed his hand. "Thank you."

"No thanks needed," he said.

"So," Dutch said as he pulled up a chair beside me, "before you even ask, no, Sheriff Barnes isn't going to be an issue."

I blinked. "How did you--?"

"It's part of his charm," Range said as he brought a plate of fruit out for all of us to munch on.

"Dutch and I are already on it," Troop said as he scooted a chair up to my other side, "so by the end of today, things will be settled and everything will be back to normal."

"Well, hopefully not *everything*," I said.

"Good to hear you feel that way," Range said as he dragged a lounge chair in front of all of us and climbed his big ass into hit.

I swear, the chair groaned out for mercy as he leaned back with his two plates of food steadied on both of his thick thighs.

"What?" he asked when he saw me staring. "Boy's gotta eat."

"Here, here," I said as I lifted a piece of crispy bacon from my plate.

As we all ate and sipped our drinks, I found my gaze locked with the horizon. With the watery world stretched out before me and all the bullshit finally behind me. I felt invigorated. Empowered. Ready to take on the world and all it had to offer.

But it was Range's voice that pulled me from the depths of my mind.

"So, what are you going to do about your nursing job?" he asked.

I shrugged. "I don't know, really. But, for once, that doesn't scare me."

Range chuckled. "Good girl."

The sentiment made me shiver as I reached for my coffee.

"You know," Troop said as he slid a finger up and down the puckered skin of my arm, "I think someone likes that nickname."

Dutch leaned into my ear and purred like a damn cat. "Such a good girl for us."

My eyes fluttered closed. "You guys will be the death of me."

"Naomi," Range said curtly.

My gaze flew open. "What? What's wrong?"

His stone-cold stare locked with mine. "You know we'd never hurt you. Ever. Right?"

"You know that's just a figure of speech, right?" I asked.

"Naomi."

I nodded softly. "I know. I know you guys won't."

He turned his attention back to his food. "Good."

"Any idea what you're going to do from here?" Troop asked before he sipped his coffee.

I reached for mine and took a long pull of its creamy goodness, giving myself time to think. For the past couple of weeks, I had done nothing but take things day by day. And each day that unfolded, I found myself succumbing to the life that had been thrust upon me without my permission. What had once been a life sentence had turned into a life changer, and I didn't know much of anything any longer. Things that used to give me happiness no longer did, and things I used to hate brought me joy. And pleasure. And respect.

"Well," I said as I set my coffee mug off to the side, "I can't really go home. Home was Gordon's place, and I sure as hell don't want to go back there."

Dutch settled his hand on my shoulder. "I'll go back today and get the rest of your things."

I smiled at him. "I'd really appreciate that... if that's what I wanted you to do."

"You don't want your things?" he asked.

I shook my head. "It all feels dirty now, if that makes any sense."

"Well," Troop said as he shoveled food into his face, "then I guess we'll just have to send you on some shopping sprees."

I snickered. "Don't tempt me. I'll spend all of your money if you give me the chance."

I swear on my life, I heard someone knocking somewhere, and my suspicions were confirmed when Range stood.

"Trust me, you couldn't do that. We have too much of it," he said mindlessly as he made his way back inside.

I furrowed my brow. "Wait, how much money do you guys really have?"

Troop barked with laughter. "Hell of a question, don't you think?"

"Is it who I think it is at the door? Because if it is, we might want to put on clothes," Dutch said.

"Wait, who's at the door?" I asked.

Troop placed his food on his chair as he stood. "Good idea. Let's go, Dutch."

"Wait a second," I said as I craned my neck over my shoulder. "seriously. Who's at the door?"

Range appeared once more, only that time he had a shirt thrown over his torso. "We figured you might want to talk with someone who has advice for you."

"And who's that?"

"Naomi?"

My entire body froze. "Dad?"

"Oh, my God. Naomi!" he exclaimed as he rushed outside.

"Dad!?" I yelped as I shot up from my seat.

My food tumbled to the ground, but I didn't care. I opened my arms for my father, and he raced into them, wrapping me up in the tightest hug I had ever received.

"Oh, Dad," I choked out as I started crying against his shoulder.

"It's okay. I'm here. I'm right here, baby," he whispered.

"I missed you... so... so much," I choked out.

He peppered kisses along my head. "I missed you, too. Are you okay? Did they hurt you? Are they feeding you regularly? Have they let you go? Can you come home?"

"Sh-sh-sh-sh," I whispered as I picked my head up and gazed into his tired eyes. "I'm okay, Dad. I'm... I'm very okay."

His gaze dropped to my neck before his lips down turned into a frown. "Where did you get those?"

My cheeks blushed, and I used my hair to cover them up. "Let's take this conversation one step at a time. Yeah?"

"Are they taking advantage of you? Because if they are--."

I cupped his cheeks. "Gordon was the one taking advantage of me, Dad. Not them."

His eyes widened. "He what?"

I held my arm out to where Dutch had been sitting. "Come and sit. There's fruit, and I can get you some coffee, and we can just talk. Okay?"

He eyed me carefully. "You sure you're all right?"

I smiled, and I swear my heart came alive. "I'm more than all right, Dad. I'm fantastic."

He shook his head. "I haven't seen that smile in so long."

"I haven't had it in so long."

His gaze searched mine. "What the hell has happened? Some sheriff came by my house yesterday asking questions about Gordon, and you, and—."

I moved him by his shoulders and sat him down before

pulling up another chair in front of him. With our knees touching, I took his hands within mine, studying the worry and relief that cascaded over his face at the same time. I couldn't imagine how confused he must feel, and I wanted to answer all of his questions.

I just hoped it didn't overwhelm him.

"Is it going to be easier for you to ask questions and me to explain? Or do you want me to just dive into the story and you can interject with questions as we go?" I asked.

He squeezed my hands. "Let me ask my questions. You know I love my questions."

I snickered. "You sure do, Dad."

He sighed. "Why is Gordon's face all over the news right now as a missing person?"

I didn't know it was, but that didn't shock me. "He's a dirty cop."

He gasped. "What!?"

I nodded. "He was in bed with Tommy Gun Griggs, and has been for quite some time."

"You're joking."

"Not one bit."

"So, he's going to prison?"

I smiled. "For a very, very long time. They've got enough evidence on him to put him away for life, if that's what they want to do."

The last thing Dad needed to know was that he was sitting with Gordon's murderers. Or, more specifically, the woman who took solace in his murder.

"So, is that why a Sheriff Barnes came by asking about Gordon yesterday? Because he didn't seem to know where to find the man."

I had to tiptoe around that question softly. "Okay, maybe it's better if I explain, because a lot of these answers are sort of knotted around each other."

"How long have you known about Gordon working for the mob?"

And that was my intro to the story I had concocted in my head. "I suspected things about a couple of years ago, but when I came across a lockbox in our bedroom while cleaning up one day, I found proof."

"What kind of proof?"

I shrugged as I heaved a heavy sigh. "There was a gun in there with a filed-off serial number, a bunch of money in all sorts of different currency, a journal of transactions written in code—or so I found out later by Sheriff Barnes when he paid us a visit yesterday—and a passport with Gordon's face, but not his name. Or any of his other information, for that matter."

"Jesus," Dad whispered.

"When I found all of that, I took it to the police straight away. And when they saw it, they knew they had to put me in protective custody. Coming across stuff like that triggers a certain set of protocols, and one of those protocols was protective custody until Gordon was put in handcuffs and Griggs was tracked down."

Dad peered over his shoulder to find the guys standing in the kitchen, smiling to themselves as they tried their best to look like they weren't listening in.

I knew they'd be proud of my story, too.

"So, those guys are...?"

I snickered. "They're confidential informants that work for the police department. I was adamant about not leaving town because I didn't want to leave you behind, so they put me here with them. That way, they could watch over me, check up on you, and keep tabs on things if Gordon ever found me."

"Which one's Ranger?"

I blinked. "What?"

He thumbed over his shoulder. "Ranger. He kept calling me to tell me that you were okay. Didn't you ever wonder why I never came after you?"

I slowly peered in through the window and held Range's gaze for a while.

"He did?" I asked.

Dad picked up my hands in his. "You never once wondered why I didn't come after you?"

I shrugged as my attention returned to him. "I figured you understood that giving myself up for you meant that you couldn't come after me with their threats and stuff. That's all."

He brought my hands to his lips to kiss. "Those daily phone calls were the only thing that kept me at bay. He kept reassuring me that you were all right. That it was for your own good."

I furrowed my brow. "And when did he start those phone calls?"

"A couple of days or so after everything happened. I was so dazed and worried. Much too scared to go to the police for fear that their threats were real. And then he called, and explained that it was for your own safety, and that whatever you had gotten caught up in, they'd make sure you got out of it."

"I'm so sorry, Dad," I whispered.

Gordon. Ranger started calling my father after we figured out Gordon's dirty little secret.

I couldn't have loved that man more if I actively tried.

My gaze gravitated back to Range, and I watched a grin cross his face. He held up his coffee mug to me before tossing me a playful wink, and my heart grew another size for him. Range had kept my father updated. That's why he never came after me. Even before I knew I was in trouble. Even before I knew what the hell was going on and the risks that sat outside the front door for me... he knew.

He kept me *and* my father safe.

I guess my men could still surprise me, after all.

"So," Dad said as he cleared his throat, "confidential informants, you say?"

I smiled back at Range. "Yeah."

"Naomi?"

My gaze returned to my father. "Yeah? Sorry, just in my head a bit. It's been a wild time."

"Are you okay, sweetheart? Honestly?"

I nodded slowly. "There was... a moment yesterday that was rough. Gordon spared no expense in tracking me down, and--."

"I do have a question, though," Dad said as he interrupted me.

I knew exactly what was coming, too. "Go ahead."

"Why were those guys in my house?" Dad asked. "Why did they attack me?"

I felt the heated presence of their gazes as the profile of my face ignited with fire. I was good at thinking on my feet, courtesy of my line of work, but I had to get this answer right. If I fumbled it up in any way, we were toast.

So, I drew in a deep breath and said the only thing that came to mind.

"The thing with WITSEC is that it's deep cover, Dad. Or so Sheriff Barnes told me. He said that if I wanted to stay in town and go with them instead, they'd have to orchestrate a way to get me into their custody that wasn't just passing me over faithfully. It had to be outside of Gordon's purview, and it had to scare you badly enough to make sure you didn't come after me. I'm so sorry, Dad. I'm so sorry for what ha—."

He cupped my cheek as tears lined his eyes. "I'm just glad you're okay, sweetheart. And I'm thankful for Ranger's phone calls. But above all else, I'm just glad these men kept you safe from Gordon."

I nuzzled against his palm. "I wish I could've told you sooner. I wanted to, so badly. But the sheriff was adamant on—."

"You know, I should've seen it sooner."

I paused. "What?"

Dad leaned back and released my hands. "With Gordon. I should've seen it sooner. He had been acting so weird, and I should have talked with you about it—."

I scooted my chair so close that my legs encompassed his. "Dad, I'm safe. We're both safe. While I was in custody with them, they were making regular routes through the neighborhood to make sure Gordon, or anyone else, came to harass you. We're both safe. Gordon is gone, and that's all that matters."

Dad stood and yanked me to my feet. "Come here. I need another hug."

I wrapped my arms around him and held him tightly. "I could use all the hugs I can get."

Then he whispered into my ear. "Are you sure these guys work for the police? Because they don't strike me as police."

I giggled. "Their confidential informants. Not police."

"So, what do they actually do?"

My gaze locked on all three of them as they stood there, watching the scene unfold. And when Range nodded his head, I knew it was okay to tell him the truth.

"They're part of a motorcycle crew that rolls around these parts. They make their money selling weapons to people who want to enact those kinds of transactions, and then they turn the information they get over to the police for a monthly stipend."

Dad sighed heavily as he gripped my shoulders and stared me down. "And they're safe for you to be around?"

I spoke my next words with truth and pride. "I've never been safer, Dad. I can assure you of that."

He breathed a heavy sigh of relief. "I swear, it's like you're glowing."

I smiled so hard my eyes almost closed. "Sometimes, you don't realize how taxing an environment is until you're out of it. I've slept and read and meditated so much while I've been here that I feel like a completely different person."

I peered over Dad's shoulder and found the guys blowing kisses at me, and it made me bark with laughter.

"God, that laugh," Dad said as he slid his hands down my arms. "I've missed that laugh."

I breathed in a breath of fresh air as the wind kicked up. "I've missed it, too."

He lowered his voice. "Wouldn't have something to do with one of those guys standing in the kitchen, would it?"

I giggled as I shook my head. "Cast off one man and off to the next?"

"Well," he said with a shrug before he sat back down, "if it makes you this happy, then why not?"

I found myself staring back at the guys through the kitchen windows, and my heart skipped a beat.

"For once in my life, I'm honestly happy," I said as I eased myself back down into the chair. "So, does it really matter why?"

Dad studied me carefully. "Are you safe now? Or do you still have to stay here for a while?"

"Well, while it's apparently now safe for you to come visit, I'll probably have to stay here until they mount their case against Gordon and Griggs."

"So, I can at least come visit you?"

"Without a shadow of a doubt," Range said as he poked his head outside. "Is Dad hungry?"

"Starving," Dad said over his shoulder.

"One plate of food, coming up," Range said.

And that's when Dad finally relaxed back into the chair.

"Well, if you're happy and you're safe, that's all a father can ask for. Just promise me one thing."

"Anything," I said as Dutch and Troop stood in the doorway, their arms crossed over their chests.

"Promise me that whatever makes you happy, you'll chase it this time. Forget about what other people want. Forget about what life tells you that you should have. Whatever is making you this happy, chase it, Naomi."

Range appeared in the doorway with a plate full of food as he stood in between Dutch and Troop. I gazed around at all three of them, feeling my heart grow three sizes just to accommodate the love I had found for them. And as I sat there, processing this newfound life of mine, I answered my father with all the confidence the world had to offer me.

"I promise."

Turn the page for a sneak peak at Twisted Glass!

I'm not who they think I am—and my life depends on making them believe it.

How does a woman without so much as a speeding ticket find herself taken hostage by a biker gang with a vicious grudge?

Ask the twin sister I never knew I had.

Staying squeaky-clean has always worked for me, and I love the life I've built—but evidently, my sister can't say the same, and her choices have led the Road Raiders MC straight to my door.

Being dragged into their world is a total shock to my system, but I can't deny the connection I feel with Axton, Dante, and Maverick. I see through their rocky exterior, and part of me wants to explore what's between us, if only I can convince them of my true identity.

Unless they kill me before I get the chance...

Twisted Glass is a complete stand-alone why choose motorcycle club romance. It is a part of the Twisted Intentions series, which features a new harem in each book. These books are not connected and can be read in any order.

SNEAK PEAK AT TWISTED GLASS
BRIELLE

Thinking about my kids was the only way to keep the pain away. But my fucking God, they did their best to break through.

"Miss Lancaster! Look!"

I turned at the sound of my name. "Way to go, Johnny! Just be careful up there, all right?"

He gave me a thumbs up. "I will!"

I cupped my hands over my mouth. "Both hands on the jungle gym!"

"Miss Lancaster?" someone asked as they tugged at my dress.

I peeked down and found little Miss Lindsey standing next to me. So, I crouched down to her eye level.

"Hey there, pretty girl," I said with a soft smile, "what's up?"

She tugged at one of the curls that I had painstakingly placed in my hair and giggled as it bounced. "Sproingy."

I touched her nose softly with my finger. "I curled my hair just for you today, cutie pie."

I had to admit, curling my hair wasn't something that I did often. My pin straight bangs matched the pin straight demeanor of the rest of my jet-black hair, and sometimes the temporary curls weren't worth the pain I went through in order to place them. But oh, the curiosity of the kids in my classroom at work made it worth the effort. A pang of pain rushed through my side, and I hissed as I snapped back up. "Johnny?"

"Yeah, Miss Lancaster!?"

"You be careful up in that tree now. I don't want you getting hurt!"

"Again."

My body grew weak as I sank to the ground, feeling the grass cushion my knees.

"Miss Lancaster!?" Johnny exclaimed.

I held my hand up as I struggled to catch my breath. "I'm okay. I'm good. Just... a bit hot."

"Again."

"Are you sure?"

"Did I fucking stutter? Again."

My eyelids grew heavy, as if they were being weighed down with lead as yet another pang of agony shot through my ribcage. I had to hold on. I had to hold onto my kids. Hold onto their smiles, laughter, and joy.

It was the only way I knew I'd stay alive.

"Hey, kids?" I called out as I shook my head.

I wanted to hold onto my little ones for as long as I could.

"Miss Lancaster, look!"

"Get the spotlight."

"Miss Lancaster! Watch!"

"Are you sure this is her?"

"Miss Ell!? Can you hear me!?"

"Miss Lancaster?"

"I love your curls!"

I swallowed hard. "And I love you."

"What the fuck did she just say?"

"Right there. Yep. Point it right at her."

"Miss Ell?"

"She has to be disassociating. No one's that good at ignoring pain."

That brought my head up from its dangling position. "Challenge accepted."

The stinging sensation rushing through my side was met only with the buzzing of the harsh light that dropped down onto my face. I winced as the bright light burned a hole into my forehead. My shoulders tensed as my mouth drew in short bouts of air. I felt it coming. Felt it brewing as something dragged its way across the floor in front of me. The hairs on the nape of my neck stood on end. My arms shivered from a cold my body didn't feel. The rough carpet beneath my feet taunted me as whatever was being dragged got closer. Then, something thudded in front of me before my seat lurched with a resounding thud.

I wanted to be back with my kids. Back at the school, where I knew that it was safe.

"Aaaa-cho!"

I sneezed all over my lap before a brutal voice hit my ears.

"Don't get snot on my fucking floors."

Panic gripped my throat. I tugged at my wrists, but they didn't come free. I outstretched my legs, or at least tried, before I realized I wasn't sleeping. The pain coursing through my body reminded me I was alive.

No. It had been a dream. It couldn't be real. There was no way that—

Oh, God. I'm really not at home.

"Where am I?" I croaked out.

A shadow cloaked me, giving my aching face a rest from its harsh light. I peeked up with one eye, managing to pry it open from the sealant of fluids and crust that had painted it shut. My ankles throbbed. My wrists ached. And for some reason, it felt like I was about to vomit.

"Who are you?" I managed to choke out.

I heard what sounded like shuffling around before the shadow abated, leaving me exposed to the harsh buzzing light.

It took my eye a second to adjust, but I found the devil himself sitting across from me when it did. The spindly chair he sat on did nothing to confine his humongous stature. He spread his legs wide as a grin slithered across his face. He looked positively murderous.

"Who are you?" I asked, trying to thread some strength into my voice.

But the man sitting in front of me with shoulders as big as the canyons simply stared. Sitting there, unwavering in his stature, while that glaring light blasted from behind him. It cloaked him in a weird sort of ambiance that would have relaxed me had it not been for the bloodlust in his eyes.

If he wasn't going to kill me, he wanted to.

And that was enough for me.

"Look," I said, shaking my pounding head, "whoever you think I am, I'm not. I'm just a schoolteacher. I work with students who need extra evaluation and care. I put together their IEPs, I get them set up with intervention tactics. I work with them on—"

"Does the name Luca ring any bells?"

I blinked. Was he serious? "Really, you've got the wrong girl. I'm just a—AH! NO!"

The thundering footsteps made me cry out before something pulsed against my lips. The chair creaked beneath a weight that shifted the arms of the chair beneath my arms. I felt his presence, even though my stare struggled to focus through the tears. His shadow loomed over me. Even though I couldn't see him—even though my eyes ached from a pain that ricocheted all the way down my spine—I felt him hovering. And when my gaze finally managed to focus on him, the disgust that curled his lips down stopped my heart in my chest.

Before he leaned me back, tipping the front two chair legs backward until I did nothing but dangle from his grasp.

"No! Stop! Please!"

My feet, moving around in the air.

"Oh, my God," I choked out as tears flooded my cheeks.

My body, suspended.

"Don't kill me, please. If I can't help, I will, I swear. Whatever it is. Just please, don't kill me."

Completely under his control.

"Please," I whispered as tears brewed in my eyes, "my parents are waiting for me. I know they must be worried. I won't say anything. I-I-If you let me go, I—"

His stare stayed still, as if torturing a woman did nothing for him. "Does the name Luca ring any bells?"

I scoffed. "I dated a Luca in college for, like, three days. Do you mean him?"

The chair's legs slammed back down before a resounding crack filled the room. It wasn't until after I'd caught my breath, however, that the searing pain ricocheted through my cheekbone.

Before something trickled down my jawline to my neck.

"Ouch," I whimpered.

"I won't ask you again," the man snarled, gripping my hair and pulled my head back.

"Ah! Please! Stop!"

His disgusting breath fanned against the shell of my ear. "Tell me the truth, you slimy little cunt, or you'll stay down here until your stomach eats away at your muscles."

I had no idea what he wanted. I had no idea what the hell he wanted me to say. But if I was going to die, I sure as hell wasn't going to die a liar.

So, I swallowed hard. "I don't know who you think I am, but you've got the wrong woman."

At first, nothing happened. Even though I braced for the pain. Even though my entire body locked up, preparing itself for the man's fists, nothing came. One by one, my muscles relaxed. One by one, the hairs along my arms and legs finally settled back down against my skin.

Until I found myself suddenly staring at the ceiling and gasping for air.

"Oh—huuuh—no."

"Do you believe her?"

I didn't recognize the voice as I laid there with heated pain rushing through the marrow of my bones. What day was it? How long had I been there? What the hell did that man want from me? I gasped to try and catch my breath. My skin tingled. My ass burned. Tears flooded the sides of my face as my lungs felt as if they were collapsing, air sac by air sac. Why couldn't I catch my breath? I forced my stomach to press out as I tried breathing through my nose. But it was no use.

My body seemed to be protesting the fact that I was still alive.

"Help," I sputtered.

From the corner of my eye, a movement caught my attention long enough to flood my body with adrenaline. My lungs set themselves on fire. It felt like my entire body was burning from the inside out. But as that shadow appeared above me, I knew I was in trouble.

I wasn't in there with one person.

I had been in there with two.

"Help—me," I managed to choke out.

"You sure we got the right one?" the voice I didn't recognize asked.

"Shut up," the brutal voice hissed.

"She doesn't match my profile. I told you this the second we—"

"If you can't handle a bit of work, then go the fuck upstairs."

Work? What the hell kind of work was this?

"She's gonna pass out if we don't sit her up," the unfamiliar voice said. "You want to do the CPR this time or are you gonna keep outsourcing that gig to—"

The room moved swiftly as my head sat upright on my body once more. The room spun around me as I leaned forward, gagging and heaving while trying to gasp for air. My body didn't know what to do. I couldn't blame it, either. It felt like I had slipped into a nightmare and didn't have a way back to reality.

For all I knew, I was already dead.

How long have I been here?

"They'll be looking for me," I murmured.

The men stopped arguing before a hand fisted my hair and yanked my head back.

"Ouch!" I yelped.

"What did you say?" the brutal man growled.

If I was going to die, he'd have to look me in the eye to do it. "My family. They'll be looking for me. And they won't stop until they've found me."

That crooked grin spread across his scarred face before a chuckle fell from his twisted mouth. He released my head, shoving it off to the side. He snorted and snarled. I heard him coughing and hocking, making my stomach turn as my mouth filled with saliva.

And when that fucking ball of snot slapped against my shin, I leaned over the edge of my chair and puked.

"Jesus, someone get her some water," yet another voice said.

Shock ran through my system as something snapped. The pitter patter of feet moved away from me, and I managed to stop throwing up onto the floor long enough to look up. Three. There were three distinct shadows moving in tandem with one another. And as their footfalls rushed up the steps, I froze.

There had been three men in that room with me.

Where the fuck am I?

Want more? Twisted Glass is out now!!

MORE BOOKS BY SAVANNAH RYLAN

Box Sets

The Bad Disciples MC Box Set
The Road Rebels MC Box Set
Marked Skulls MC Box Set
Dead Souls MC Complete Collection
Black Hornets MC Box Set
The Lost Boys MC: The Complete Collection
The Callaghan Mafia Box Set
The Black Cobras MC
Dragon Riders MC
Dirty Misfits MC
Steel Scorpions MC

Series

Twisted Metal
Twisted Glass
Twisted Hearts
Twisted Flames

Bender (Steel Scorpions MC #1)
Angel (Steel Scorpions MC #2)
Goose (Steel Scorpions MC #3)
Viper (Steel Scorpions MC #4)
Reaper (Steel Scorpions MC #5)
Fangs (Steel Scorpions MC #6)

Brooks (Dirty Misfits MC #1)
Porter (Dirty Misfits MC #2)
Asher (Dirty Misfits MC #3)
Cole (Dirty Misfits MC #4)
Tanner (Dirty Misfits MC #5)
Finn (Dirty Misfits MC #6)

Link (Dragon Riders MC #1)
Bowser (Dragon Riders MC #2)
Ash (Dragon Riders MC #3)
Knuckles (Dragon Riders MC #4)
Sly (Dragon Riders MC #5)

Declan (The Callaghan Mafia #1)
Brody (The Callaghan Mafia #2)
Gael (The Callaghan Mafia #3)
Flynn (The Callaghan Mafia #4)

Cage (Dead Souls MC: Prospects #1)
Bear (Dead Souls MC: Prospects #2)
Saint (Dead Souls MC: Prospects #3)
Ryker (Dead Souls MC: Prospects #4)
Toxin (Dead Souls MC: Prospects #5)

Texas (The Lost Boys MC #1)
Stone (The Lost Boys MC #2)

Bronx (The Lost Boys MC #3)
Notch (The Lost Boys MC #4)
Diego (The Lost Boys MC #5)
Puck (The Lost Boys MC #6)
Frost (The Lost Boys MC #7)
West (The Lost Boys MC #8)

Jace (The Black Hornets MC #1)
Maverick (The Black Hornets MC #2)
Duke (The Black Hornets MC #3)
Colt (The Black Hornets MC #4)
Thor (The Black Hornets MC #5)
Jagger (The Black Hornets MC #6)

Knox (Dead Souls MC #1)
Grave (Dead Souls MC #2)
Brewer (Dead Souls MC #3)
Rock (Dead Souls MC #4)
Diesel (Deal Souls MC #5)

Girth (Marked Skulls MC #1)
Rodeo (Marked Skulls MC #2)
Abe (Marked Skulls MC #3)
Oz (Marked Skulls MC #4)
Dash (Marked Skulls MC #5)

Hawk (The Road Rebels MC #1)
Talon (The Road Rebels MC #2)
Snake (The Road Rebels MC #3)
Fox (The Road Rebels MC #4)

Gunner (The Bad Disciples MC #1)

Hunter (The Bad Disciples MC #2)
Tank (The Bad Disciples MC #3)
Glock (The Bad Disciples MC #4)
Marco (The Bad Disciples MC #5)